EBURY PRESS

SIVAKAMI'S VOW: BOOK II
THE SIEGE OF KANCHI

Ramaswamy Krishnamurthy (1899–1954), better known by his pen name Kalki, was an editor, writer, journalist, poet, critic and activist for Indian independence. Kalki's expansive body of work includes editorials, short stories, film and music reviews, and historical and social novels. His stories have been made into films, such as *Thyaga Bhoomi* (Land of Sacrifice, 1939), the M.S. Subbulakshmi-starrer *Meera* (1945), *Kalvanin Kadhali* (The Thief's Lover, 1955), *Parthiban Kanavu* (Parthiban's Dream, 1960) and, most recently, the Mani Ratnam-directed *Ponniyin Selvan* (Ponni's Beloved, 2022). One of the most renowned names in Tamil literature, Kalki was awarded the Sahitya Akademi Award for his novel *Alai Osai* (The Sound of the Waves).

Born and raised in Chennai, Nandini Vijayaraghavan is a director and head of research at the Singapore office of Korea Development Bank. Her translation of Kalki's *Parthiban's Dream* (2021) was shortlisted for a Valley of Words award in 2022. Nandini's columns on finance and economy have appeared in *BusinessLine*, *The Hindu*, *Economic and Political Weekly* and *Financial Express*. *Unfinished Business* (Penguin Random House India, 2023) is her first India-centric business book. Nandini co-authored a non-fiction book, *The Singapore Blue Chips* (2017), with Umesh Desai. Nandini blogs at www.litintrans.com.

Celebrating 35 Years of
Penguin Random House India

SIVAKAMI'S VOW

BOOK II

THE SIEGE OF KANCHI

KALKI

Translated from the Tamil by
NANDINI VIJAYARAGHAVAN

EBURY
PRESS

An imprint of Penguin Random House

EBURY PRESS

USA | Canada | UK | Ireland | Australia
New Zealand | India | South Africa | China

Ebury Press is part of the Penguin Random House group of companies
whose addresses can be found at global.penguinrandomhouse.com

Published by Penguin Random House India Pvt. Ltd
4th Floor, Capital Tower 1, MG Road,
Gurugram 122 002, Haryana, India

First published in Ebury Press by Penguin Random House India 2023

Translation copyright © Nandini Vijayaraghavan 2023

All rights reserved

10 9 8 7 6 5 4 3 2

This is a work of fiction. Unless otherwise indicated, all the names, characters,
businesses, places, events and incidents in this book are either the product of the
author's imagination or used in a fictitious manner. Any resemblance to actual
persons, living or dead, or actual events is purely coincidental.

ISBN 9780143460039

Typeset in Adobe Caslon Pro by MAP Systems, Bengaluru, India
Printed at Replika Press Pvt. Ltd, India

This book is sold subject to the condition that it shall not, by way of trade
or otherwise, be lent, resold, hired out, or otherwise circulated without the
publisher's prior consent in any form of binding or cover other than that in
which it is published and without a similar condition including this
condition being imposed on the subsequent purchaser.

www.penguin.co.in

Contents

Characters

Mahendra Varma Pallavar	Emperor of the Pallava kingdom
Bhuvana Mahadevi	Queen consort of Mahendra Varma Pallavar
Narasimha Varma Pallavar	Mahendra Varma Pallavar's only son and the crown prince of the Pallava kingdom
Satyasraya Pulikesi	Emperor of the Chalukya kingdom
Vishnuvardhanan	Pulikesi's younger brother and the king of Vengi
Jayanta Varma Pandian	King of the Pandya kingdom
Durvineethan	King of Ganga Nadu
Thirunavukkarasar	A Saivite monk
Naganandi Adigal	A bikshu
Aayanar	A renowned sculptor of the Pallava kingdom

ix

Sivakami	Aayanar's daughter and a talented danseuse
Paranjyothi	A rustic youth from Thirusengattankudi in Chola Nadu
Kalipahayar	Commander of the Pallava army
Shatrugnan	Head of the espionage force of the Pallava kingdom
Gundodharan	A Pallava spy
Kannabiran	Mahendra Varma Pallavar's charioteer
Kamali	Kannabiran's wife and Sivakami's friend
Ashwabalar	Kannabiran's father
Rudrachariar	An exponent of music and Mahendra Pallavar's music teacher
Namasivaya Vaidhyar	A renowned physician and Paranjyothi's maternal uncle
Vajrabahu	Paranjyothi's co-traveller

l

Foreword

Naming himself after an avatar yet to come in Hindu cosmology, writer Krishnamurthy took many avatars. However, public memory is notoriously short, and he is remembered only for his historical fiction. His participation in the freedom struggle and shouldering the Tamil Isai (music) movement, where he insisted that Carnatic concerts should also have Tamil songs (ironically in Madras at the peak of the Justice Party/Dravidian movement), and his magazine editorship are often forgotten. However, Kalki draws parallels to his life and times in his writings. I would like to remember him as a mirror to Tamil life, as one who echoed the happenings of the first half of the twentieth century.

His writings take us back to those days with authenticity. Funnily though, even his historical fiction set 1000 years ago often reflect current events.

Sivakamiyin Sabadham was distinctly Kalki's masterpiece. We can find parallels in the novel to the turbulent years of the Quit India movement of 1942. Written as a radio play without some of its priceless characters, Kalki rearranged the story to suit print media. And Kalki couldn't get over the novel either. We can find distinct parallels in *Ponniyin Selvan* and *Sivakamiyin Sabadham*, though they were written nearly a decade apart. Nandini (in *Ponniyin Selvan*), considered perhaps his best character, has so many parallels with an unlikely character in *Sivakamiyin Sabadham*, Naganandi. They both were one of a royal twin with serpentine characteristics.

Tamil is not an easy language to learn. It is hedged in by its own complexities which, while rendering it alluring for those who know it, makes it very exacting for others to venture in to enjoy its intricacies.

It is an irony that those who lose out on this aspect of Tamil are not only the millions who need to access it but are fenced out, but also its own proponents. Many geniuses like Kalki did not get the renown they deserved because of this rigidity. A novel is timeless and like a magical mirror—it reflects the writer's genius for eternity long after he has gone. A writer's thoughts are timeless and should not be inscrutable to a reader who does not understand the language.

Some of the earliest translators of Tamil were British civil servants and missionaries who, frustrated that the great works of Tamil were not available to the rest, took great efforts to translate them into English. Three hundred years ago, Whyte Ellis, a collector of Madras, not only translated the Tamil book of social law, *Thirukkural*, but also trained many Indians in the art of translating in the Madras college he founded.

A language is just a conduit for a storyteller. The magnitude of his story is much bigger. A good translation will take Kalki's works to a larger audience who should not be denied the greatness of a novel because they can't understand the language it was written in. I am happy Nandini Vijayaraghavan has come out in flying colours in her effort.

It is not easy to translate Tamil either. And that too a story written almost a century back with a storyline that is a millennium old.

Ever since civilizations started mingling, interpreters have always been the most skilled in history. The *dubashes* of the Madras Presidency rose to be the neo nobility because of their capacities to interpret. To be skilled in two languages could make one an interpreter. But a translator's job is much more deep-rooted. A translator is a bridge who possesses the capacity to understand the feelings that inspired these words from a writer's pen. Also, the ability to reach out to somebody who wants to understand the story as it was written.

The Siege of Kanchi was a section in *Sivakamiyin Sabadham* that is close to historical truth. The Chalukyas did lay a cordon of forces around the Pallava capital and tried to starve them out. If they had buckled, Tamil history would have changed forever. The resilient Pallavas, at great human cost, persisted and created a space for future dynasties to spurt forth in the next centuries. Though historians would consider the Chola period as the golden age of Tamil civilization, their very origins were determined by the historical event of the Chalukya siege of Kanchi.

This volume of the novel deals with bravery, resilience, love and sacrifices, where Kalki takes his characters to their crescendos. Nandini Vijayaraghavan has brought forth all these emotions onto the page, creating vivid imagery in the readers' minds. I am certain this book would be more than a bridge for those who do not know the language to read the novel in the original. I am sure that there are thousands who earlier could not access these stories, hedged in by a language they haven't learnt. And I am certain that Nandini's writing will be the conduit for those thousands to join the legions of Kalki lovers.

Chennai   Venkatesh Ramakrishnan
                    Bi-lingual novelist and historian, author of
                    Kanchiyin Tharakai and *Gods, Kings and Slaves*

The Story Thus Far

Paranjyothi, a brave youth from the village of Thirusengattankudi in the Chola kingdom, travels to Kanchi, the capital of the Pallava kingdom, by foot to enrol himself as a student at the Saivite saint Thirunavukkarasar's monastery. He meets Naganandi, a bikshu, on the way. Naganandi, who saves Paranjyothi's life by killing a cobra that was about to bite him, predicts that Paranjyothi will get into trouble that very night. Paranjyothi does not believe him. By the time the duo reach Kanchi, the fort gates are sealed. However, a security guard named Marudappan, who is a Naganandi loyalist, lets them in.

On entering the fort, Marudappan informs Naganandi that the arangetram of danseuse Sivakami, daughter of the renowned sculptor and painter Aayanar, had come to an abrupt halt that evening and that he had received orders to seal the fort gates. Speculation of an impending war is rife in the city. After listening to this news, Naganandi and Paranjyothi part ways. While Naganandi heads to the royal viharam, Paranjyothi strolls around Kanchi in search of Navukkarasar's monastery.

Meanwhile, the temple elephant has run amok and charges towards Aayanar and Sivakami, who are returning to their forest residence in a palanquin. The palanquin bearers set the palanquin down and flee. Paranjyothi, who fortuitously arrives there, wields his spear deftly at the elephant, which turns and starts chasing him. Aayanar and Sivakami are, however, rescued. Paranjyothi manages to escape the elephant, but loses the bundle he is carrying. The bundle contains, amongst other things, some money and messages from his maternal uncle, a renowned physician, to Thirunavukkarasar and Aayanar, requesting them to enrol Paranjyothi as their student.

Due to the impending war, the Pallava emperor Mahendra Varmar imposes a curfew at night. The city guards who find Paranjyothi wandering around aimlessly imprison him. Naganandi bikshu helps Paranjyothi escape from the prison, takes him through a secret route out of the Kanchi fort and introduces him to Aayanar, who is willing to take Paranjyothi under his tutelage. When Aayanar is in the midst of a conversation with Naganandi and Paranjyothi, Sivakami heads to the lotus pond near their home in the forest. There, she meets her lover, the crown prince, Narasimha Varmar, Mahendra Pallavar's only son.

Meanwhile, Naganandi persuades Aayanar to send Paranjyothi to Nagarjuna mountain to learn about the secret of the indelible paints used in the Ajantha caves. This, he says, can be Paranjyothi's 'guru dakshina'. Aayanar, who is extremely keen to know about the indelible paints used in the Ajantha caves, readily agrees and secures a high-breed steed and travel permit from Mahendra Pallavar for Paranjyothi. Naganandi hands over a written message to Paranjyothi to carry with him.

As Paranjyothi heads to Nagarjuna mountain carrying Naganandi's message, he befriends a brave and mysterious warrior, Vajrabahu, on the way. That night, Vajrabahu drugs Paranjyothi, causing him to fall asleep, and replaces the message Paranjyothi is carrying with one that is penned by him.

Unaware of this, Paranjyothi continues his journey and stops at the Buddhist monastery on the banks of the North Pennai River, as instructed by Naganandi. The senior bikshu of that monastery sends Paranjyothi with six horsemen who are supposedly heading to the Nagarjuna mountain. Paranjyothi, suspecting the horsemen were heading elsewhere, tries to escape. The horsemen imprison him and lead him to the Chalukya army camp.

At the Chalukya army camp, Paranjyothi runs into Vajrabahu, who asks him to state the truth to the Chalukya emperor, Pulikesi. Paranjyothi is produced before Emperor Pulikesi, who reads the message Paranjyothi is carrying. Pulikesi is unable to comprehend the message and cannot understand what Paranjyothi is saying, as he does not know Tamil. So, he solicits Vajrabahu's assistance. Vajrabahu states that the message may be for Pulikesi's brother, Vishnuvardhanan, who is the ruler of Vengi.

The whimsical and cruel Pulikesi commands that Paranjyothi be escorted by nine horsemen to Vishnuvardhanan, and that he be killed if Vishnuvardhanan cannot decipher the message. Vajrabahu assures Paranjyothi that he will meet him on the way before he is taken to Vishnuvardhanan.

The following day, Paranjyothi, accompanied by the horsemen, sets out to meet King Vishnuvardhanan. They stop at an isolated hut occupied by an old man for the night. When everyone is asleep, the old man wakes Paranjyothi up and escorts him to the two horses waiting outside. Paranjyothi realizes that the old man is Vajrabahu in disguise. Vajrabahu and Paranjyothi ride away, pursued by the horsemen. In the fierce combat that follows, Vajrabahu and Paranjyothi kill all the horsemen. Vajrabahu also finds a message one of the horsemen was carrying for King Vishnuvardhanan and retains that message.

Vajrabahu offers to take Paranjyothi along with him to the Pallava army camp. Paranjyothi surmises Vajrabahu is a spy to Emperor Mahendra Varma Pallavar. As Vajrabahu and Paranjyothi travel for several days together towards the Pallava army camp, their friendship grows. During their conversation, Vajrabahu informs Paranjyothi that the whereabouts of Mahendra Pallavar, who left Kanchi purportedly for the army camp, were unknown. Paranjyothi expresses his desire to join the Pallava army to Vajrabahu, who promises to assist him.

On reaching the Pallava army camp, Vajrabahu asks Paranjyothi to wait outside, and says that he will secure Emperor Mahendra Varmar's consent to allow Paranjyothi inside the camp. While Paranjyothi is waiting restlessly outside, he observes that the Pallava army turns jubilant suddenly. On enquiring, he is informed that Emperor Mahendra Varmar has reached the army camp.

Chapter 1

Northern Entrance

One evening during the monsoon, the sun was setting behind the ramparts of the Kanchi fort, and the golden rim of the clouds in the northwest was progressively fading. When the sun had finally set, the clouds turned a deep blue, reminiscent of Tirumal's skin tone.

Trees and creepers rustled in the strong wind blowing from the northeast. Birds nesting in the fort walls, temple towers, palace roofs and art halls of Kanchi were returning home, flapping their wings. The Kanchi fort's imposing northern entrance was bereft of activity in the twilight.

The gates of the fort had been sealed after Mahendra Chakravarthy had left for the battlefield eight months ago. They were fastened with heavy iron chains from the inside and sealed with a big lock.

Two soldiers, armed with spears and swords, stood guard outside the gates. Horns were suspended from both their necks. The highway, which led to the entrance of the fort, twisted and turned like a moving snake and covered a long distance.

There was not a soul visible on the highway, yet the guards were observant. It seemed as though they were expecting someone. Suddenly, a cloud of dust rose in the distance. The trotting of horses was also heard. The guards became even more alert.

The sound of the warning drum on the upper storey of the fort entrance reverberated in the air. The cloud of dust and sound of horses neared the fort in no time. In the dim evening light, the horses were not clearly visible.

The two warriors who rode in the front were holding flags that bore the insignia of a rishabha, a bull. The lone warrior who followed them was clad in battle attire and was riding a high breed horse. He looked majestic. A few more horses followed them at a distance. All the horses came to a halt on the other side of the bridge, across the moat.

One of the warriors holding the flag called out, 'The commander of the Kanchi fort, Paranjyothi, is coming. Open the fort gates!' Another soldier repeated the first soldier's call.

Several voices cheered in unison, 'Long live Commander Paranjyothi!'

The two soldiers who were guarding the fort hastened forward. They bowed before the lone warrior seated on the high breed horse. Yes, the warrior seated on the statuesque black horse was indeed Paranjyothi! He had transformed completely in the last eight months.

He had been a naïve youth when he had arrived in Kanchi. His face had exuded a childlike innocence. Now, it was marked with the injuries suffered on the warfront, and the maturity that worldly experience endowed. Hence everyone accorded him the respect and honour he deserved.

Paranjyothi, the newly appointed commander of the Kanchi fort, proudly displayed the lion insignia to the guards standing deferentially in front of him. After seeing the insignia, the guards bowed to Paranjyothi again and walked back. As they neared the moat's bridge, they blew the horns that hung around their necks.

Immediately, a small door built within the gates of the fort opened. A soldier looked out of that door. He asked the guards something, to which they responded. The next moment, the sound of iron chains and locks being unfastened was heard. The gigantic fort gates opened noisily, allowing the horsemen in.

Paranjyothi raced ahead of the soldiers holding the flags and entered the fort. There was another smaller entrance approximately two hundred feet away from the main entrance of the fort. In the area that spanned the two gates ran a path tiled with black granite. Soldiers holding spears stood on both sides of the path. They were interspersed with soldiers holding illuminated torches.

Amidst them was a decorated chariot with two horses harnessed to it. Several soldiers stood by the chariot holding rishabha flags. The flags fluttering in the strong gust of wind that blew through the open fort gates seemed to welcome the newly appointed commander of the fort.

Kumara Chakravarthy Narasimhar was seated in the chariot. The charioteer, Kannabiran, was standing, holding on tightly to the reins.

As soon as Commander Paranjyothi rode through the fort gates, Mamalla Narasimhar jumped down from the chariot. When he gestured, a soldier announced in a thundering tone, 'Here comes Commander Paranjyothi, the bravest of the brave, who demoralized the demonic forces of the Chalukya, Pulikesi! Welcome! Welcome!'

The din of hundreds of soldiers who echoed, 'Welcome, Commander Paranjyothi!' reached the sky.

Along with these cheers, conches, horns, drums, trumpets and bugles were played in unison, inspiring the soldiers present.

It was obvious from Paranjyothi's expression that he had not expected such a tumultuous welcome. He immediately jumped down from his horse and approached the kumara chakravarthy.

Paranjyothi was about to prostrate before the crown prince when Mamallar prevented him from doing so and hugged him. Both were unable to speak for some time. It was the kumara chakravarthy who spoke first.

'Commander, you seem to have travelled non-stop all day! You're so tired that you're unable to speak!'

'Prabhu, it is not fatigue that has rendered me speechless, but your boundless affection. I did not expect to meet you at the entrance of the fort!'

'Great warrior, had the chakravarthy not prohibited me from leaving the fort, I would have travelled one kaadam to meet you outside the fort! Do you know how eager I have been to meet you for the last eight months?' Saying this, the kumara chakravarthy mounted the chariot and made Paranjyothi sit next to him.

'Shall we head to the palace, commander? What do you wish to do?' asked Mamallar.

Paranjyothi responded, 'Prabhu, as we ride to the palace, I wish to look around the city of Kanchi. I do not want to waste any time. We will send these soldiers ahead.'

As commanded by the kumara chakravarthy, the soldiers stationed at the Kanchi fort along with those who had accompanied Paranjyothi, rode ahead swiftly.

The charioteer Kannabiran skilfully tugged at the reins of the horses. The chariot also moved ahead.

The gates of the fort were sealed again. The fort's northern entrance, which had been lively for some time, fell silent again.

Chapter 2

Old Friends

Old memories flooded Paranjyothi's mind when the chariot crossed the inner gates of the fort and rode through the beautiful and wide streets of Kanchi. Eight months ago, on one such full moon night, he had entered Kanchi, though through the southern gates. He was reminded of what had happened that night. The difference between his entry then and now was stark.

When Mamallar observed, 'Commander, why are you so silent?' Paranjyothi was shaken out of his reverie.

'I beg your pardon, prabhu. Your affection has rendered me speechless. I cannot believe that I am travelling in a chariot sitting shoulder to shoulder with Mamallar, the Pallava crown prince and the great wrestler who defeated all other wrestlers in Dakshina Bharata!'

'Why is it so incredible? It's an honour for me to travel sitting by your side! Aren't you the great warrior who—like Mount Mandara—churned the demonic Pulikesi's ocean-like

5

army? Didn't you cause the massive elephant force of the Vatapi army to disperse like a cyclonic wind dispersing dark clouds?'

'Has news of the heroic feats of the Pallava cavalry already reached Kanchi?' asked Paranjyothi, attributing his success to his men.

'Why not? We came to know of the gallant acts of the cavalry through the weekly messages the chakravarthy sent. We disseminated the information we knew across the country,' observed Mamallar.

'Ah! See how your affection has enthralled me. I forgot to hand over the message the chakravarthy has sent for you!' Saying this, Paranjyothi handed over the tube containing the palm leaf missive that was carefully fastened to his waist.

'Commander, are you sure that this is the message the chakravarthy gave you? I hope it was not changed en route,' teased Mamallar, laughing.

When Paranjyothi smilingly remarked, 'Do you know that story too?' his embarrassment was evident.

'Yes, I know! I know everything from the time you befriended Vajrabahu on the way . . .' When Mamallar revealed this, both of them burst out laughing.

Mamallar continued, 'It is eight months since the chakravarthy left Kanchi. I was adamant about accompanying him. The chakravarthy categorically refused. I then requested him to send me weekly updates on the war from the battlefield. He agreed and has been sending me weekly messages since then. Commander, today is the first day I am seeing you, but you are no stranger to me. I have been acquainting myself with you through the messages the chakravarthy has been sending for the last eight months. Today, when I saw you,

you did not seem unfamiliar. I feel as though I have met an old friend whom I have known for long!'

'Prabhu, I too share your sentiments. Don't think I am repeating what you just said like a parrot. It is truly so. Not a day passed without the chakravarthy talking about you during the last eight months. So you too are no stranger to me.'

The kumara chakravarthy held Paranjyothi's hands firmly and stated enthusiastically, 'Commander, in that case, both of us are fortunate. The divine poet Thiruvalluvar's couplet is apt for us. Didn't he say: *When emotions connect, friendships blossom / Making meetings meaningless.* The title *"poyya mozhi pulavar"* is so appropriate for the author of *Thirukkural.'*

Paranjyothi responded, 'Pallava kumara, I beg your pardon. I am illiterate and have not even stood in the shadow of a school. I neither know Thiruvalluvar nor his *Thirukkural.* The chakravarthy has given you the responsibility of educating me. You will understand once you read the message.'

The kumara chakravarthy was embarrassed by those words. 'So what, commander! I will happily abide by the chakravarthy's commands . . .'

Paranjyothi interjected saying, 'It is not with my interests in mind that the chakravarthy has commanded you thus. It is with your interests in mind!'

Mamallar stared at Paranjyothi, unable to comprehend what he was saying. Paranjyothi then observed, 'Yes, prabhu. The chakravarthy believes that while you are virtuous, you lack patience and decisiveness. He said that you will develop

---

* Scholar whose words are always true/never go wrong.

patience when you start teaching me! The chakravarthy is so confident of my intellectual capability!' Hearing this, Mamallar burst out laughing and Paranjyothi followed suit. The charioteer Kannabiran, unsuccessful in his attempts to suppress his laughter, also laughed heartily. The horses harnessed to the chariot, unable to understand the reason for this gaiety, neighed aloud.

Hearing the horses neigh in their naturally 'tuneful voices', the three of them burst out laughing again.

Chapter 3

Vow of Friendship

Even as Paranjyothi was conversing with Mamallar, he eagerly observed the wide main roads of Kanchi, the crowded markets interspersed with temples dedicated to Lord Shiva and Lord Vishnu illuminated by lamps, the Saivite and Vaishnavite monasteries that taught the divine language of Tamil, the Samana and Buddhist temples, the schools that imparted Sanskrit and the Vedas, and the art schools that taught painting and sculpture.

The city was livelier than it had been eight months ago when he had entered Kanchi for the first time through the southern gates of the fort. Paranjyothi thought that, as the news of war had suddenly broken out that day, the gates of the fort had been sealed and spies were active in the city, Kanchi had been sombre. After people had recovered from the initial shock and mustered courage, life had returned to normal. But how long would this last? Very soon, a dark, grave mood would supplant the gaiety of this beautiful city.

Such thoughts occurred intermittently to Paranjyothi as he and Mamallar rode in the chariot through the city.

As they approached a massive temple, Paranjyothi guessed that it must be the Ekambareshwarar temple from the appearance of the beautiful sanctum sanctorum. He confirmed his conjecture with Mamallar.

'Yes, commander. Haven't you visited this temple before?' asked Mamallar.

'No, I have not. The previous time I was in Kanchi, I went looking for the Ekambareshwarar temple, but I did not reach this spot that day. Please ask him to stop the chariot. I would like to take a close look at the heart of Kanchi,' requested Paranjyothi.

Paranjyothi observed the seemingly endless rows of illuminated lamps in the temple, the majestic temple chariot that stood opposite the temple at the street junction, the wide roads in all four directions that led to the temple chariot, the mounds of flowers, coconuts and plantains that lay in the surrounding shops, and the temple mandapam supported by a hundred exquisitely sculpted pillars. He exclaimed, 'Ah! Pulikesi's love is not unfounded!'

'Pulikesi's love? What are you saying, commander?' asked Mamallar.

'The brave Vajrabahu told me of the love Pulikesi had for beautiful Kanchi. Apparently, when the name Kanchi was uttered, the change in Pulikesi's face was similar to that of a man in love with a woman!'

'Commander, no matter how shrewd the gallant Vajrabahu is, don't you think that he ought not to have met Pulikesi? What is your opinion?' asked Mamallar.

Paranjyothi avoided responding to that query. Instead, he asked, 'Prabhu, where is Thirunavukkarasar's monastery located?'

'Look . . . that vacant building is his monastery.'

'Ah! I came to enrol in this monastery and learn Tamil. It's my ill luck that the monastery shut down the moment I arrived to educate myself!' moaned Paranjyothi.

Narasimhar smiled slightly and replied, 'When you were destined to be of great service to the Pallava dynasty, how could you have become Navukkarasar's disciple? Also, it is God's wish that you learn Tamil from me!'

'I wonder if the elephant that ran amok that night foresaw this. It was only because of that elephant that my life took this turn,' quipped Paranjyothi. He then suddenly recollected that night's incidents and enquired, 'Aiyya! How are Aayanar and Sivakami doing?'

Paranjyothi was not blind to the change in Mamallar's face when Sivakami's name was mentioned. He thought, 'Ah! Mamallar himself is an example of the love Vajrabahu spoke of!'

There was a perceptible change in Mamallar's voice when he responded. 'I am told that they are well, commander, but it's been several months since I saw them. They are residing at Aayanar's old forest residence. The sculptors who were working in Mamallapuram were sent to build Bharata mandapams as commanded by the chakravarthy. After that, Aayanar left Mamallapuram and returned to his forest residence.' Mamallar's voice betrayed his feelings as he spoke.

Once again, Mamallar held Paranjyothi's hand firmly and acknowledged in an emotional tone, 'Commander, you have rendered stellar service to the Pallava empire in the last eight months. You will be of greater service in the future. But nothing can be greater than the valorous service you rendered that night. Didn't you rescue Aayanar and Sivakami? This is proof of how much I value that act of yours!' Saying this,

Mamallar showed Paranjyothi the spear he had flung at the mad elephant.

Paranjyothi's heart melted listening to Mamallar's emotional speech. Unable to speak, his hand gripped the base of the spear Mamallar was holding. He had intended to retrieve the spear from Mamallar.

Narasimha Varmar continued to hold the spear and remarked, 'I have prayed at Ekambarar's sannadhi several times for a true friend. I believe that your arrival at Kanchi is in response to my prayers. Commander, let's take an oath of friendship in this very sanctum. Let us establish our friendship by swearing on the spear that saved Aayanar and Sivakami.'

The temple bell at Ekambarar's sacred sannadhi rang then, resonating with the sound, 'Om, Om.'

* * *

That night Kannabiran told Kamali, 'My dear! There is a competitor to Sivakami for the kumara chakravarthy's attentions! I ferried both of them through the streets of Kanchi today. As I think about it, I feel very sad!

'Why are you blabbering? If what you're saying is true, reveal her identity immediately! I will poison her and kill her right now,' cried Kamali.

'It's not a she, it's a he! The youth who saved your friend by flinging the spear at the mad elephant has returned from the battlefield. He has now been appointed the commander of the Kanchi fort. Looking at the affectionate way in which the kumara chakravarthy chatted with him, it seemed as though he would forget even Sivakami.'

'Is your understanding so limited? Shall I tell you why Mamallar is so fond of that boy? It is because that boy rescued my friend! Isn't this proof of how steadfast Mamallar is!' retorted Kamali.

'Your razor-sharp mind cannot be praised enough! Why did you have to marry a mere charioteer? You ought to have married a minister who rules the kingdom,' quipped Kannan.

'Haven't you heard the proverb, "Love is blind"?' responded Kamali.

Chapter 4

Sivakami's Birthday

Ah. It had been a long time since Sivakami and Mamallar had met, because the chakravarthy had prohibited Mamallar from leaving Kanchi. One might wonder about her present condition.

On nearing Aayanar's house, the change in the environment compared to eight months ago was shocking. The lively environment prevalent then was conspicuous by its absence. The *kal kal* noise from the chisels was no longer heard. Aayanar's disciples who used to work on sculptures were no longer around.

The trees in the surrounding forest looked different too. Then, it was spring. New buds had been sprouting from the trees. The mango trees had been covered with flowers and tender buds. Banyan trees and fig trees had been covered with golden-hued leaves. Now, the trees were covered with deep green as well as half-dry leaves. The earth was covered with dry leaves. Rainwater stagnated in some places.

The leaves atop the trees retained some of the water from the previous night's rains. Whenever there was a strong gust of wind, the water dripped and fell on the ground. It seemed as though the trees were shedding tears observing the changes that had occurred in that part of the country.

However, the birds that resided in the trees continued to chirp tunefully. Several melodies were heard in different tones. But there was a difference even in those tones. The liveliness was missing. It seemed as though the birds were singing mournful songs with a heavy heart, recollecting happier times!

As one neared the house, one could see two men working under a tree.

Yes, one of them was the sculptor, Aayanar. But where was the tranquillity that was so characteristic of him? When had this obsessiveness gripped him? What were he and his accomplice doing?

They were grinding a mixture of green leaves using a mortar and pestle and extracting its juice. A vessel containing the extract of green leaves was boiling on the stove next to them. Seeing all this, we can guess that Aayanar was researching paint additives.

The chakravarthy had sent orders from the battlefield asking Aayanar to stop the works at Mamallapuram and assignments at other places. On receipt of these orders, Aayanar returned to his forest residence along with his daughter. He sent away all his disciples to build Bharata mandapams at all the temples in Thondai Mandalam. He had retained an assistant to help him.

For some time, Aayanar had not been fully engaged in sculpting. He was eagerly awaiting Paranjyothi's return from Nagarjuna mountain. After a few months, he had received some puzzling news about Paranjyothi. He had heard rumours that Paranjyothi had joined the Pallava army and was performing extraordinary acts of gallantry as the head of the Pallava cavalry.

Naganandi adigal had also stopped visiting him. Aayanar's desire to learn about indelible paints had increased multifold. So he stopped carving sculptures and began to research paint additives. His focus on Sivakami's dance training also diminished. Sivakami found this convenient, as she now had enough time to reflect upon the all-encompassing love that had blossomed in her heart. She believed that she was blessed with a good fortune no one else in the world had been blessed with thus far. She was immersed in thoughts about her love and her lover. She fantasized about her future with him and built castles in the air! She derived immense pleasure from these fantasies. In her imaginary life she experienced both happiness and disappointment, and spent a lot of time with her lover. It must be said that the intensity of the joy and sorrow Sivakami had felt living this vicarious life during the last eight months was comparable to the intensity of emotions one experienced in a lifetime.

Was Sivakami all alone in the house now?

It appeared that she was not alone, for one could hear voices. Whom was she talking to? Was it to her mute aunt, her athai? No, for two to three male voices could be heard. One could actually overhear the conversation.

'Ammani! What's the point in losing your temper with us? We are just carrying out the Pallava kumarar's orders,' remonstrated an usher.

'I care neither for the Pallava kumarar nor his orders! It seems that Mamallar is idle today! That's why he suddenly remembered the existence of this sculptor's daughter. All right, open that ivory box and show me its contents!' commanded Sivakami in an angry tone.

'There is a necklace made from invaluable pearls obtained from the seaport in south Pandya Nadu! Ammani, even Emperor Harshavardhana's consort does not wear such pearls. See how the pearls dazzle!' stated another usher.

'Enough! I don't want this pearl necklace. Convey this message of mine to your kumara chakravarthy. There is a punnai tree on the banks of the pond near Aayanar's house. The ground beneath the tree is covered with pearl-like punnai flowers in the morning. Tell him that the beauty of those punnai flowers far exceeds the beauty of this pearl necklace. If he so desires, he may come to see the flowers one morning. What does that golden casket contain?' asked Sivakami.

'Ammani, these corals were hidden in the depths of the sea by the goddess of beauty. Our men had to trick the god of the oceans to appropriate these. Emperors are keen to embed these in their crowns. The Pallava kumarar opined that this peerless coral necklace is fit to adorn the queen of Bharata Shastram . . .

'Well, your Pallava kumarar may be impressed by this coral necklace, but tell him this. The coral necklace fades in comparison with the red beak of the parrots reared by Aayanar's daughter in their house. He can come in person and have a look. Take it away! What's in that basket?'

'Golden champa, jasmine and pichi flowers from the palace garden . . .'

'No need! Take everything away. Tell your Pallava kumarar that, once upon a time, Sivakami used to love flowers. Now, for some reason, she dislikes flowers. Why has the Pallava kumarar sent all these things?'

'He has sent these because today is your birthday, Ammani!'

'Is that so? I am very happy. I am extremely happy that the kumara chakravarthy remembers the birthday of this humble sculptor's daughter. But his memory must be faulty. Take these things back and tell him that it's not Sivakami's birthday today. Tell him that no woman by the name Sivakami was ever born on the surface of this earth!'

How surprising! Wasn't Aayanar working outside the house just some time ago? Now his gentle voice could be heard from inside the house. 'My child, Sivakami! Why are you chiding them like this? When the kumara chakravarthy himself remembered your birthday and sent gifts . . .'

'Keep quiet, appa! Don't treat the kumara chakravarthy lightly. He is trying to deceive us by sending pearl and coral necklaces and flowers. You can trust anyone but Mamallar. Ushers! Why are you still standing here? Pick up all these things and leave right away! Are you going to take these things or not?'

'We will take them back, amma!'

One would have expected the ushers to leave the house carrying the gifts they had brought, but there was no sign of anyone coming out of the house!

How mysterious! One could hear the sound of people talking inside the house, but actually there was no human movement.

Sivakami was sitting alone inside the house. She was seated on the throne Aayanar had sculpted for the chakravarthy. With whom had she been conversing all along?

The mystery was soon revealed. Sivakami had been playacting by herself. 'Ushers, come here!' she instructed.

No one came. But she continued to speak, imagining someone was in front of her.

'Also tell your Pallava kumarar this. "The day that Mamallar's heart melts and he comes to see this sculptor's daughter is her birthday." Do you understand?'

After saying this, Sivakami kept quiet for some time. Then she spoke again, but in a different voice. Now the male voice of an usher could be heard.

'Ammani! I beg your pardon. The Pallava kumarar who sent all these gifts also conveyed that he himself would come after some time in his golden chariot.'

Once again Sivakami spoke, this time in a happy tone and her natural voice. 'Ah! Did Mamallar say that he himself would come after some time? If so, today is indeed my birthday! . . . Appa! Today is your daughter's birthday. Did you know? Why are you keeping mum? At least today, please refrain from grinding the green leaves . . . I can hear the sound of the chariot approaching!'

Sivakami leapt up from the throne. At that point of time, the sound of a chariot coming towards the house was indeed heard. She ran to the entrance of the house with indescribable eagerness.

The chariot was nearing the house. It was the kumara chakravarthy's golden chariot. The charioteer was also Kannabiran. But who was seated in the chariot? It seemed like someone else!

Ah! What a disappointment! It was certain that the person in the chariot was not Mamallar. Sivakami held on to the pillar at the entrance of that sculpted house and stood like a stone statue.

Chapter 5

Tempestuous Love

When the chariot came to a halt in front of the sculpted house, Paranjyothi looked down, unable to face Sivakami. The very first time Paranjyothi had visited that house, he had come to the conclusion that Aayanar's daughter was no mere mortal and was endowed with divine qualities. He had already conjectured the profound love that Sivakami and Mamallar shared. The Pallava kumarar had himself confirmed the same the previous night.

In the courtyard of the palace, the two friends were engaged in deep conversation, soaking in the intoxicating moonlight. It was then that Mamallar had divulged his innermost feelings to Paranjyothi. All these days he had suppressed his feelings towards Sivakami like water in a dam. Now he had found a trustworthy friend, and the barriers broke down and Mamallar's revelation of his love flowed like a river in spate. Paranjyothi was rendered speechless, inundated in that flood. This obsessive love was entirely new to him. It was true that he too was in love with Thiruvengadu Namasivaya Vaidhyar's daughter. But Paranjyothi experienced peace and happiness when thought of her. Paranjyothi observed that Mamallar's love was akin to a cyclone repeatedly striking a mountainous region, a volcano that emits fire and smoke without warning, or a turbulent ocean where the waves rise as high as the mountains. The intensity of Mamallar's love shocked as well as frightened Paranjyothi.

Paranjyothi's heart melted when he thought of all the obstacles that stood in the way of the successful culmination of their love. The greatest barrier was Mahendra Chakravarthy, who had other plans for Mamallar. Would Mamallar be able to overcome this barrier?

For the last eight months, Paranjyothi had shared an intimate relationship with the chakravarthy, who had reposed a lot of trust and affection in him. Paranjyothi, who knew the chakravarthy's innermost views on most issues, also knew that he was aware of Mamallar's love and was not supportive of it.

So, Paranjyothi was now in an awkward situation. On the one hand, the chakravarthy, who was like a father to him and whom Paranjyothi worshipped, was keen to divert Mamallar's attention away from Sivakami. On the other hand, Mamallar had shared his most intimate thoughts with Paranjyothi and was expecting his assistance in fulfilling his love. If he acted in accordance with the chakravarthy's desire, he would be betraying his friend. If he acted in accordance with his friend's desire, he would be betraying the chakravarthy.

He had also to think of Sivakami's position, in addition to his own predicament. What was good for her? Would this unsuitable romance do her any good? What were Aayanar's views on this issue?

Amidst all this confusion, one thing was crystal clear. Paranjyothi's feelings for Sivakami were a combination of reverence, concern, respect, loyalty and pure affection. His feelings for Sivakami were similar to those of Lakshmana towards Sita.

***

When Sivakami realized that Mamallar was not in the chariot, she did not even want to know who the visitor was. Her attention was diverted to the charioteer, Kannabiran.

Kannabiran alighted from the front seat of the chariot and walked ahead. Paranjyothi got down from the rear and followed him. When they neared the house, Sivakami asked, 'Anna! Is everyone well at home?' Disappointment was evident in her voice.

'No, thaye! No! Nobody is well at home. Kamali has a headache. My father's legs are aching. I am also not keeping well . . .'

'What happened to you, anna?' asked Sivakami.

'I don't know. Something is wrong with my stomach. Kamali says that the only remedy for my illness is a cat.'

'The remedy is a cat! What nonsense is this?' exclaimed Sivakami.

'Yes, thaye! Nowadays I feel incredibly hungry. Last night I ate the nine appams, seven dosais and twelve kozhukattais that Kamali had made and asked her for more food! She opined that there were mice in my stomach. "Only if you eat a cat will your hunger be satiated", she quipped!'

Hearing this, Sivakami burst out laughing. Paranjyothi was also unable to suppress his laughter.

Hearing Paranjyothi laugh, Sivakami turned towards him. 'Ah! Who's this?'

Paranjyothi mustered his courage and asked, 'Ammani, don't you recognize me?'

'Aren't you from Thiruvengadu ...?'

'Yes, that's me! I am Paranjyothi, who had brought a message for your father from Thiruvengadu Namasivaya Vaidhyar—'

Kannabiran interrupted saying, 'I beg your pardon! I forgot the groom at the wedding, thaye! Let me introduce him. He is the commander of the Kanchi fort! The chakravarthy himself has sent him to safeguard the fort. Henceforth, there is no place safer on earth to hide than the Kanchi fort. Without his orders, even Lord Yama cannot enter the fort!'

Kannabiran was an artist of sorts. Paranjyothi knew that even Mamallar gave him the latitude to speak in this manner. So Paranjyothi ignored him and enquired, 'Where is your father? Is he inside?'

Sivakami's expression indicated that she too hadn't liked what Kannabiran had uttered in jest. She exclaimed, 'There—Appa is coming!'

Paranjyothi looked around. Aayanar was walking towards the house from under the tree.

When he came close to them, Commander Paranjyothi asked, 'Aiyya, do you recognize me?'

Immediately, Aayanar asked eagerly, 'Who is this? Paranjyothi?' He rushed towards Paranjyothi and hugged him. He then asked him in a low tone, 'Thambi, what about the task for which you set out? Did you succeed or not?'

Observing Aayanar's animated expression and his eager tone, tears filled Paranjyothi's eyes. He admitted in a soft, choked voice, 'This time I failed. But someday I will definitely find out the secret of the Ajantha paint additive and inform you.'

'No need, thambi! I heard that you joined the Pallava army. I thought that the news might be untrue. But that's not an issue. I myself will discover the secret of indelible paints soon. Thambi, I am conducting some new experiments. Would you like to come with me? I will show you,' asked Aayanar, pointing to the tree under which he had been sitting.

Sivakami interjected. 'Appa! Anna has come after eight months. Ask him to come in and sit down. Let's hear what he has to say.'

'Oh yes, of course! Come in, thambi!' invited Aayanar and ushered Paranjyothi into the house.

Chapter 6

Obsession

When Paranjyothi looked around the sculpture mandapam at Aayanar's house, he realized that there had been no progress since his previous visit, and that the statues Aayanar had been working on then were still incomplete. He felt totally disheartened. The valorous man thought, 'Why did this war break out?'

Aayanar and Paranjyothi sat in one corner of the veranda. Sivakami stood leaning against a pillar, just as she had when Paranjyothi visited their house the first time.

'Do you know, appa, he is now the commander of the Kanchi fort!' remarked Sivakami.

'Is that so? Naganandi adigal had predicted after observing thambi's physiognomy that he would rise to a senior position . . .' Saying this, Aayanar thought for a moment and then asked, 'Thambi, what did you do with the missive?'

'Aiyya, I was cheated in that matter. Despite you and Naganandi cautioning me, it came to naught. The message—'

'Ah! The chakravarthy—'

'Yes, aiyya, it fell into the emperor's hands.'

'Ah!' exclaimed Aayanar. 'Did Mahendra Varmar mention anything about it?'

'Mahendra Varmar? I wasn't referring to the Pallava chakravarthy; I was talking about the Vatapi emperor. The Vatapi soldiers captured me on the way and produced me before Pulikesi, who forcibly extracted the missive from me.'

Aayanar was only able to exclaim, 'Ah!'

Just then, one could hear someone heaving a deep sigh somewhere close by.

Paranjyothi thought it was a snake hissing. But neither Aayanar nor Sivakami seemed to have heard the sound.

At that moment, Sivakami—who was facing the entrance—saw Kannabiran standing there and gesturing to her.

'Thambi, did you actually see the Vatapi emperor?' asked an amazed Aayanar.

'Yes, aiyya! I saw him from the same distance as the Buddha statue is from here.'

'What did he say?'

'Who knows? He spoke in a language I do not understand. You seem to be eager to see the Vatapi emperor!'

'Yes, thambi! I wish I had not sent you. Instead, I ought to have gone with the missive!'

'Why are you so keen, aiyya?'

'It seems that the Vatapi emperor spent two years of his childhood in the Ajantha mountains. So he is probably aware of the secret additive. Isn't that possible?'

Paranjyothi was reminded of Vajrabahu deriding the arts. How right he was! Aayanar's obsession with art had turned him crazy. It had caused him to forget that Pulikesi was an enemy, and had instilled in him a desire to meet that emperor.

'Aiyya! I haven't yet told you the important task on account of which I came here. The chakravarthy has commanded me to convey a message to you.'

'Which chakravarthy?' asked Aayanar.

'Mahendra Pallavar!'

'Ah! Mahendra Pallavar! I had thought so highly of him! Once upon a time, all the sculptors in the Pallava empire had congregated and conferred the title "Vichitra Siddhar" on him. It would have been more appropriate to confer the title "Sabala* Siddhar".'

'Why are you talking thus, aiyya?'

'Look, thambi. He asked me to go to Mamallapuram, leaving this place. He insisted that five temples must be sculpted out of mountains in six months. Within a month, he commanded, "Stop working on the temples!" Chakravarthy was not like this before; he has changed a lot.'

'He has not changed, aiyya! He has to do a few things because of the war . . .'

'War! Destructive war! As if the ongoing war is not enough, we have been ordered to keep the old Bharata War in mind! Thambi, shall I tell you something? The true reason for the chakravarthy suspending work in Mamallapuram is not to construct Bharata mandapams. He wants to save on the provisions provided to the sculptors and workmen! I heard that all the provisions in the harbour granary have been transported to Kanchi!'

'These are essential tasks to be performed during war time, aiyya. The Kanchi fort should be ready to withstand a year, or even two years of siege. If you had only seen the ocean-like Vatapi army advancing . . .'

---

* Fickle

'There have been rumours of the Vatapi army coming here for the last eight months!'

'But do you know why that gigantic army has not reached here yet? If Mahendra Pallavar had not reached the battlefield eight months ago, the city of Kanchi would have been razed to the ground by now, aiyya. I myself saw thousands of huge war elephants in the Vatapi army. The Pallava army has not more than a hundred war elephants. Despite this, do you know how we have prevented the Vatapi army from advancing beyond the North Pennai River? The Pandavas owe their victory in the Bharata War to Lord Krishna's razor-sharp mind and Arjuna's skill with the bow. Both Lord Krishna and Arjuna have together incarnated as one person in Mahendra Pallavar!'

'Thambi, your devotion to the chakravarthy makes me very happy. Tell me, what message has the chakravarthy sent for me?' asked Aayanar.

Paranjyothi responded: 'Pulikesi's army has crossed the North Pennai River, aiyya. The army of Vishnuvardhanan, Pulikesi's brother, which conquered Vengi, has also joined the Vatapi army. Now it's impossible to prevent them from advancing for long. That's why the chakravarthy has sent me to prepare the Kanchi fort for the siege. The siege may continue for a year or two. So, we are going to evacuate people unnecessarily staying within the fort and also those living in villages around the fort. The chakravarthy has ordered me to seek your views on this. It is not advisable for you to stay here when the enemy army is approaching Kanchi.'

'Ah! Is the chakravarthy trying to chase me away from this forest house too? What do I care which king comes here and which king leaves this place? Who is going to come to this forest searching for me? Even if they come, are they going to abduct me? If they want to, they can take these stone statues and chisels away. If they want to, they can also scratch the paintings and remove them from the wall!'

'Aiyya, your speech reflects your anger. You speak without realizing the danger the Pallava empire is facing . . .'

'What has the chakravarthy commanded us to do?'

'You and your daughter may come and live within the Kanchi fort. Alternatively, you may go to Chola Nadu and live with your friend Namasivaya Vaidhyar for some time. If you decide to go to Thiruvengadu, he has commanded me to send you with adequate security. You may act according to your wishes,' reported Paranjyothi.

Aayanar looked around and asked, 'Sivakami, what do you wish to do?' But Sivakami was nowhere to be seen.

Chapter 7

Infant Kannan

Kannabiran had gestured to Sivakami when Aayanar and Paranjyothi were conversing. Sivakami had discreetly slipped away, unnoticed by her father and Paranjyothi.

'Anna, why did you call me? Is it something important?' she asked.

'Yes indeed!' replied Kannan.

'Did Kamali akka send me a message?'

Kannabiran lowered his tone and quipped, 'She said that the youth who is sitting with your father ought to be poisoned and killed immediately.'

Sivakami smiled as she asked, 'What kind of a joke is this, anna? Why should he be poisoned?'

'Ammani, is administering poison to someone a joke?'

'No; that's why I asked for the reason.'

'He is competing with Mamallar, thaye!'

'What is he competing for?'

'For the kingdom! Everyone is saying that the chakravarthy has adopted Paranjyothi. It is Paranjyothi who will inherit the kingdom, not Mamallar.'

'Ah! If only it were true ...'

'Thangachi, it seems that you will be extremely happy if that happens!' exclaimed Kannabiran.

'Indeed, anna! It is this kingdom that is coming between us. It would suffice if we lived for each other. What is the necessity for a kingdom?'

'All women are the same! Kamali too said the same thing.'

'What did she say?'

'She said what you just uttered. "Kanna! Isn't it enough if we live for each other? Why do you have to be employed as the kumara chakravarthy's charioteer? Come, let's go to some village and live in peace", she suggested.

'Are you going to act in accordance with her wishes, anna?'

'I too would like to do that. But the infant Kannan stands in my way.'

'Who is the infant Kannan, anna?'

Kannan winked and urged, 'Why don't you think a little harder, thangachi?'

'What do you want me to think of?' asked Sivakami.

'Despite being so intelligent, can't you figure out who the infant Kannan is?' He lowered his voice further and stated, 'Infant Kannan is in Kamali's stomach.' Kannabiran smiled embarrassedly as he uttered these words.

When Sivakami realized that Kamali was pregnant, she exclaimed, 'Is that so, anna? I'm very happy.' She felt inexplicable emotion. She felt a deep urge to see Kamali immediately and hug her.

Kannabiran remarked, 'Thangachi, it would be good if you could convey your happiness in person. Kamali cannot leave Kanchi for some time. It seems that she has a lot of news to share with you.'

'I too am eager to see akka, anna! But how is that possible?' asked Sivakami.

'True, thangachi. It's not possible. I too said this to Kamali. Will they come and stay with us in our humble hut . . .?'

'Anna! Don't say that! How can there be poverty in the place where you and Kamali live . . .? Your hut is a thousand times dearer to me than a palace . . .' As Sivakami was speaking, she suddenly paused. It seemed that a random thought had interrupted her speech.

'I will try to visit you, anna. I will tell appa . . . Is there any other news?' she asked.

'There's nothing important. It's just a small thing. This morning when I rode the chariot to the palace, Mamallar took me aside. I asked, "Prabhu! What is it?" He replied, "Nothing Kanna. I didn't sleep all night." I observed, "Your face gives the fact away. Why didn't you sleep?" He revealed, "I was speaking to the new commander." I asked, "Is that all?" He answered, "Then I wrote a message." I asked, "To whom?" He replied, "My father." I responded, "Fine." Then he slowly admitted, "I wrote another message too."'

Sivakami's voice was choked with emotion when she exclaimed, 'Anna! Give me the message!'

'I will, thangachi! I certainly will! But once you receive the message, you should not run away and put me in an awkward position . . .'

'What awkward position, anna?'

'Last time you fled as soon as Mamallar's message reached your hands. Do you know how much I suffered as a result? "What did Sivakami do on receiving the message? How did she look? How were her eyes?" When Mamallar asked these questions, I blinked ignorantly . . .'

'Stop joking, anna! Give me the message!'

Kannabiran delayed on purpose for some time and finally handed the message over to Sivakami.

Sivakami did not stand there for even a second after that. She ran down the path that was to the right of the house towards the lotus pond.

Chapter 8

The Snake Hisses

Sivakami sat on her wooden throne on the banks of the lotus pond amidst the woods. She then looked at the message she was holding close to her chest.

'Wicked message! Isn't it enough that the Pallava kumarar's love has pierced my heart? Do you have to poke me too?' As she chided thus, she reverently brought the epistle to her eyes. Hesitating for a moment, she quickly moved it to her ruby red lips. She then removed the top blank leaf of the missive. Small neat handwriting resembling pearls was now visible. Sivakami started reading the message eagerly. She was taken aback when she heard someone call out, "Akka! Akka!" from the back. She turned around and saw a green parrot sitting on the hand rest of her wooden throne, observing her intently.

Sivakami burst out laughing. Her laughter resembled the sound of anklets. She told the parrot, 'Suga Brahma Muni, what are you doing here? Can rishis be present in an anthapuram where young women reside? Why do you have to come here when a young lady is reading a message from her lover? Go away!' Saying this, Sivakami rebuffed the bird, like a young woman brushing away her lover as he tried to caress her cheeks.

Suga Muni responded aptly, 'I will not!'

Sivakami once again laughed out. 'You deceptive rishi! I don't know how, in stories, princesses spoke secrets with you around! Never mind. When I become the queen of the Pallava empire, I will ensure that you have no place in the palace . . .'

Then that mischievous Suga Muni chirped in a shrill voice, 'Mamalla! Mamalla!'

'Oh! Is that so? Are you telling me that if I were to chase you away from the palace, you will approach Mamallar to intercede? There is no use, muni! The moment Sivakami devi ascends the Pallava throne, she will banish paupers carrying begging bowls, bikshus, ochre-robe-clad sanyasis and kabalikas sporting garlands made of human skulls. Only married people who carry out their household duties conscientiously will have a place in the Pallava kingdom. Will you keep quiet till I finish reading this message . . .?'

Suga Brahmar, unable to keep quiet, called out, 'Rathi! Rathi!' Sivakami looked around. Rathi, the fawn, was running towards her.

'Rathi, you are the right companion at the anthapuram. You will listen to everything without opening your mouth. Suga Muni will not listen to anything completely. He will then say something embarrassing in the presence of others. Once this deceptive muni leaves this place for good, I will read out Mamallar's message to you, Rathi!'

Sivakami then stroked Rathi's jaw and looked at the message again. Sometimes a child with a tasty eatable in her hand is hesitant to eat it as she is scared that it will get over. Similarly Sivakami, after postponing the pleasure of reading the message, finally started reading it. The following message was written in Prakrit.

To Sivakami devi, the dear daughter of Bharata's renowned sculptor, the damsel whom the goddess of beauty bows to and lauds and the maiden who rules the heart of Mamalla Pallavan:

I had written in my previous message that I would no longer write messages to you and that I myself would come in person. I am acting in contradiction to my previous message for two reasons.

My dear! I had a dream last night, which caused my body to tremble with pleasure. The dream gave me unimaginable pleasure.

I dreamt that I was floating across the sky. In the dream, my sleep was interrupted for some unknown reason. I tried to open my eyes in vain without realizing that they were already open. As pitch-black darkness enveloped me, I felt they were closed.

As I was thinking about the darkness that was blacker than the kohl applied to your eyelids, I observed a circular beam of light appearing above me. The circle of light expanded and intensified. That golden glow came closer without hurting my eyes. When that light neared me, I realized that it was your divine countenance. Words cannot describe my amazement and joy.

Sivakami, soon I could see your entire form. As I was watching your glittering form amidst limitless darkness, a strange thought occurred to me.

It occurred to me that your form was not that of a mere mortal made of blood, flesh, bones and skin. I believe that Brahma must have created you by fusing the tender rays of the moon, the fragrance of jasmines, the delicate feathers of the swan and melodious music.

As I stood intoxicated, you came close to me. I saw your radiant countenance next to mine. Two teardrops glistened at the corners of your wide eyes like the dewdrops that settle on a water lily at dawn. Your breath caressed my face. I was longing to embrace you, who were so close to me. But I did not do so.

A doubt arose within me. I was scared that if I touched you, your body would morph into the tender rays of the moon, the fragrance of jasmines, the delicate feathers of the swan and melodious music.

It seemed as though you sensed my fear. Your red lips parted slightly and the tips of your pearly white teeth were visible as you smiled slightly! I became even more intoxicated as your lustrous form came closer.

Ah, do you know how unfortunate I was! At that time, I heard the sound of a cobra hissing in the background. I immediately turned around. Two birds perched on the branch of a tree were playfully pecking at each other's beaks. There was a black-and-yellow cobra on a lower branch of that tree, slithering its way up towards the two birds. I realized it was the hissing of this snake that I had heard. I drew out my sword, even forgetting your presence.

That was it; I woke up.

Radiant princess residing forever in my eyes! I don't believe in dreams and their interpretations. However, I often wonder what this dream implies. I am concerned if this is a warning of an impending danger you may face.

As the war is nearing Kanchi, you must be careful. But don't be scared or worried. As long as I am able to wield a sword, you and your father will face no danger.

It is almost dawn; the east is turning bright. I will give you another piece of information and conclude.

I have a new friend. Do you know who he is? He is the youth who flung his spear at the mad elephant and rescued you and your father. The chakravarthy has sent him to safeguard the fort. We were conversing a lot last night; we mostly spoke about you.

He bears a message from the chakravarthy for you and your father. You must either live within the Kanchi fort or move to Chola Nadu. But do not take any decision till I visit and discuss the matter with you.

The imminent war is good in one respect. I will soon be freed. The day of my departure from the fort may come soon. When that happens, I will immediately visit you and then attend to other tasks.

My dear! Sometimes this war and kingdom seem to be of no consequence to me. I wish all this were a dream! How happy I would be if I woke up one day and realized that I was no longer the chakravarthy's son but one of your father's disciples. Then nothing could come between us. If it were so, would I have refrained from meeting you for the last eight months?

Sivakami read the message all over again. Then she remarked, 'Rathi! Haven't I read every message that came from the Pallava kumarar to you? This time I will not! Even if I did, you would not understand.'

She climbed the magizham tree holding the message. Two feet above the ground, there was a hollow close to the branches. She put her hand into the hollow and removed seven to eight missives. She counted the old messages, placed the new one along with the others and put all of them back into the hollow. She then climbed down the tree.

'Rathi, come, let's go. Suga Brahma Rishi, please come. Let's go home. It is lunchtime; appa will be waiting for us.

Are you angry with me because I did not read Mamallar's message out to you? I will read out the message to both of you tomorrow. Why only tomorrow! As long as I live, I will read the messages out to you every day. Rathi, what do you think of the kumara chakravarthy? Suga Mamuni,* do understand that Mamallar is a great poet like Kalidasa and Bharavi. Do you know who his inspiration is? This humble sculptor's daughter, Sivakami!' Sivakami was speaking in this manner to Rathi and Suga Muni as she walked towards the house.

When Sivakami had walked away and was out of sight, Naganandi adigal emerged from his hideout. He noiselessly walked over and pulled out the missives Sivakami had hidden in the hollow of the tree. He quickly opened them and read them one by one. The deep sigh he heaved as he read the messages resembled a cobra hissing.

---

*Great saint.

Chapter 9

Rathi's Smile

Sivakami repeatedly recollected Mamallar's message, particularly the last section, and rejoiced. Didn't Mamallar say that he would rather be Aayanar's disciple than the chakravarthy's son? Ah! The son of the chakravarthy who rules one-third of this expansive Bharata Kandam was willing to give up his claim! Why? All for the sake of the daughter of Aayanar, who depended on royal largesse for his livelihood! This kingdom stood in the way of his love for her! Such a profound thought was beyond imagination.

'Rathi, no other woman in this entire universe is as fortunate as your friend Sivakami,' boasted Sivakami, holding the face of the fawn that followed her. Rathi widened her beautiful eyes and looked up at Sivakami.

'Look here, Rathi. You too are fortunate. Forget about me deriding Mamallar eight months ago. At that time I had told you, "Today he is restraining me from visiting Kamali's house. Tomorrow he will ask me not to bring Rathi along to the palace. A relationship with such aristocrats will not suit us." The very same Pallava kumarar says today, "I don't need the kingdom. It is enough if Sivakami is with me!" What he says is only fair, Rathi! Isn't it enough if we are there for each other? Why do we need a kingdom?'

Sivakami kissed Rathi's head and continued. 'Rathi, you're going to be very happy! Mamallar and I will build a thatched hut in a virgin forest and live there happily. I will chase away Suga Brahma Rishi and retain only you. You will have a lot of work to do, Rathi! You will have to act as an emissary between Mamallar and me!'

Rathi smiled through her eyes and nodded her head as if to say, 'Enough of this nonsense!' She then extricated herself from Sivakami's hands and moved away to graze.

Just then, Sivakami heard a voice calling out, 'Amma, Sivakami!' She looked around, startled. She saw Aayanar emerging from the bushes. She felt embarrassed thinking he might have heard her talking to Rathi.

But what Aayanar smilingly stated next dispelled her fears. 'My child! I was taken aback hearing you talk to someone in the middle of the forest. Were you talking to Rathi? Poor girl, what will you do? There is no one to even talk to you in this place. You are finding it difficult to spend your time here. At Kanchi, your friend Kamali gave you company . . .'

As Aayanar approached Sivakami talking in this manner, she hugged him. She then hesitantly remarked, 'Appa, do you know? Kamali . . . Kamali . . .'

An agitated Aayanar asked, 'What happened to Kamali? Is she unwell?'

Sivakami teased, 'Yes, appa! Kamali is unwell,' and burst out laughing.

Seeing this, Aayanar realized there was nothing to be concerned about. He asked, 'Then what is it, Sivakami? Did she send a message that she would be coming here?'

Sivakami replied, 'No, appa,' and then whispered into his ears, 'Kamali is bearing infant Kannan in her stomach!'

Aayanar understood the matter, tenderly hugged his daughter and remarked, 'I am so happy! I gave my blessings during Sivakami's marriage . . .'

'Appa, when did your dear daughter get married?' asked Sivakami.

Aayanar realized that he had inadvertently said Sivakami instead of Kamali. He stated in embarrassment, 'What did I say, my dear? Did I mention Sivakami's marriage? So what? You will also get married one day. What I meant to say was that I had blessed Kamali during her marriage that a son should soon be born to her and he must learn sculpting from me.'

After saying this, Aayanar lapsed into silence. He started thinking about Sivakami's marriage. He was reminded of his intention to get her married to Paranjyothi, who was was now a famous warrior and the commander of the fort. Would he consent to marrying a mere sculptor's daughter?

Sivakami asked, 'Appa, what are you thinking of?'

He responded, 'Nothing, my dear! Where did you disappear when Paranjyothi and I were talking? The chakravarthy has sent an important message through him. I looked for you to get your opinion. Come let's go home and discuss it at length. Your athai must be wondering where we have disappeared to without having lunch!'

Both of them walked down the narrow path in silence. Aayanar was thinking about Sivakami's future. Sivakami's heart, like a bee that swarms around the honeysuckle, was hovering around Mamallar's messages in the hollow of the magizham tree.

Chapter 10

Blissful Dancing

'Appa, it's been a long time since I danced. Shall I dance today?' asked Sivakami.

Both of them were sitting on a rock under a tree that lay at a short distance from the house. Under the tree adjacent to them lay the mortar and pestles, stove and utensils to prepare colour dyes.

Aayanar looked in amazement at Sivakami.

'What happened today, my child? Your face is glowing,' he enquired.

Sivakami, taken aback, was unable to respond. She then admitted that she had been feeling happy ever since she had heard about Kamali. 'Appa! Shall we go to Kanchi and visit Kamali?' she asked. Then, realizing her mistake, she bit her tongue. 'What was the message the chakravarthy sent us?' she asked.

'It seems that the enemy forces have crossed the North Pennai River. They may lay siege to Kanchi. It seems that the chakravarthy has asked us to either move to Kanchi or to Chola Nadu. What do you say, amma?'

'What do I have to say, appa? What do I know? Do as you wish . . .'

'My desire is to remain here. I will not be at peace if I leave this forest house,' admitted Aayanar.

'I too feel that way, appa! Shall we continue to live here?' asked Sivakami.

Mamallar had written to her asking them not to take any decision till he visited them, and Sivakami had this in mind when she spoke to her father.

She was also extremely eager to visit Kanchi and meet Kamali, but she was reminded of the message Mamallar had sent her eight months ago, after she had visited Navukkarasar at Kanchi. The Pallava kumarar had written, 'My heart bleeds when I think of you—who ought to be lying down in the nila muttram* of the palace, under a pearl-embedded silk canopy on a jasmine-strewn golden bed—sleeping on the floor of my charioteer's house on a mat!' This demonstrated not only his tender love for Sivakami, but also indicated that he did not appreciate her staying at Kannabiran's house.

Reading this message, Sivakami battled between her kinship with Kamali and her ardent love for the Pallava kumarar. Finally, it was love that won.

'Ah! What kind of a woman am I? After daring to fall in love with a world-renowned sovereign's son, how can I behave in a manner that affects his stature?' Regretting her action, she decided not to go to Kanchi without knowing the Pallava kumarar's preference. This was another reason why she spoke as she did.

---

*Loosely translated as moonlit courtyard

Aayanar responded in a worried tone, 'But Mahendra chakravarthy is an astute man. What if we encounter peril after flouting his command? There is no one to turn to for advice. Wouldn't it be good if Naganandi adigal were here? He left eight months ago and has not yet returned. I wonder what happened to the bikshu.'

Understanding Aayanar's dejected state of mind, Sivakami in an attempt to enthuse him asked, 'Appa, it's a long time since I danced. I will dance today; will you watch?'

A voice asked, 'May I also watch Sivakami dance?'

Both of them turned around together. Naganandi adigal was standing some distance away.

'Buddham saranam gacchami, dharmam saranam gacchami, sangam saranam gacchami.'

When Naganandi completed his chanting, Aayanar remarked, 'Adigal! Welcome! Welcome! Elders say that God appears when you think of him and blesses you. Like God, you too have come here.'

'Is that so? Were you reminded of this ochre-clad mortal? Did Sivakami also condescend to utter my name? No one is more fortunate than me if that were the case. Aayanar, your daughter's fame has spread far and wide across the nation. I had been to Thiruvadhigai, Thillai, Uraiyur, Vanchi, Nagai, Madurai and Korkai harbour. Sivakami's fame preceded me in all these places. When people realized that I had come from Kanchi, they enquired about Sivakami's prowess in Bharatanatyam. Bikshus, Samana monks, Saivite elders, Vaishnavite devotees, the Uraiyur Chola king and Chinese monks visiting Nagapattinam enquired about Sivakami. Aayanar, you are fortunate to have the very embodiment of art as your daughter . . .'

Aayanar and Sivakami were dumbfounded as the bikshu effusively showered praise. Naganandi finally concluded saying, 'Oh great sculptor, during the last eight months Sivakami must have become even more proficient in dancing. Today, will I have the fortune to watch the queen, whom the the southern country lauds, dance?'

Sivakami's opinion of Naganandi changed to some extent after he showered this praise on her. So when Aayanar asked, 'Will you dance, amma?' Sivakami immediately acquiseced.

When the three of them reached home, Sivakami changed into her dancing costume and stood ready to dance. A newfound joy was evident in her face and body. Mamallar's loving words and Naganandi's praise had made her glow. Sivakami started dancing to the beat Aayanar chanted.

There was no music in the chanting, no meaning and no abhinayams to demonstrate emotions. Only the joyous exuberance of dance prevailed, radiating from every organ of her body and from every movement of hers.

Ah! There were so many different types of movement in that joyous dance. Ananda nrityam! The stately gait of an elephant, the amorous gait of a horse, the sprightly gait of a deer, the bewitching gait of a peacock and the graceful gait of a swan—they all featured in Sivakami's dancing.

After some time, it did not seem as though Sivakami was dancing at all. She appeared to have lost all consciousness and was immersed in an ocean of joy. Aayanar too had lost all sense of time and had reached a timeless state of mind.

Chapter 11

Cowardly Pallavan

Fortunately, there was one person who was not completely spellbound when Sivakami was dancing. Needless to say, it was Naganandi bikshu.

'Enough, Aayanar! Stop! Sivakami's mortal body cannot withstand her passionate dancing anymore. Neither will the world withstand this.' Hearing Naganandi speak, Aayanar came back to reality and stopped chanting the thalams. Sivakami also stopped dancing.

The bikshu exclaimed, 'Aayanar, you are treacherous. How can you conceal such divine talent in the middle of the forest? Your behaviour is similar to that of a miser who locks a priceless gem he possesses in a chest! An illuminated lamp should be placed in the middle of a hall. If you keep the lamp in a corner and cover it with a cloth, not only will the lamp get extinguished, but the cloth too will be burnt. The world will be enthralled by your daughter's talent. The world is waiting to watch her dance. Please pay heed to what I say.

Let us go to Thillai. Let Sivakami dance there like Parvati, who competed with Paramasivan. But Sivakami will not lose like Parvati. Lord Nataraja will lose in the first instance. He will lower his raised leg to the ground and relax.

'From Thillai, let's go to Nagapattinam. A large sangam of bikshus is convening at Nagapattinam. Buddhists from Kanyakubja, Kashi, Kailai, Javaha Islands and China will be participating in this sangam. Expert sculptors, music maestros and dance exponents from all over the world are congregating there. Allow your daughter to dance at that sangam. Both she and you, who gave birth to her, will become world renowned. From Nagapattinam, let's proceed to Uraiyur. It is true that, today, the glory of the Uraiyur Cholas has diminished and that they are vassals of the Pallavas. But they are descendants of an ancient and prestigious clan. They are connoisseurs of art. The Chola prince, Parthiban, is a proficient painter. He will be extremely happy when he sees Sivakami's dance performance. We will then take Sivakami to Siddhar mountains to visit the monks, and then go to Madurai. Maravarma Pandian recently passed away and his son Sadaiyavarman has ascended the throne. Sadaiyavarman is a great admirer of the arts. If Sadaiyavarma Pandian watches Sivakami dance, he will not leave you desolate in this forest house. He will make you stay in the best of the Madurai palaces and honour you . . .'

Aayanar and Sivakami were hypnotized by Naganandi's speech, like snakes mesmerized by the music from a snake charmer's magudi.

When Naganandi finally asked, 'What do you say, Aayanar?' Aayanar did not know what to say. He was thinking, 'The chakravarthy's command and Naganandi's views are so similar.' Yet, he felt an inexplicable reluctance.

He remarked, 'I have nothing to say. I have to ask Sivakami,'. Aayanar looked towards Sivakami.

In her mind's eye, Sivakami saw herself visiting Chidambaram, Nagapattinam, Uraiyur and Madurai, dancing before thousands of people and being applauded by them. But she too felt a hesitation she was unable to comprehend.

So when Aayanar sought her opinion, she replied, 'What do I know, appa? Please decide in the manner you deem fit.'

Naganandi asked, 'Well, Aayanar, how is your work progressing? I don't see new sculptures of dance postures. Haven't you sculpted even one statue since the time I visited you last?'

Aayanar admitted in a wistful tone, 'No, it has been ages since I even touched the chisel.'

'Why? What crime did the art of sculpture commit? Why should the foremost sculptor of the southern country not touch the chisel?' asked the bikshu.

Sivakami interjected saying, 'It's all because of you, adigal! Appa is keen to find out the secret of the Ajantha colour dyes. For the last seven months he has been collecting various kinds of green leaves and grinding them.'

'Ah! Unnecessary work! Haven't I promised you that I will find out the secret at any cost and share it with you?'

Aayanar asked impatiently, 'It's true, you had promised. But there are no signs of your fulfilling it. Your sending a message was of no use. Haven't you heard that Paranjyothi has joined the army and has become a famous commander?'

'I heard so too. It seems he came to Kanchi only yesterday.'

'Yes, that boy had come here this morning. It seems that the chakravarthy has sent him to safeguard the Kanchi fort. My god! He has changed so much in the last eight months.

When he came with you he was so humble, shy and tongue-tied. Today, he is so proud and haughty!'

'Appa, he was not arrogant at all. His behaviour towards you was so deferential. He hesitated so much even as he communicated the chakravarthy's command,' interjected Sivakami.

'Aayanar, may I know what the chakravarthy's command is?' asked the bikshu.

'He has commanded us to leave this house! Mahendra Pallavar used to be so appreciative of sculptures. I thought so highly of him,' complained Aayanar in a forlorn tone.

'I thought lightly of your chakravarthy—his intelligence is evident only now. Aayanar, do you know the kind of activities your chakravarthy has indulged in? The strength of the Pallava army does not exceed fifty thousand warriors. With this minuscule force at his disposal, he has managed to restrain the ocean-like Vatapi army on the banks of the North Pennai River for eight months. Mahendra Pallavar is extremely astute, Aayanar! Never mind! What did Paranjyothi say about the task for which he was sent? Didn't you enquire about that?' questioned the bikshu.

'Would I not have asked? That poor boy faced great danger on the way. Apparently, the Chalukya warriors captured him. He somehow managed to escape from them. Fortunately, when he was imprisoned he threw the missive into the river that flowed through the mountain ravine.'

'He is not only intelligent but also lucky! When I saw him for the first time sleeping under a tree by the highway, I realized that he was very lucky. But I had anticipated that he would be lucky in a different sense. Ah, I have committed a great mistake!' acknowledged Naganandi, sighing slightly.

'Adigal, I don't see how luck has not favoured Paranjyothi now.'

'You don't know, Aayanar. He could have been far more fortunate. But due to some unfavourable planetary position ...'

'Thank god! This fortune is adequate. If he gets any luckier, it will go to the boy's head!' retorted Aayanar. As Paranjyothi had returned without ascertaining the secret of the Ajantha paints, Aayanar had begun loathing him.

Sivakami interrupted, saying, 'Appa! Appa! Did you hear this news? It seems that Mahendra Chakravarthy may anoint Paranjyothi instead of Mamallar as his successor. The charioteer Kannabiran stated that the people were talking in this manner.' Dimples appeared in her cheeks as she laughed heartily.

'Who, Kannabiran? Ignore him, he is crazy! He keeps blabbering like this,' opined Aayanar.

Then Naganandi remarked, 'No, Aayanar, that's not so! Kannabiran was not blabbering. I will not be surprised if things pan out in the manner he described. The valorous Mahendra Pallavar may have decided that it is better to give the kingdom to Paranjyothi rather than instating a cowardly Pallavan on the throne.'

Chapter 12

The Storm Within

When Sivakami heard the words 'cowardly Pallavan', she felt as though lightning had unexpectedly struck her head and that its effect was transmitted throughout her body.

Aayanar was also taken aback and he asked, 'Adigal, what are you saying? Who are you referring to as "cowardly Pallavan"?'

'The entire world knows of the cowardly Pallavan. He is discussed in towns and villages, don't you know? But you reside in the middle of the forest! You probably don't know!' shot back the bikshu.

'What is it that I don't know? Who are the people talking about in this manner? I find this mysterious!' exclaimed Aayanar.

'There is no mystery. Why shouldn't I tell you something the whole world knows? I am referring to the Kumara Chakravarthy Narasimha Pallavan, who bears the title 'Mamallan'. The entire world knows that he is very cowardly and is a weakling. When Mamallan initially heard that the Vatapi army was invading the Pallava empire, it seems that he started shivering and then fainted. At that time, he was at the palace anthapuram surrounded by women. The chakravarthy was extremely embarrassed. Aayanar, why do you think Mamallar did not accompany the chakravarthy to the battlefield? Why did Mahendrar leave for the battlefield after sequestering Mamallar in the Kanchi fort?'

'Oh, wicked bikshu! How can you say such defamatory things? What you're saying is slanderous! Aren't you embarrassed to talk in this manner about someone who vanquished all the renowned wrestlers in the south and won the title Mamallar before he was eighteen years old?' asked Aayanar angrily.

'Great sculptor, I didn't know you were so ignorant. These are matters that concern royalty; why should we worry? Nevertheless, since you don't believe my words, I will explain. The title "Maha Mallan" is fabricated. All the wrestlers who were supposed to combat with Narasimha Varman were commanded to lose even before the contest began. The chakravarthy tried to infuse valour and courage in his son by resorting to such acts. Poor man! It was of no use! When he heard of the war, he was shaken. Narasimha Varman is an incarnation of Utthara Kumaran. Do you know why the chakravarthy has arranged for Bharata mandapams to be built across the country and the Mahabharata to be read there? This was done keeping his dear son in mind . . .!'

'Adigal, stop! I cannot bear to hear such disparaging remarks about the kumara chakravarthy,' protested Aayanar.

'I wonder how you will react if you heard more details about him. But I don't want to mention those things in your daughter's presence,' said Naganandi, looking towards Sivakami.

When Sivakami was around seven to eight years old, she had placed her hand in a bee hive. The bees had stung her all over her body. For an entire day, she had experienced intense pain. Sivakami's anguish when she listened to Naganandi's disparaging remarks about Narasimha Varmar was a thousand times greater than the pain she had felt when the bees had stung her. The impact of every word that the bikshu uttered was akin to molten lead being poured into her ears.

When the bikshu said, 'But I don't want to mention those things in your daughter's presence,' she realized that it was an opportune moment and stood up. Without looking in their direction, she entered the second courtyard of the house.

Seeing Sivakami's feet, adorned with red dye, from under the door, the bikshu said the following in a loud voice.

'Aayanar! Not only is your daughter a great artist but she is also very well-mannered. Look how she walked away in an instant. What I was about to say was that the chakravarthy was worried about his son on another count. In the Pallava dynasty, no one has been as great a womanizer as him at such a young age. Apparently, an erotic message written by Mamallan to a woman fell into the chakravarthy's hands. The chakravarthy forbade Mamallan from leaving the Kanchi fort keeping all this in mind . . .'

As Naganandi was speaking thus, the feet that had been visible from under the door disappeared. Then Naganandi resumed speaking in a low voice.

Sivakami fled to the backyard of the house as though she were being chased by a thousand ghosts. She ran aimlessly into the forest. She continued running till she was tired and then sat on the prop root of a tree.

The parrot and the fawn followed Sivakami. She did not notice them. After some time, Rathi came close to her and placed her nose gently in her hands. Sivakami pushed Rathi away shrieking, 'Get lost! You despicable creature!'

Oblivious to the situation, Suga Rishi stupidly chanted, 'Mamalla! Mamalla!' Sivakami scolded the parrot and raised her hand to hit it. The parrot flapped its wings and flew away, escaping Sivakami's blow.

She was suddenly reminded of the messages in the hollow of the magizham tree on the banks of the lotus pond. She ran towards the lotus pond, intending to incinerate the messages to ashes by setting fire to them. She quickly reached the pond, stood on the wooden plank-seat, and put her hand into the tree hollow.

Oh no! Was there a cobra in the hollow that bit her? Why was there such a horrified expression on her face? Why did she remove her hand in such a rush? Why did she climb up and look intently into the hollow?

The reason was that the hollow of the tree was empty!

Where could the messages, which had been there in the hollow that morning, have disappeared to?

The bikshu too rushed to the lotus pond. He observed, from across the pond, Sivakami putting her hand into the hollow of the tree and failing to find the messages there. Naganandi Adigal was taken aback by the shock and fear evident on Sivakami's face.

Chapter 13

Shatrugnan's Story

At the Pallava war camp on the banks of the Papagni River, seated in a tent atop which the rishabha flag fluttered majestically, was Mahendra chakravarthy. His personal spy, Shatrugnan, was standing in front of him. It was evident that Shatrugnan had travelled a long distance. He was drenched in sweat. His appearance had changed beyond recognition during the last eight months.

The chakravarthy stared at him and asked, 'Is it Shatrugnan?'

'It's me, Pallavendra!'

'You look very different!'

'Yes, prabhu. No matter how much difficulty I face in your service, my body becomes stronger!'

'No, I meant that you have become thinner. I recollect assigning an important task to you eight months ago. Do you remember the task?' asked Mahendrar.

'I remember it very well, prabhu. No other thoughts distract me,' stated Shatrugnan.

'It was I who forgot! Please remind me,' remarked the chakravarthy.

'You had asked me to shadow the bikshu.'

'Oh! Then?'

'You asked me to appoint someone to watch Aayanar.'

'Is that all?'

'You had given me another difficult task, prabhu. You had commanded me to monitor the kumara chakravarthy's movements!'

'Yes! Yes! I remember that.'

'You had asked me to send any important message through a trustworthy person. If the message were extremely important, you had asked me to come myself.'

'So it seems that you have brought extremely important news.'

'Yes, Pallavendra. It was a message that could not be sent through anyone else. So I came myself.'

'Tell me everything, one by one.'

Shatrugnan first reported what he had come to know by shadowing Naganandi.

After sending Paranjyothi along with a message to Nagarjuna mountain, Naganandi had headed southwards. Shatrugnan had followed him. He had reached a viharam located amidst a dense forest and surrounded by small hills on the banks of the Kedil River. Naganandi had then conveyed a message to some of the bikshus there and sent them in all four directions. It came to be known that one of them had gone to Uraiyur and another had reached Thalaikkadu, the capital of the Kanga kingdom.

Then, Naganandi had travelled further southwards.
He had crossed the Kollidam and Kaveri rivers and reached
Nagapattinam. From there, he had gone to Madurai. When
Naganandi and Shatrugnan reached Madurai, Maravarma
Pandian had been extremely sick and on his deathbed.
His successor had commanded that all foreigners be imprisoned.
Naganandi and Shatrugnan had happened to be in the same
prison cell. There, he had befriended the bikshu. When they
were in prison, Maravarman had passed away and Sadaiyavarman
had ascended the throne. Then both of them were released.
Naganandi had met the new Pandya king and had parleyed with
him for several days. Amidst this, emissaries who had gone to
Kanchi carrying a marriage proposal for Mamallar had returned
to Madurai. Once again, Naganandi and Sadaiyavarman had
held talks, after which the Pandian had commanded that an
army be mobilized from across the country.

Naganandi had left Madurai and travelled northwards.
Shatrugnan had accompanied him. On the way, it had seemed
as though Naganandi was immersed in deep thought. They
had crossed the Kaveri and Kollidam rivers and reached the
viharam at Kedil. By then, Shatrugnan had begun wondering
whether Naganandi had realized that he was a spy. At that
time, a young bikshu who used to be at the Kanchi royal
viharam was present at the Kedil viharam. The young bikshu
had kept staring at Shatrugnan, confirming his suspicions.
So when the young bikshu offered him dinner, Shatrugnan
had not eaten it immediately but had dropped some food
into the river. He observed that the fish that ate the food had
immediately turned blue and their dead bodies had floated
to the top of the river. That night, unnoticed by Naganandi
and the young bikshu, he had conducted a reconnaissance of
the viharam and the hills surrounding it. He had observed

that a lot of weapons lay amassed in the concealed caves in the hills. As he went around the hills, he had heard a scary hissing noise, and his heart had almost stopped! Despite his best efforts, he had been unable to find out where the noise had come from.

The next day at dawn, the bikshu had left the secluded viharam and proceeded northwards, crossing an ocean-like dam called Thiru Paarkadal on the way. Unknown to the bikshu, Shatrugnan had followed him. Finally, Naganandi adigal had reached Aayanar's forest residence.

Shatrugnan had appointed a man named Gundodharan to watch Aayanar during his absence. Gundodharan had become Aayanar's disciple, learning sculpture and painting from him; he had stayed with Aayanar at his house. Gundodharan had no special news to report. He only informed him that the charioteer Kannabiran and his wife Kamali had visited Aayanar's house a few times.

Shatrugnan had arranged for Kannabiran's father to monitor Mamallar's movements. He reported that Narasimha Varmar had obeyed the chakravarthy's orders completely. For the last eight months, Mamallar had not left the Kanchi fort. He had been fully absorbed in readying the fort for the impending siege.

After Shatrugnan finished relating the above information, the chakravarthy observed, 'Shatrugna! You have executed my orders excellently. Is this all the news you have? Looking at your face, it seems there is some other important news!'

'Yes, prabhu. I found a few messages. I brought them along personally so that no one but you gets to see them.'

'Messages? What messages?' asked a surprised chakravarthy as he extended his hand.

'Pallavendra, please forgive me if I have committed a mistake ...'

'You fool! Have you intercepted the message that Pulikesi sent to Durvineethan?' roared the chakravarthy angrily as he leapt up from his seat.

'No, Pallavendra! Please forgive me. The messages are not war-related!'

'Thank god! I thought that you had stupidly intervened and messed things up. Which messages are you referring to?'

'Pallavendra, I have brought along messages professing love.'

'Ah!' exclaimed a surprised chakravarthy as he sat down. His eyebrows knotted and creases appeared on his forehead. 'Give me the messages. I'll read them,' he commanded. Shatrugnan removed his turban and took the bunch of eight missives from it. He hesitantly handed them over to the chakravarthy. Mahendrar took the missives and, holding them, was pensive for some time.

Then he admitted, 'Shatrugna! Nothing can be more excruciating than ruling a kingdom. I have to indulge in this base act for the good of the kingdom! I am about to commit the heinous crime of tearing open Narasimhan's child like heart.'

Chapter 14

Mahendrar's Mistake

When Mahendrar read the messages Shatrugnan had given him, his hands started trembling. He read the first few messages slowly. He read the remaining ones rapidly.

Finally he told Shatrugnan in a sad tone, 'Shatrugna, you ought not to have brought these and given them to me.'

'Pallavendra, please forgive me!' replied Shatrugnan.

'You are not at fault, Shatrugna. You do not have to apologize for performing your duty. How could you know that your act would cause me so much sorrow? In the palace garden sprouted a beautiful flowering shrub. In the middle of the forest grew an exquisite flowering creeper. As they grew, they developed tender buds. When they attained youth, they were in full bloom. I am now dutybound to uproot the shrub and the creeper and set them on fire. Shatrugna, it is evident from the epistles you have brought that this duty is so vicious . . .'

Mahendra Pallavar repeatedly sighed and then asked, 'Shatrugna, do you know how much hurt I will cause to

Narasimhar's tender heart? Listen to this.' He then read the following extract from one of the messages.

'My dear! My life, body and soul are eager to come and meet you. Even if I were incarcerated in a place where the security is a hundred times greater than that of the Kanchi fort, I would overcome all obstacles and fly across to meet you. Even if someone were to imprison you in an island in the middle of the sea, like Ravana imprisoned Sita, I would come there looking for you. Even if Indra were to imprison you in Svarga Loka or if Virudhirasuran imprisoned you in Pathala Loka, they could not prevent me from meeting you. But I am facing an obstacle that far exceeds these; it is my father's command. Mahendra Pallavar has commanded me not to leave the Kanchi fort till further orders, Sivakami.

'If there is one thing in this world I am incapable of doing, it is flouting my father's command. Even if Lord Shiva were to appear in front of me and ask me to contravene my father's orders, I will never do so. Do you know why my father, to whom I am so devoted, has subjected me to so much cruelty? He has prevented me from meeting my two lovers, who are dearer to me than my life. One of my two lovers is the daughter of the sculptor Aayanar, Sivakami. I want to meet her all alone on the banks of the lotus pond in the middle of the forest. Do you know who my other lover is? May I mention her name? If I tell you, you should not feel envious. Her name is the goddess of victory, Jayalakshmi. I am keen to meet my second lover on a blood-soaked battlefield. I want to come and meet you after she garlands me with victory!'

As Mahendrar read, Shatrugnan stood with his head bowed, looking at the ground.

'Did you hear that, Shatrugna? I am so fortunate to have given birth to a son like him. Am I not more fortunate than Rama's father, Dasaratha? What was so great about Rama's sacrifice? He gave up the throne and went to the forest with Sita and Lakshmanan. Is it surprising that Rama preferred strolling around the forest over ruling a kingdom? But doesn't restraining oneself from going to the battlefield to obey a father's command require a hundred times more resolve than going to the forest? Not going to see your first love calls for a thousand times greater strength of character. I feel extremely happy that Narasimhan has emerged successfully from such a harsh test. But I, who put him to the test, stand summarily defeated. I had thought that if Narasimhan and Sivakami were separated, Narasimhan would be able to escape Sivakami's web of love. It is so appropriate to compare love with fire, Shatrugna! While a gust of wind can extinguish a weak fire, that very wind will fan and intensify a strong fire. I think the relationship between separation and love is akin to that of wind and fire. Infatuation subsides on account of separation. True love intensifies over a period of separation and smoulders like an inferno! This is true in Narasimhan's case. It seems as though Kama Deva will bring my elaborate plans to naught using one of his flower arrows. Shatrugna, it is acceptable to lose to the Vatapi emperor. Can Mahendra Pallavan afford to be defeated by the mere flowers of Manmadan? Never!' Saying this, Mahendra Chakravarthy laughed again. His laughter echoed with joy.

'I am changing my command to Narasimhan this very instant. Shatrugna, the communiqué I am going to give you should reach Kanchi at the speed of wind and thought. Durvineethan's army is advancing towards Kanchi from Thalaikkadu. Let Narasimhan proceed to the battlefield to combat that army and decimate it. Narasimhan may visit Aayanar's house and meet Sivakami before going to war. I am not going stand in the way!'

Hearing this, Shatrugnan smiled inexplicably, seeming to enquire, 'Are you enacting your deceptive plays even with me?'

Chapter 15

The Parrot and the Kite

'Kamali'

'Kanna!'

'Nothing is interesting anymore!'

'Why is that so?'

'The new commander's good fortune infuriates me.'

'What is the use of getting angry? He has been recognized as the bravest amongst the brave, thanks to his deeds on the warfront.'

'I too am eager to proceed to the warfront.'

'Who stopped you from doing so?'

'Who else? It was Mamallar! I regret being Mamallar's charioteer. It is because of him that I'm also incarcerated in the fort.'

'As if you would have engaged in astonishing heroics hadn't you been his charioteer!'

'Anyway, Mamallar is bound to go to the warfront one day. Then no one can stop me! If I die as a brave warrior in the war, will you tell our little Kannan about me?'

'Sure! Sure! I will tell Kannamal that when it comes to championing bravery while sitting at home, you are peerless in the entire Pallava kingdom.'

'What did you say? Kannamal?'

'Yes! Why can't it be Kannamal?'

'Enough! I am convinced that no more women should be born on earth. Never.'

'True! God ought not to have created women in a world inhabited by men who are such blockheads. You are incapable of even understanding the difficulties you put us through.'

'This is a baseless accusation, Kamali! How have we caused you difficulty?'

'Didn't you mention some time ago that you would go to war and that I should comfortably stay at home? Wouldn't that trouble me? Mamallar has not visited my sister Sivakami for the last eight months. Wouldn't that upset Sivakami?'

'You're always concerned about your sister. You don't think of anything else.'

'Yes, Kanna! For the last few days, I have been thinking only of her. The more I think about her, the sadder I feel. I wonder why Sivakami had to fall in love with Mamallar. Parrots should live with parrots and cuckoos should live with cuckoos. How can a parrot living on the branches of a tree aspire to marry a kite soaring in the sky?'

'What is this, Kamali? Why are you talking like this? It was you who insisted a few days ago that your sister is peerless and that emperors would die to fall at her feet!'

'Yes, Kanna. I said so out of love for my sister. Affection clouds your intellect, doesn't it? When you sit back and think about it, you realize that no good will come out of this relationship. I ought not to have spoken supportively to Sivakami and fanned her desire. You also committed the mistake of delivering Mamallar's messages to her ...'

'How did this enlightenment dawn on you?' asked Kannan mockingly.

'Don't you shamelessly refer to the little Kannan? It is only after I started bearing him in my stomach!' Kamali retorted.

'What is this, Kamali? What is the connection between your sister marrying Mamallar and little Kannan? I don't understand!' Kannabiran burst out laughing.

'Are you done with laughing, Kanna!'

'Yes!'

'In that case, respond to my query! Why did the chakravarthy command Mamallar not to leave the Kanchi fort?'

'What is so surprising, Kamali? There is no secret in this. Isn't Mamallar Mahendra chakravarthy's only son? He commanded thus to protect his heir from the perils on the battlefield. Everyone knows that this is the chakravarthy's command to the Ministers' Council ...'

'Does a person have to hide in the fort in order to be safe, Kanna? Is Mamallar such a coward? Is he incompetent? Or is he a naïve child?'

'I can only think of this reason. If you know the actual reason, why don't you tell me, Kamali?'

'Shall I tell you? The chakravarthy somehow got wind of Mamallar's love for Sivakami. He does not want this love to grow. As Mamallar is bound to visit Sivakami if he goes outside the fort, he commanded Mamallar to stay within the fort.'

'In that case, it seems that your Mahendra chakravarthy has not understood our Mamallar. Is it so easy to change Mamallar's mind, Kamali?'

'You are not aware of Mahendra chakravarthy's crafty capabilities, Kanna! The entire world knows that once he sets his mind on a goal he will achieve it by hook or by crook.'

'But even the chakravarthy is very fond of your sister, Kamali! Why should he prohibit Mamallar from seeing her?'

'Stupid Kanna! It is one thing to be fond of the sculptor Aayanar's daughter. It is another thing to get her married to the kumara chakravarthy. Think of all the complications that would arise when my sister bears a male child! Now do you understand why I admitted that all these thoughts occurred to me due to little Kannan?'

'I don't understand, Kamali!' replied Kannan.

'You will never understand anything, Kanna! Since you handle horses all the time, your intellect has become akin to that of a horse!' quipped Kamali.

'Look here, Kamali! Say whatever you want about me. I will listen to it. Don't say anything about my horses! If only humans had the intellect of horses, the world would have been a better place to live in!' remonstrated Kannan.

Kannan was enraged that Kamali had spoken derogatorily of horses. He looked away without speaking. Kamali was also immersed in thought. So Kannan was forced to compose himself. 'What are you trying to say, Kamali? What stops Mamallar from marrying your sister?' he asked.

'Kanna, you have been engaged in royal service all these days. Despite this, you are unaware of royal customs. The marriages of kings and princes are not like that of commoners like you and me. Wouldn't Mamallar's son ascend the Kanchi throne one day?'

'You don't require a sharp intellect to understand this. A horse's intellect would suffice!'

'Then, why don't you use that intellect and think further! How can the son born to a sculptor's daughter ascend the Pallava throne?'

'Why not? What is the difficulty in that? The throne in our palace is not so high. I myself could lift him and seat him on the throne!'

'You are being frivolous, Kanna. Would the public consent to the sculptor Aayanar's grandson ascending the Pallava throne?'

'It is my responsibility to get the public to acquiesce, Kamali! Why don't you watch! I will whip all the citizens till they consent!'

'That's not all, Kanna. A grandson of Mahendra Pallavar's uncle is growing up at Vengipuram. Don't you know that? Wouldn't that Aditya Varma Pallavan compete for the throne?'

'He will not, Kamali! Vengipuram has been razed to the ground. Along with Vengi, Aditya Varman has also been vanquished. He will no longer compete for the throne.'

'Moreover, Mamallar is not like other crown princes! He will not marry Sivakami for love and another princess to be his queen consort. Mahendra chakravarthy understands his character well. Isn't our Mamallar, like Rama, so steadfast that he will marry only once?'

'Yes, Kamali, there is no doubt about that. In that respect Mamallar is like Rama and Kannan. I wasn't referring to the Kannan of Gokulam. He is like the Rama of Ayodhya and this Kannan of Kanchi!' When Kannan pointed to himself, Kamali burst out laughing. After pausing for some time,

Kannan asked, 'Kamali, one thing amazes me! How did you come to know of such highly confidential royal matters?'

'Everything did not occur to me, Kanna. Certain things occurred to me as I thought about these issues. I came to know of other things by eavesdropping.'

'Where did you eavesdrop? When did you eavesdrop?'

'A man had come here four to five days ago when you were not at home, Kanna. He and your father were conversing for a long time. I heard Sivakami's name being mentioned, so I stood by the corner of the wall and listened. They were discussing these issues. Also . . .'

'Also what, Kamali?'

'They also discussed another important matter.'

'Tell me!'

'Your father is aware that Mamallar is writing messages to Sivakami and that you are carrying those messages to Sivakami. He was mentioning this to that stranger!'

'Ah! That crafty fox, that fake sanyasi, that cat who pretends to be peaceful! Has he been watching me?' asked Kannabiran. It was his father whom Kannabiran was describing in such "glowing" terms! Kamali closed his mouth with her hands. 'Do you know who that new man was, Kamali?' asked Kannabiran.

'I don't know. I have never seen him before,' admitted Kamali.

At that moment, the sound of horses galloping was heard. Both Kannan and Kamali looked out through the window at the street. A man was riding a horse swiftly past their house. His face turned for a moment towards Kannan's house and then he looked ahead.

Kamali exclaimed, 'Kanna, that's him! That rider was the one who was speaking to your father the other day! Do you know who he is?'

'I do, Kamali! He is the head of the spies, Shatrugnan. He has returned after visiting Mahendra chakravarthy. He is bearing important news. I will go and find out what it is.' Saying this, Kannan left the house.

***

Within a nazhigai, a chariot came to a noisy halt in front of that house. Kannabiran jumped down from the driver's seat of the chariot and ran into Kamali as he rushed towards the kitchen. 'Why the rush?' asked Kamali.

'Why the rush? It's the rush to get to the battlefield!' Kannabiran revealed.

Exclaiming, 'What! Are you going to the battlefield?' Kamali sprinted towards Kannan and embraced him.

'Yes, Kamali! The head of the spies, Shatrugnan, has brought a message from Mahendra chakravarthy. The chakravarthy has now consented to Mamallar proceeding to the warfront. Mamallar is leaving in another half nazhigai. Kamali . . .'

'Are you leaving too, Kanna? Truly?'

'What kind of a question is this, Kamali? If Mamallar goes to war, how can I not accompany him?'

'Mamallar is the only son of the chakravarthy; he will ascend the Pallava throne one day. It is necessary for him to wage wars. Why do you have to go? Why should we be concerned about politics?'

'What is this, Kamali? Till yesterday, you never spoke in this manner. When our motherland is in danger, how can we remain at home, unconcerned? The Pallava kingdom is facing dangerous times, Kamali. Pulikesi is advancing from the north, at the head of a gargantuan army. The chakravarthy is impeding the advance of that army. Meanwhile, the king of Ganga Nadu seems to be in a hurry. He is coming from the west with a large army, eager to reach Kanchi before Pulikesi does. Do you know the name of the king of Ganga Nadu, Kamali? Durvineethan! It seems that he is an incarnation of Duryodhanan! Mamallar is leaving to confront this Durvineethan, and I will also go, Kamali. The opportunity I was yearning for all these days has now come. Please bid farewell to me whole heartedly and cheerfully!'

'Kanna, what can I do? I somehow do not feel happy. I feel even more depressed when I think of my sister, Sivakami. I wonder what fate has in store for her.'

'Ah! I omitted to convey an important matter. Didn't you raise all kinds of doubts about Mahendra chakravarthy, Kamali? Do you know what the chakravarthy has written in his message? He has asked Mamallar to meet Aayanar and Sivakami before proceeding to the battlefield and to send them to the Kanchi fort. I will probably bring them here in my chariot. What do you now have to say about Mahendra Pallavar, Kamali? Is he a good man or a wicked one?' asked Kannabiran proudly, his head held aloft.

'I hope everything ends well. Kanna, you too should return unhurt from the battlefield!' When Kamali stated this, tears welled up in her eyes.

Chapter 16

Preparations for the Siege

Even as Kannabiran and Kamali were arguing, Mahendra Pallavar's queen consort, Bhuvana Mahadevi, Mamalla Narasimhar and Commander Paranjyothi were engaged in serious discussion in the front hall at the entrance of the anthapuram.

'Devi, the kumara chakravarthy has been complaining about being confined within the fort for the last eight months. He has no reason to complain. I have inspected the fort's ramparts and the city. He has more or less renovated the Kanchi fort. Even if Devendran and Virudhirasuran together invade the Kanchi fort, they will not be able to enter. The kings of Vatapi and Thalaikadu—Pulikesi and Durvineethan—are bound to fail,' complimented Commander Paranjyothi.

'What has Narasimhan done to bolster the fortress? It is you who have to tell me, Paranjyothi. Narasimhan does not tell me anything. He thinks that a helpless woman confined to the anthapuram will be ignorant of war-related matters,' remarked Mahendra Pallavar's queen consort.

'Amma, are you truly a helpless woman confined to the anthapuram? In fact, I feel much more helpless being confined! I never imagined that Mahendra Pallavar would cheat me in this manner!' Saying this, Mamallar clenched his fists.

'My child, don't blame your father. Caution and foresight characterize his words and actions—'

Paranjyothi interrupted Bhuvana Mahadevi saying, 'True, devi! I swear that no one in the entire universe is endowed with the razor-sharp intellect and foresight that Mahendra chakravarthy possesses!'

'Have you both teamed up? In that case, I will join you. There is no doubt that Mahendra chakravarthy acts with foresight. But his father, Maharaja Simha Vishnu, was endowed with even greater foresight. That is why he crowned Durvineethan's father. He personally went to Ganga Desam and crowned Durvineethan's father! Isn't Durvineethan's gratitude evident in his actions now? Like a fox interrupting the combat between two lions, he has chosen to invade the Pallava kingdom when Pulikesi is attacking us! Durvineethan is hurriedly advancing towards us, without even halting at night! Despite being aware of this, I have to remain confined within this fort! My blood boils when you speak of the chakravarthy's razor-sharp intellect and foresight!' As Mamallar spoke, his eyes reddened with anger.

'My child, don't feel disheartened. I too am enraged with the Gangapadi king's ungrateful and treacherous act. What can be done? The right time has to come,' counselled Bhuvana Mahadevi.

'Devi, there is no doubt that the chakravarthy would have planned to punish Durvineethan appropriately,' remarked Commander Paranjyothi.

'The chakravarthy will not only have planned, he will also execute the plan. But where is the necessity for me, who bears the titles Yuva Maharaja, Kumara Chakravarthy and Mamallar? Amma, if there is someone who is inferior even to Utthara Kumaran in the Mahabharata, it is me. At least Utthara Kumaran went to the battlefield and then fled. I have not even left the palace. If someone were to pen the story of our times like the Mahabharata, would he be able to laud my might and valour? Yet, both of you advise me to remain calm!' The brave Mamallar's eyes were filled with tears as he spoke thus.

Unable to face him, Paranjyothi spoke to the chakravarthini. 'Devi, it is incorrect for the Pallava kumarar to compare himself with Utthara Kumaran. What was Utthara Kumaran doing when everyone else had left for the battlefield? He spent his time watching his sister Utthara Kumari learn dancing. Mamallar did not spend his time in that manner!' As Paranjyothi spoke, all three of them were reminded of Sivakami's dancing. Mamallar's face fell.

Paranjyothi, realizing that he had committed the gross mistake of mentioning the word 'dancing' observed, 'Moreover, war has not yet begun. War of a much larger scale than the Mahabharata war is about to break out only now. The opportunities for Mamallar to perform his gallant acts will arise only now.'

'Enough! Enough! Does it matter how many wars break out? Does it matter what kinds of opportunities arise? How can you be sure that my father will not imprison me within this fort?' asked Mamallar furiously.

Understanding her son's state of mind, the mother tried to change the topic saying, 'Paranjyothi, you have not mentioned anything about Narasimhan's efforts to strengthen the fort.'

'Devi, haven't you seen the moat that surrounds our fort?'

'Yes, I saw it eight months ago. I have not stepped out of the palace ever since the chakravarthy left for war.'

'I too saw it eight months ago. Previously, it was like a small canal. Now it is as large as an ocean. Crocodiles with their jaws wide open thrive in the moat. I wonder how many soldiers of the Vatapi army are going to attain moksha in this moat!' pondered Paranjyothi.

'Only if they enter the moat. What if they build bridges or cross the moat using boats?'

'Five thousand archers are waiting camouflaged within the fort walls to shower arrows on our foes, devi. Those who cross the moat despite this will have several surprises waiting for them. They will break their legs by falling into concealed pits. They will be ensnared in invisible nets and traps. Even if they overcome all this and try to climb the fort walls, boulders placed on the fort walls will fall on their heads!'

'I heard that the Vatapi army is as large as an ocean, Paranjyothi! If lakhs of soldiers apply their minds, won't they be able to cross the moat?'

'Yes, they may cross the moat. But they will not be able to scale the fort walls so easily!'

'What will happen if elephants cross the moat at the fort entrance? How can the wooden gates of the fort withstand the might of mad elephants?' When the queen consort raised this query, Paranjyothi smiled as though he was reminded of something.

'Why are you smiling?' asked the chakravarthini.

'I smiled hearing your query. True, devi! The Vatapi warriors are going to act in the manner you described. They are going to cross the moat at the location of the fort gates. Alternately, they may fell large trees and use the trunks as bridges. They are going to use elephants to force open the fort gates. Prior to that, they will intoxicate the elephants by making them consume liquor. But those elephants will be shocked. Our warriors will fling spears at lightning pace from the upper storeys and walls adjacent to the fort gates: the intoxicated elephants will retreat howling and trample the Vatapi warriors to death. I was amused imagining this sight. Not only that. Certain elephants may escape the spears and bang their heads against the fort gates. When the fort gates break, another shock awaits those elephants, devi. When the outer gate breaks, the inner gate, embedded with spear tips, will pierce the elephants' skulls and they will hastily retreat,' revealed Paranjyothi.

'Is that so?' asked Mamallar's mother in an surprised tone.

Mamallar, who had been silent till then, joined the conversation. 'Yes, amma. Do you know the key reason behind all these arrangements? It is Commander Paranjyothi. The day he arrived at Kanchi, he flung a spear at a mad elephant, which hastily fled. The very next day, all the blacksmiths in Kanchi started making spear tips! It was the commander's act that inspired my father to devise the right strategy to combat the Vatapi army's elephants. Father himself recounted all this to me,' acknowledged Mamallar proudly as he hugged Paranjyothi.

'Devi, yesterday I inspected the work done by Kanchi's blacksmiths during the last eight months. They have manufactured lakhs of spears. Kanchi's blacksmiths are extremely skilful, amma! All the spears are exactly like the one I brought from Chola Nadu. Even I could not make out that the spear I carried while travelling to the north was not mine. I carried it thinking it to be mine. It was only when I returned that I realized that Mamallar had safely preserved my spear. Mamallar's thinking that he has wasted eight months is completely incorrect. He has not only strengthened the fort walls, he has also done a lot to ready the fort for the siege. Grains enough to sustain the Kanchi citizens for two years have been accumulated here. All unnecessary people have been evicted from the city. Evicting the kabalikas who were a disgrace to Kanchi was a monumental task. The kumara chakravarthy employed a great ruse to achieve this, devi. Yesterday, he passed an order to shut down all the liquor shops in Kanchi. Today all the kabalikas, carrying their skulls and cow hides, left Kanchi through the northern entrance!'

As Paranjyothi was talking, a maid entered the anthapuram from the front quarters of the palace, approached Bhuvana Mahadevi, and whispered something.

After listening to her, Bhuvana Mahadevi joyously exclaimed, 'Narasimha! Shatrugnan has come with a message from your father!'

When Mamallar hurriedly stood up, his mother observed, 'My child, let Shatrugnan come here. I will also listen to the message.'

Chapter 17

Freedom

Three pairs of eyes steadfastly gazed at Shatrugnan, who walked in breathless and drenched in sweat. The queen consort, without even giving him a moment to regain his breath, asked, 'Shatrugna! What message have you brought?'

'Thaye, I have brought messages for all three of you,' reported Shatrugnan, and bowed to them. 'Devi, Mahendra Pallavar's first message is for you. He asked me to convey to you that, till now, you have been known as the wife of a valorous man. Now the time has come for you to be known as the mother of a valorous son. Eight months ago you had wholeheartedly and smilingly sent your husband to the battlefield. Now you must bid farewell to your son as he leaves for the battlefield in a similar fashion,' conveyed Shatrugnan.

Inexplicable emotions flooded over Mamallar. His shoulders straightened and goose pimples sprouted all over his body. He leapt up and prostrated in front of his mother.

'Amma, do fulfil the chakravarthy's wishes and grant me unequivocally the same freedom he has granted me,' urged Mamallar.

'Wait, my child! Let's listen to all the messages,' advised Bhuvana Mahadevi.

Mamallar immediately asked, 'Shatrugna, what message do you bear for me?'

'Good news, prabhu! It's a message that will gladden your heart. The ungrateful king of Ganga Nadu, Durvineethan, is rushing towards Kanchi, in an attempt to reach here before Pulikesi. He is engaging in this treacherous act, forgetting that the Ganga dynasty is indebted to the Pallava dynasty. The chakravarthy has given you the responsibility of punishing Durvineethan appropriately. He has asked you to take the army stationed at Kazhukunram and vanquish Durvineethan before he reaches Kanchi.'

Mamallar ran like one possessed towards Shatrugnan and hugged him. He excitedly asked, 'Shatrugna! Is this true? Am I dreaming? Has the chakravarthy truly asked me to wage a war against the Ganga Nadu army?'

'Yes, prabhu! This is not a dream, this is reality. Here is the royal decree,' remarked Shatrugnan, and handed over a communiqué to Mamallar. As Mamallar read the message, which was embossed with the symbols of the Pallava dynasty, that is, the ram and the spear, enthusiasm was evident in his face. As he finished reading the message, his eyebrows became slightly knotted. 'Shatrugna! The chakravarthy has written that he has also sent a verbal message through you. What is that?' he asked.

'Yes, prabhu. Even amidst all the worries related to the kingdom, the chakravarthy was unable to forget the responsibility of safeguarding artistic treasures. He asked me if the sculptor Aayanar and his daughter were in Kanchi. I replied in the negative. He asked you to personally visit Aayanar's house and send them to Kanchi before proceeding to war.'

Mamallar's joy was complete. He was desirous of taking leave of Sivakami before proceeding to the battlefield. Now, a clear opportunity to visit Aayanar's house had arisen.

For a moment, he wondered if the chakravarthy had acted in this manner as he was aware of Mamallar's feelings for Sivakami. But how could the chakravarthy be aware of his feelings? Ah! His dear friend Paranjyothi must have sent a message. This thought intensified his feeling of comradeship towards Paranjyothi. He gripped Paranjyothi's hand firmly to convey his gratitude.

However, Paranjyothi was confused. He asked Shatrugnan, 'Aiyya, you said that you also had a message for me. What is it?'

'He asked you to follow Mamallar, just like Lakshmana followed Rama. The chakravarthy assured that he himself would return to Kanchi soon and assume charge of the security of the fort.'

'Ah, is my dear friend accompanying me?' asked Mamallar, brimming with happiness. He hugged Paranjyothi.

He then prostrated before his mother and requested, 'Amma, please bid me adieu.'

Tears filled the eyes of the chakravarthini of the Pallava kingdom. 'My child! Come back victorious!' she remarked.

Mamallar stood up. He hesitated as though he wanted to say something. 'Narasimha, is there anything else you want to say?' asked his mother.

'Yes, amma. Did you hear what the chakravarthy has said about Aayanar and Sivakami?'

'I heard that, Narasimha. What about it?'

'I am sending them to Kanchi and then going to the battlefield, amma.'

'Do that, my child.'

'When Sivakami is here, you should look after her like your daughter-in-law.'

'Daughter-in-law? Never! I will look after that motherless girl like my own daughter, Narasimha.'

Hearing this, Mamallar smiled and quipped, 'No, amma. It would suffice if you looked after her like your daughter-in-law.'

Bhuvana Mahadevi's eyebrows knotted. She asked, 'Why do you say that, my child? Why do you contradict me when I say that I will look after her like my daughter? Probably . . .' Saying this, she looked at Paranjyothi.

'Oh! I understand now! When Paranjyothi went to learn sculpting from Aayanar, did he steal the heart of Aayanar's finest sculpture?' she asked.

Both Mamallar and Paranjyothi looked distressed.

'That's all right, amma! We have no time to waste. We have to leave now. Please give us leave,' stated Mamallar.

Within two nazhigai of Shatrugnan reaching Kanchi, the kumara chakravarthy and Commander Paranjyothi left the fort through the northern gate. They went to Thirukazhukunram and issued orders to the forces stationed there to get ready to leave the following dawn. Mamallar and Paranjyothi, mounted on high-breed horses, then rode to Aayanar's house, accompanied by a small cavalry. They intended to meet Aayanar and Sivakami that very evening and join the forces the following day at dawn.

Mamallar dreamt of sharing his innermost thoughts with Sivakami as he rode towards Aayanar's house. But when he reached, all the castles he had built in the air crashed to the ground! Pin-drop silence prevailed within and outside the house!

Chapter 18

Journey

That Karthikai evening, an uncovered bullock cart was traversing the road from Kanchi to Chidambaram. Sivakami and her athai were seated in that cart. Following them at a distance was Rathi, who was frolicking around and grazing the grass that grew on both sides of the road. Suga Brahma Rishi was travelling happily, alternating between sitting on Rathi's back and flying over the cart. Aayanar and the bikshu were walking behind the cart, talking to each other.

* * *

That year, it had rained nonstop for fifteen days during Aippasi itself, so all the ponds and dams were brimming with water. Waves rose and ebbed in the roadside streams. In the wet paddy fields, the second round of cultivation had just begun. Millet and ragi grew abundantly in the dry lands.

The trees on both sides of the road, the coconut groves and the banana plantations that interspersed the paddy fields were a feast to the eyes.

Though heavy rains had ceased several days ago, clouds were still visible. Like travellers who rushed when they had no time, these clouds flitted across the sky swiftly. Sometimes they caused a light drizzle and then dispersed. The breeze, laced with raindrops, glided over water bodies and lush green groves and caused people to shiver. It was a rare kind of pleasure.

It seemed as though the birds had developed sore throats after coming into contact with the draft. A raw edge was audible in their chirping.

* * *

A strange conversation was underway inside the cart. 'Will it rain today, Sivakami?' asked her athai.

'Mountain?' Where is it?' replied Sivakami.

'True, the peacocks are happy when it rains!' observed her athai.

'There is no dearth of celebration when the sun shines in the evening,' Sivakami remarked.'

'What did you say?' asked her athai.

'What did you ask?' countered Sivakami.

Sivakami's athai, though hard of hearing, loved to talk. She would talk and pose questions to Sivakami, who—while daydreaming—would provide irrelevant answers without really listening to the questions. As her aunt was unable to hear

---

'The Tamil words for 'mountain', 'rain', 'peacock' and 'evening' are 'malai', 'mazhai', 'mayil' and 'maalai' respectively.

properly, she would say something else. Their conversation had continued in this fashion as they travelled.

They had travelled almost eight kaadam from Kanchi.

Sivakami felt a hot rage within herself in sharp contrast to the cool weather outside. What Naganandi had said about Mamallar had caused intense turmoil within her.

When deeply in love, one is easily dismissive of others who bad-mouth one's object of desire. But if one is already seized by doubts, others' criticism only fuels one's own anger and results in a rage directed towards one's love and the world at large. Apparently, lovers are subject to these emotions manifold times. The cause for this is the lovers' conviction about the 'infallibility', 'perfection' and 'divinity' of each other. This trust and conviction, when shaken, results in monumental fury. There is also frustration and a sense of loss.

Sivakami had evidently built a temple in her heart and had consecrated Mamallar as the primary deity, above all the other gods of her pantheon. Naganandi's treacherous words had razed that temple to the ground in a moment! The idol of the deity consecrated in it had also been smashed to smithereens.

The scandalous words Naganandi had cunningly uttered about the kumara chakravarthy were so credible that Sivakami was completely taken in. What else could be the reason for Mamallar hiding in Kanchi when such a major war was underway in the kingdom?

Stories of Paranjyothi's brave deeds had spread far and wide and had even reached their forest residence. When Sivakami saw Paranjyothi in person, she realized that what she had heard must be true. The rustic boy who had come to learn Tamil and sculpting had become a commander. His flinging the spear at the elephant and rescuing them on the night of the arangetram had left an indelible impression on her. Sivakami thought that when one compared Paranjyothi's valorous deeds with Mamallar hiding within the fort, it was not surprising that everyone in the country called him the 'cowardly Pallavan'. Her insecurities made her believe Naganandi's words.

It is only natural to believe that a person guilty of one lapse may have committed many other misdemeanours. So, Sivakami found Naganandi calling Mamallar a womanizer convincing too. She had heard of decadent princes born to brave kings in stories. She had not even imagined that Mamallar could be one such prince. Now she thought that it must be true. Ah! He must be an expert in misleading and cheating poor girls! He had sweet-talked and tricked an innocent girl like her. He had spoken as though he would instate her on the throne of the Pallava kingdom! Men could be such cheats! And princes in particular could be such cruel demons!

Such thoughts tormented Sivakami during the journey.

Sometimes she thought that, as the castle she had lovingly created in her heart had crumbled, her life going forward would be sorrowful. When the monsoon clouds showered raindrops as they dispersed, she felt that the whole world was shedding tears, sympathizing with her situation. She also felt that, not just in this birth, but also during all her previous births, her life must have been sorrowful.

But after a night's rest, when Sivakami resumed her journey at dawn, the sight of sunlight playing on the dew drops, making them shine like diamonds, would lift her spirits a bit.

She would think that there was no need to ruin her life now that it had been established that Mamalla Pallavar was a coward and a womanizer. 'It is a large world. Doesn't the world extend beyond the Pallava kingdom? Don't I possess the wonderful talent of dancing? As Naganandi observed, isn't the world waiting to watch and appreciate my dancing? Why should I think that my life is ruined?' Sivakami would try to motivate herself by thinking in this manner. She would derive happiness by imagining that she would perform in far-flung countries and win accolades.

In a state of conflicting emotions, Sivakami had compelled her father to undertake the journey as suggested by Naganandi. But it was no use, however much she tried to divert her mind and lift her spirits. She was unable to overcome the sorrow that welled within her from time to time. She was unable to extinguish the flames of fury that surged within.

More importantly, during twilight, the distress and sorrow Sivakami felt were considerable.

* * *

That evening, when Sivakami was travelling in the bullock cart immersed in sorrow, an incident diverted her attention. The signs of a large army marching down the road were apparent.

The din of conches, trumpets, bugles and drums was heard. The marching of men and horses, warriors' conversations and their war cries were nearing by the minute. Soon, they saw the front line of soldiers.

Chapter 19

Enter Gundodharan

Hearing the sound of the army approaching, Aayanar and the bikshu, who were walking at a distance behind the cart, hastened towards the cart.

When the front line of the army came into sight, the cart came to a halt by the roadside. Sivakami and her aunt alighted from the cart. As the aunt was unable to hear the army advancing, she was not agitated like the others. The bikshu hid himself behind a roadside tree. As the rest of the group knew that he had vowed not to come face-to-face with royalty, they were not surprised by his behaviour.

But the fact was that everyone was unsettled. Which army was approaching? Where was the army headed to? Why? As the army was coming from the south, it was certain that the army was not the Vatapi army. Then, whose army was it?

***

Ever since the travellers had left Kanchi, they had been discussing the progress and outcome of the war. Sights that reminded them of the ongoing war were present everywhere.

There was a lot of human traffic on the roads. People were moving towards the south. Mostly, they were those who had left Kanchi and were headed towards the neighbouring villages due to the impending war. The crowd was predominantly composed of women, children, the aged, mendicants, the physically challenged and the kabalikas.

The kabalikas were cursing the Pallava kingdom as they left. They showered the most acerbic of their curses on the kumara chakravarthy, who had ordered the closure of the arrack shops, which had forced them to leave Kanchi. Many of them vowed to behead the 'scoundrel' Mamalla Narasimhan. Being bloodthirsty, they also vowed to drink his blood. Some of them threatened that they were going to burn Mamalla Narasimhan and Paranjyothi alive to appease Rudran, and cool themselves by smearing their ashes all over their bodies. As these curses were uttered in Prakrit and other related dialects, it was obvious that the kabalikas hailed from the northern and western provinces.

As Sivakami was travelling in the bullock cart and was mentally wandering across several countries, she did not hear those terrible curses. But those curses pierced Aayanar's ears. Unable to hear them, he shut his ears with his hands.

It seemed as though the bikshu was unaffected by those curses. Instead, he smiled occasionally, and this accentuated the harshness of his face. Once, the bikshu talked to the kabalikas and then approached Aayanar saying, 'Aayanar! If I were to ever renounce Buddhism and embrace Saivism, I will definitely join the kabalikas!'

Aayanar, who was surprised to hear this, exclaimed, 'Swami! Why should such a thought occur to you? Why are you angry with Buddhism? After seeing the troubles and difficulties caused by wars, I now think that the path of ahimsa taught by Buddha Bhagavan is supreme!'

Aayanar was even more confused when Naganandi argued, 'That's why I'm telling you this. If you were to renounce Kala Bhairava Murthy and seek refuge in Buddha Bhagavan, wouldn't Rudra Murthy require a follower to replace you?'

Whenever they saw the rare sight of a few travellers coming from the south, they would stop them and ask, 'What's the news from the south?' The travellers would respond and then enquire about the situation at Kanchi. Naganandi listened to these conversations with great interest.

After listening to one such conversation, Naganandi loudly exclaimed within earshot of Aayanar and Sivakami, 'I think that the intentions of Yuddha Devan, the god of war, are in direct contradiction to ours. It seems as though our journey will not proceed as per our plans!'

'Is that so? What mercy is Buddha Devan showering? What are his divine thoughts?' asked Aayanar.

'Appa is also becoming hard of hearing like athai!' quipped Sivakami and smiled.

Naganandi, who enjoyed the joke, remarked loudly as though he were addressing a deaf person, 'Aayanar! I wasn't referring to Buddha Devan, I was referring to Yuddha Devan.'

'Is that so? What is the Yuddha Devan saying? Is he going to impede our travel?'

'That's the case!' confirmed Naganandi. He then lowered his voice and stated, 'The Pallava kingdom is facing unanticipated dangers. It seems that the Ganga Nadu army is advancing from the west and has assembled at the border. The Pandya king has mobilized a large army and is advancing from the south. The Pandya army has reached the southern border of the Chola kingdom. You are aware of the Vatapi army advancing from the north. The Pallava army can now flee and escape in only one direction . . .!'

'Which direction are you referring to?' asked Aayanar.

'I was referring to the eastern direction. Mahendra Pallavar can seek refuge with Samudra Rajan in the east.'

'Are you suggesting that he should drown himself in the ocean? Adigal! When did your heart become barren like a desert, completely devoid of kindness?' asked Aayanar angrily.

'Oh, great sculptor! Why do you consider me to be a person of such base character? Hasn't the Pallava dynasty descended from a child bestowed by the sea? I asked if that sea would not shelter the Pallava dynasty, which is now in danger. Does seeking refuge in the sea imply drowning in the sea? They can escape by boarding a ship to Lanka! But even that is fraught with danger. The present king of Lanka is a dear friend of Mahendra Pallavar, but it seems that there is a major revolt to depose him. Poor man! The misfortune that befell the Pallavas has now spread to their friends,' declared the bikshu, and laughed obnoxiously.

Aayanar defended Mahendra Pallavar saying, 'Why should he flee to Lanka? He can stay within the Kanchi fort.'

'True, the Kanchi fort is there. The father can emulate the actions of his cowardly son, who has been hiding in the fort for eight months. Had the Vatapi forces advanced without stopping, the fort would have been destroyed in a moment. Now the fort has been buttressed, so he can be secure within the fort for some time. I am unable to understand what the Vatapi army was doing on the banks of the North Pennai River for the last six months!' wondered the bikshu.

The impact of these words on Sivakami was akin to a rod being wielded on a wound. 'God! Won't you humble the arrogant, venomous Naganandi?' she prayed.

Sivakami had conflicting opinions about the bikshu. She felt a baseless disgust and an inexplicable fear towards him. After hearing his comments about Mamallar, she felt even more disgusted.

On the other hand, she respected him and was devoted to him due to his worldly experience and knowledge of the arts. Moreover, the bikshu encouraging her often to dance at the courts of far-flung countries and earn the title 'the peerless queen of dancing in Bharata Kandam' caused her to indulge in grandiose daydreams. Sivakami was aware that all this could be achieved only with the bikshu's assistance, and that her naïve father would be of no help. So, she decided to suppress the disgust she felt towards the bikshu and develop friendly feelings.

However, the bikshu's derogatory remarks about the Pallava dynasty and Mamallar intensified her disgust and made it difficult for her to develop amicable feelings towards him.

When the bikshu commented about the Vatapi army lingering on the banks of the North Pennai River for six months, Sivakami enquired in an angry tone, 'Swami! It seems as though you yourself will go to the banks of the North Pennai River and lead the Vatapi army here!'

'Why should I harbour anger towards the Pallava dynasty? I regretted the fact that we are unable to continue our journey as planned due to their incompetence. Didn't I mention that we would visit Chidambaram and then the temples in eastern Chola Nadu before proceeding to the colossal Buddha sangam that is to be held at Nagapattinam? Now we have come to know that the Pandya army is invading the Chola kingdom. I am wondering if it is wise to visit Chola Nadu at this time,' explained the bikshu.

'Then what do you think we ought to do?' asked Aayanar.

'There is a peaceful place on the banks of the Kedil River. There are enough facilities for you to continue with your sculpture works. There are several hills and boulders. I think you should stay there till all this war-related commotion subsides,' opined the bikshu.

Aayanar, who increasingly had doubts about the bikshu, replied, 'We will decide as we proceed, swami.'

As the conversation between them had progressed in this manner during the last two days, hearing the sound of an army approaching, Aayanar and Sivakami were concerned that it was the Pandya army. But when everyone saw the rishabha flag fluttering at the head of the army, they realized that it was the Pallava army. The slogans raised by the soldiers confirmed this.

'Destruction to Vatapi!'

'Destruction to Thalaikkadu!'

'Destruction to Pulikesi!'

'Disgraceful death to Durvineethan!'

'Long live Kanchi!'

'Long live Mahendra Pallavar!'

'Long live the valorous Mamallar!'

The soldiers raised the above slogans as they majestically marched past. The sound of bugles and other war-related instruments interspersed these slogans and echoed in all four directions. When these slogans were heard, no one observed Naganandi who was hiding behind the tree. His face resembled that of a cobra with its hood raised and eyes emitting fire sparks.

The army was small, consisting of a cavalry of forty to fifty horsemen and an infantry of two thousand foot soldiers. So, this army crossed the travellers within half a nazhigai.

Silence enveloped the road which had been throbbing with activity till some time ago. It seemed as though one had come from a large city to an eerie forest.

The soldiers chanting 'Long live Mamallar!' and 'Long live the valorous Mamallar!' had lifted Sivakami's spirits. Had Mamallar been a coward, would the Pallava soldiers have cheered him thus?

Naganandi's voice was heard asking, 'Aayanar, shall we proceed? It will take us one nazhigai to reach Ashokapuram!'

'Ah! Let's go! Sivakami! You and athai get into the cart,' instructed Aayanar.

Sivakami continued to stand and asked, 'Appa, where is this army headed to?'

'I don't know. It seems as though this army is proceeding to a battle. Hearing those soldiers chant war slogans, I was inspired to fling the chisel away and pick up the sword. I am ashamed we are fleeing our city out of fear,' admitted Aayanar.

'Aayanar, when did you develop this vacillation? Some time ago hadn't you professed your immense devotion to the embodiment of mercy, Lord Buddha?'

At that time, from the direction in which the army had proceeded, the sound of a lone horse approaching was heard. The sound of horse hooves neared them.

Everyone stood rooted to their spot, eager to know who was coming.

The horse came close to them. When they recognized the rider, Aayanar and Sivakami felt boundless surprise.

The reason was that the rider was the person who had vanished into thin air from their forest residence on the day Paranjyothi had visited them.

'Guru! What fault did I commit? You abandoned me like an orphan and left without telling me!' cried out Gundodharan.

Chapter 20

Gundodharan's Story

Gundodharan jumped down from the horse and prostrated before Aayanar who was standing on the road. He then stood up and remarked, 'Aiyya, please bless me. It is by your grace that I was able to find you.'

'I am very happy, Gundodhara. I am happy that you came searching for us and found us. But it was not we who abandoned you. Wasn't it you who abandoned us and mysteriously vanished? Where did you go?' asked Aayanar.

'Guru, what could I have done? Didn't Kannabiran come the other day riding a chariot? He told me that my grandmother had found me a bride and wanted me to come to Kanchi immediately. I ran to Kanchi, concerned that matters would go out of hand, to tell my grandmother that I do not want to marry. I wanted to take leave of both of you, but neither of you was in the house. I searched for you by the lotus pond, you were not there. This bikshu was standing on the banks of the lotus pond,' Gundodharan stated and looked intently at Naganandi.

'What are you saying, thambi? Am I the only bikshu in the Pallava kingdom? You probably saw someone else,' retorted Naganandi adigal.

'No, swami. It was you whom I saw. You were holding seven to eight missives in your hands and reading them one by one. The sound of your sighing resembled a cobra hissing.' Sivakami felt a prick in her heart. She was reminded of Mamallar's messages that had gone missing.

Then Naganandi shot back, 'Why are you blabbering? It wasn't I who was standing on the banks of the lotus pond and reading the missives!'

Aayanar also acknowledged, 'It must have been someone else, Gundodhara. You continue relating your story.'

'No, Guru, it was he whom I saw. Do you know what I thought of when I saw his face and heard him hissing? Ah! I should not reveal that! If I do so, the bikshu may get angry and bite me.'

Sparks emanated from Naganandi's eyes. Aayanar, realizing that the situation was becoming precarious, remarked, 'Look at him, swami. With such an intelligent disciple, how can I craft sculptures? That's why I have done no work for the last eight months. Leave that matter aside, Gundodhara. What happened to the bride whom your grandmother found for you?'

'Guru, I told my grandmother, "Paati, despite several kings being keen to get their daughters married to our crown prince, Mamallar, he continues to be a bachelor. The dear daughter of my guru is also unmarried. When the two of them are unmarried, what is the necessity for me to get married? If you want to, you get married. I will arrange for it".'

When Gundodharan spoke in this manner, everyone burst out laughing. Sivakami's athai also laughed and then asked, 'Why are you laughing?'

'Gundodharan is getting married!' observed Sivakami.

Aayanar asked, 'All right, thambi! How did you come to know that we were headed in this direction?'

Gundodharan replied, 'Guru, I hurriedly explained things to my grandmother and came running back to our home. The house was locked. I thought now that my guru has deserted me, God is my sole guide. I went to sleep under a tree thinking along those lines. Do you know what happened then? By divine intervention, the kumara chakravarthy and our new commander, Paranjyothi, came there.'

'Who came?' asked Aayanar and Sivakami in unison.

'Mamallar and the commander Paranjyothi came there riding horses. Ah! Those horses were high-breed horses . . .'

'Then?' asked Aayanar.

'Several horsemen came riding behind them. Kannabiran came riding a chariot.'

'All right, what happened then?' asked Aayanar.

When Sivakami heard that Mamallar had come, she felt dizzy. She shivered. Her heart and lips itched to ask several questions. Nevertheless, after asking, 'Who came?' she was dumbstruck. As Gundodharan was aimlessly chattering without conveying the message, she was annoyed.

Gundodharan reported, 'Guru, the kumara chakravarthy was thrice as angry as I was when he saw the locked house. You ought to have seen the speed at which Mamallar turned his horse and rode away. Oh god! I never realized that the kumara chakravarthy was so short-tempered. When the kumara chakravarthy turned his horse around and rode away, the horsemen followed suit. Why the rush? Why this frenetic activity? By the time I woke up and emerged from behind the tree rubbing my eyes, all the horsemen had disappeared.'

Feelings of happiness, fear, anger and worry rose within Sivakami, tormenting her like cyclonic winds churning the ocean. She was happy that Mamallar had come looking for her. His anger instilled fear in her. She was angry with Naganandi for pressurizing them to leave before Mamallar's arrival. She was worried, wondering how she was going to rectify her mistake. One incident which aroused several emotions within her instilled in her an eagerness to know more.

She strengthened her resolve and asked, 'Appa! I don't think Gundodharan is stating the truth. Why should the kumara chakravarthy visit our house? Isn't he hiding inside the fort, fearing war?'

Aayanar, unable to respond to her query, looked at Gundodharan, who exclaimed, 'Guru, I cannot believe that Sivakami ammai spoke so "graciously". How can you say that the valorous Mamallar hid inside the fort, fearing war? Which charlatan poisoned Sivakami ammai's ears by uttering such slanderous words? Mamallar stayed within the fort in deference to the chakravarthy's orders, and proceeded to the battlefield as soon as the chakravarthy commanded him to do so!'

'Battlefield? Which battlefield?' asked Aayanar.

Gundodharan responded, 'Don't you know, guru? The entire country knows about it. Don't you know that the king of Ganga Nadu, Durvineethan, is invading the Pallava kingdom, emboldened by the fact that Mahendra chakravarthy is tied up at the banks of the North Pennai River? To vanquish him and his army, Mamallar has proceeded to the battlefield along with the army stationed at Thirukazhukunram for our self-defence. Didn't you observe the army that marched past this road some time ago? That army was stationed on the banks of the South Pennai River. It is going to join Mamallar, who is headed to the battlefield. Aren't you aware of all this?'

Aayanar was extremely surprised that Gundodharan, who had seemed to be a docile, dim-witted and tongue-tied person thus far, could speak so articulately. He was about to ask Gundodharan about something else when Naganandi intervened in a panic-stricken voice, 'Aayanar! Darkness has set in. Shouldn't we resume our travel and reach Ashokapuram to stop for the night? Gundodharan is coming with us. There is ample time to talk with him and get all the news.'

In truth, as it was dark, no one was able to closely observe Naganandi's face. Had they been able to do so, they would have been taken aback that his already harsh face had turned even harsher.

Aayanar told Sivakami, 'My child, the adigal is stating the truth. Get onto the cart. We will get all the details from Gundodharan later on.'

Sivakami had several questions to ask Gundodharan, but there was one that was at the top of her mind. How had Gundodharan secured a horse? A comforting thought occurred to her: that kumara chakravarthy's anger had subsided and that he had provided Gundodharan with a horse to fetch them.

So, she stated, 'Appa, let athai travel in the cart. I will walk with all of you for some time.'

Chapter 21

How the Horse Was Secured

The cart started moving as soon as athai sat in it. The others followed. Gundodharan also walked, holding the horse by its reins.

'Appa, ask Gundodharan how he obtained the horse,' urged Sivakami.

'I did not even know that Gundodharan could mount a horse. Gundodhara, when did you learn to mount a horse?' asked Aayanar.

'Guru, even ochre-clad bikshus who have renounced the world mount horses these days! It was a young bikshu who initially rode this horse, Guru. I pushed that young bikshu into the dam and mounted this horse!' confessed Gundodharan and laughed heartily.

Observing that Gundodharan's speech had annoyed Naganandi, Aayanar chided, 'Gundodhara! What is this? You claim to be my disciple and behave in this manner. It does not reflect well on you.'

Sivakami remarked, 'Appa, Gundodharan would not have behaved in that manner. He is joking.'

'No! No! I am stating the truth. Didn't you observe the dam by the road two kaadam away? I pushed the young bikshu into that dam,' admitted Gundodharan.

Naganandi told Aayanar in a low and anxious tone, 'Respected sculptor, ask him what transpired in detail!'

When Aayanar complied with this request, Gundodharan revealed, 'I did not find you at home and went to sleep under a tree, dejected that you had deserted me. When I heard the sound of several horsemen approaching, I woke up, hid behind a tree and watched. All those who came left hastily. I yearned for a horse so that I could catch up with you. It would be impossible to find you if I were to travel by foot. Just then, a young bikshu emerged from behind another tree. He asked me if Naganandi adigal had visited that house. I then recollected seeing this bikshu by the lotus pond. I stated, "I don't know his name, but I saw a bikshu by the lotus pond." The bikshu thought for a moment and started walking. I too walked with him, happy that I had a companion to travel with. But that young bikshu cheated me. After walking for some time, he mounted this horse which was hidden in the forest and sped away without even informing me. I decided that bikshus are not to be trusted. That includes the bikshu who is walking with us.'

Aayanar scolded, 'Gundodhara! Don't speak ill of elders like the bikshus! Tell us what you did after that!'

'What did I do? What can I do after that? I thought that it was fine if I did not have a horse as long as I had my two god-given legs. After walking for two days, my legs were aching. This afternoon I was sitting on the road by the side of the dam. Then that young bikshu came riding the horse. I said, "Adigal! You left before me. But you have come here after me!" He was surprised to see me. He agreed, "Yes! These days, travelling is dangerous. Isn't the Pallava kingdom in a penurious state? What if they seize the horse and send it to the battle? So, I had to travel cautiously!" Then the bikshu continued riding the horse and I accompanied him, walking. As we travelled, the bikshu repeatedly complained, "I am unable to bear this thirst." I felt immense pity for him. I told him, "Adigal! You should quench your thirst by consuming the waters of this divine dam," and knocked him off the horse. The bikshu fell into the dam. Ah! Do you know how joyously he was consuming the waters of that dam?'

Hearing this, Sivakami was unable to suppress her laughter. Aayanar chided her, saying, 'Why this inappropriate laughter?' He then questioned Gundodharan, 'You sinner! What did you do after that?'

'Guru, is it a sin to quench the bikshu's thirst by offering him water?' asked Gundodharan.

'State what you did thereafter!' asked Aayanar, in a very harsh tone.

'What did I do? When I realized that the bikshu did not know how to swim, I tied one end of his upper cloth that lay on the banks to the roots of a tree. As soon as he grasped the other end, I advised, "Bikshu, why don't you patiently swim to the banks? I am leaving." Then he shrieked, "Aiyya, the missive! The missive!" I asked, "Which missive?" He pleaded, "The missive I brought for Naganandi. See if it is on the banks!" I looked around the banks. The missive lay there. I showed it to him and assured him, "It is safe. Don't worry," and then mounted the horse. That's all, I reached here,' stated Gundodharan, concluding his story.

Naganandi angrily demanded, 'Aayanar! For heaven's sake, take the missive from your disciple and give it to me.'

Aayanar remarked in a troubled voice, 'Gundodhara, did you enrol as my disciple to bring me disrepute? How dare you behave in this manner! Let bygones be bygones; this is Naganandi adigal. Have you brought that communiqué along? Give it to me!'

'Guru, is this true? My guess was right. Is he Naganandi adigal? Swami! Here is the communiqué!' remarked Gundodharan, and handed over the missive to Naganandi. The bikshu silently accepted the epistle and attempted to read it in the moonlight that streamed through the trees. But it was evident that he was unable to do so.

The pace of the bikshu's walking accelerated. Barring the sound of carts, horse hooves and footsteps, silence prevailed on that road. The sound of human conversation had completely ceased.

Chapter 22

At Ashokapuram

There was a town named Ashokapuram seven kaadam from Kanchi, en route to Thillai. In this town, there stood a majestic pillar erected by one of the most benevolent rulers to have reigned over Bharata Kandam, Emperor Ashoka. Once upon a time, one thousand bikshus used to reside in the viharams that surrounded this pillar. There were also thousands of households that practised Buddhism here. Fragrant smoke from incense sticks used to envelop the town during the evening aradhanais to Lord Buddha at the chaithyams.*
Hundreds of bells would resonate at that time. At Buddha's sanctum, thousands of lamps would glitter. Devout bikshus and householders, carrying plates filled with flowers, used to head to the chaithyams.

---

*Viharams comprise a temple dedicated to Buddha and a monastery in which bikshus reside. A chaithyam is a standalone temple dedicated to Buddha.

Now, Ashokapuram lay in eerie ruins. The glow of a single lamp was visible in the building in which the chaithyam and the viharam coexisted. The rest of the buildings had been razed to the ground. Those buildings that were intact were enveloped in darkness. However, the pillar of dharma erected by Emperor Ashoka nine hundred years ago glowed in the moonlight, proving that 'Dharma can never be destroyed.'

It was this Ashokapuram that Aayanar, Sivakami and the others reached two nazhigai after night set in. When they neared the Ashoka Pillar, Aayanar looked at the erect pillar drenched in moonlight. He broke the silence that had prevailed amongst them thus far, remarking, 'Ah! What a virtuous soul Emperor Ashoka was! Wouldn't this world be joyous if all the emperors and kings were like Ashoka? What is the necessity for wars? Why harbour enmity? Why should one cause another to bleed? Isn't it possible for human beings to love one another and follow the path of ahimsa?'

Then, Sivakami interrupted saying, 'Appa, what is this? Sometime ago you expressed the desire to wield a sword and proceed to the battlefield. Now you're talking of love, ahimsa and joy. I've never seen you vacillate thus.'

'True, Sivakami. I am not in a balanced state of mind these days. I am troubled thinking that Lord Buddha's attempts to establish the kingdom of love in this world were in vain,' admitted Aayanar.

The bikshu responded saying, 'Aayanar, the human race is not yet mature enough to accept Buddha Bhagavan's teachings. What can we do?'

Gundodharan suddenly jumped into the conversation saying, 'Why do you generalize about the human race, adigal? Though all are animals, there are differences between the lion, the calf, the snake and the squirrel. Similarly, there are several differences amongst human beings. Like Ashoka, who was a descendant of the Maurya dynasty, Mahendra Pallavar too attempted to establish the faith of love in his kingdom. He tried to shun war. If a Pulikesi, a Durvineethan and a Pandian sprout to thwart this, what can Mahendra Pallavar do? In this world, as long as snakes exist, so will mongooses. If there were no mongooses, wouldn't man have to wield sticks at snakes?'

'My god, I never realized that Gundodharan was so articulate!' complimented Aayanar, while the bikshu looked at Gundodharan with disgust and anger.

Sivakami quipped, 'What Gundodharan says is fair, appa! As long as belligerent people exist in this world, isn't it necessary that those who can control them also exist?'

'True, Sivakami. Not only that. If the world is filled will love, valour will become extinct. How will a world devoid of valour be? Then there will be no inspiration for literature, poetry and the arts,' acknowledged Aayanar.

Gundodharan observed, 'Guru, may I say something? If this Ashoka Pillar is only a pillar, of what use is it to anyone? Who will read the message inscribed on the pillar and follow the same? Shall I tell you what to do with this pillar?' He then tapped the pillar and a metallic sound emanated from it. Gundodharan then suggested, 'It is made of good-quality iron. It should be melted in a blacksmith's furnace and swords and spears should be made from it.'

As this conversation was taking place near the Ashoka Pillar, Naganandi walked ahead and reached a nearby viharam. At the same time, an aged bikshu emerged from the entrance of the viharam holding a lamp. Naganandi read the message Gundodharan had brought in the light of that lamp. The others fortunately did not observe the fear on the aged bikshu's face on witnessing Naganandi's changing expressions as he read the message.

By the time Naganandi had finished reading, Aayanar and the others had reached the entrance of the viharam. Immediately, Naganandi assumed a composed tone and a calm expression. He then told the other bikshu, 'Swami, these people may have to stay here for five to six days. Please make the necessary arrangements. Then he disclosed, 'Aayanar, this missive bears an extremely important message. I must thank your disciple. Though he pushed the bearer of this message into the dam, didn't he bring the message? I need to leave urgently to attend to the message. It may take me two to three days to return. Till then, you may stay here comfortably. This bikshu will make the necessary arrangements for you. Moreover, wouldn't Gundodharan be helpful?'

As Naganandi uttered the last sentence, he shot a piercing look at Gundodharan, but in a gentle tone told Sivakami, 'Sivakami, please don't mistake me thinking that I am leaving you mid-way! I am leaving on account of a very urgent task. I will join you soon.'

As in most other viharams, there was a sanctum for Buddha at the centre of this decrepit viharam. There were rooms for the bikshus to reside in, on both sides. The rooms on one side were vacated for Aayanar and his family to stay.

After they had gone to their rooms, Naganandi entered one of the two rooms on the other side.

Chapter 23

Who Was Defeated?

That night, Sivakami was unable to sleep for a long time. She recollected Gundodharan's words. She was ashamed that she had believed in all the slander that Naganandi had uttered about the kumara chakravarthy. She decided to question Naganandi about the lies he had said and denounce him for that.

Amidst all these thoughts, she was also concerned that she had incited Mamallar's anger by leaving the forest residence against his wishes. She consoled herself thinking that he would not find this unforgivable. Assailed by several such thoughts, fatigue overcame Sivakami and she involuntarily closed her eyes.

When she was half asleep, she woke up with a start hearing someone call out from a distance. She listened intently. The sound of Gundodharan shrieking and a horse trotting away were heard simultaneously.

Sivakami woke up Aayanar, who was fast asleep. When they both reached the entrance, Gundodharan howled, saying, 'Aiyyo! Guru! The bikshu stole my horse.'

Aayanar attempted to console him, saying, 'Appane! That horse was never yours!'

Gundodharan then hollered, 'Naganandi stealing my horse is at least acceptable. Why did he have to fling a snake at me as he was leaving?'

When Aayanar asked, 'What was that about?' Gundodharan responded as follows: The bikshu had woken up and come to the entrance stealthily. He had unfastened the horse and mounted it. Coincidentally, Gundodharan had woken up then. He had run and held on to the horse. The bikshu had unfastened his bundle and flung an object from it at him. Realizing that it was a cobra, Gundodharan had shrieked as he ran away. The bikshu had then sped away on the horse.

Aayanar and Sivakami were unable to believe Gundodharan's narrative. They thought that he was blabbering in the aftermath of a dream.

Gundodharan remarked, 'Guru, I cannot bear to be parted from my dear horse. I will somehow get it again and return.'

So saying, he ran in the direction in which Naganandi had ridden away.

* * *

Five days had passed since the bikshu had left them. The first three days went by without any incident. Time weighed heavily on both Sivakami and Aayanar. But as they had undertaken this journey on the bikshu's counsel, Aayanar was unable to definitively decide where to go next without his advice. After listening to Gundodharan, Sivakami had lost all enthusiasm for continuing with the journey. She frequently thought about returning to Kanchi.

On the fourth day, a few strange incidents occurred at Ashokapuram. At sunset, what seemed to be the sound of incessant thunder was faintly heard in the distance. The sound became progressively louder. Soon, it resembled the sound of a roaring sea, and appeared to be nearing the viharam.

Suddenly, the sound became amplified. Then it changed into the din of thousands of people running.

Aayanar and Sivakami came rushing from inside the viharam to the entrance to observe what was happening. At a distance, amidst the trees, the road to Chidambaram was visible. Several people were frantically running down that road. In the middle of that crowd, a gigantic elephant with a howdah fastened to its back was rushing. Seven to eight armed horsemen were riding around the elephant. A few people carrying a tall flagstaff were also running. The flag hoisted on the flagstaff was torn to shreds.

After that, groups of ten, fifty and hundred people could often be heard running down that road all night. Sivakami observed that sometimes people walked or ran around the Ashoka Pillar, and then down the desolate road on which the viharam was located.

When Sivakami enquired about all this to Aayanar, he opined, 'A battle must have been fought somewhere, my child! It is obvious that one side has lost the battle. The vanquished side is desperately fleeing!'

'Appa, our foes must have lost the battle. The people who are fleeing don't seem to be Pallava warriors, do they?' asked Sivakami.

'How would we know, my dear? Nothing is visible in the night. But I too think that the army Mamallar led must have won the battle,' stated Aayanar.

All this frenetic activity ended before dawn. After dawn, there was no sign of noise, commotion or running. Sivakami stood at the entrance of the viharam and looked at the road. She was waiting for someone to pass by so that she could enquire about the previous day's events. It must have been a jaamam since daybreak. The silence that had prevailed till then was shattered.

The sound of horses rapidly galloping down the road was heard.

Then, the horses were also seen. My god! How many horses? Ten, fifty, hundred . . . It seemed as though there might have been one thousand horses! Animated warriors armed with swords and spears were seated on those horses. Sivakami's heart overflowed with joy when she noticed a warrior amidst the horsemen, seated on a majestic black horse holding the rishabha flag aloft. She concluded that she was right in thinking that the foes must have lost the battle and that the Pallava army was pursuing the fleeing adversaries.

Sometime after the cavalry had crossed the road, two lone horses followed by a chariot were seen. What a miracle! The two horses and the chariot took a diversion from the road, crossed the Asoka Pillar and approached the viharam in which Sivakami was staying. It seemed as though they were taking this shortcut to catch up with the cavalry which had crossed the road some time ago.

Ah! Who was riding the first horse? She could not believe her eyes. Sivakami felt as though her heart had stopped beating!

Yes; the person riding the horse was Mamallar Narasimhar!

Sivakami, who was standing at the entrance of the viharam, saw Mamallar. Unexpectedly, her eyes brimmed with tears. As she was overcome by emotion and felt inexplicably shy, she turned around and took a step with the intention of entering the viharam.

Then, she heard a voice say, 'Ah!' and someone pulling at the reins of the rapidly galloping horse that abruptly skidded to a halt. Sivakami turned around and looked towards the street.

Mamallar's sharp look pierced Sivakami's heart. That look was filled with indescribable happiness and surprise, boundless affection and anger.

All this lasted only for a moment. The very next moment the horse started galloping as swiftly as the wind. Though Commander Paranjyothi, who was following Mamallar, saw Sivakami, he continued riding his horse without stopping.

When Sivakami observed that Kannabiran was riding the chariot that followed the horses, she again stood by the pillar at the entrance of the viharam and gestured to the chariot to stop.

Kannabiran pulled back the reins of the horses and brought the chariot to a halt. As the horses stopped abruptly, the chariot came screeching to a halt, as though the axle had broken.

Chapter 24

The Pullalur Battle

Kannabiran continued to hold on to the reins of the horse as he jumped down from the chariot and hurriedly asked, 'Thangachi! What is this? When did you come here? What is the name of this place?'

'Anna, we intended to go to Chidambaram! We stopped here on the way. This place is called Ashokapuram. Didn't you notice the pillar erected by Emperor Ashoka there?'

'I don't have the time for all that now. But why did you folks embark on a journey in such haste?'

'We undertook this journey so that we did not have to stay in that forest residence all by ourselves during the war. The kumara chakravarthy has completely forgotten us!'

'How can you say that? It is impossible for Mamallar to forget all of you! As soon as we received the chakravarthy's orders to proceed to the battlefront, we first came to your house. Do you know how angry Mamallar was when he saw the locked house?'

'Why should someone who did not visit us for the last eight months get angry? That's all right. Where are you all headed to at such a furious pace?'

As he mounted the chariot, Kannan enquired, 'Didn't you hear of the Pullalur battle?'

'Oh! Are you fleeing because you are afraid of fighting?' asked Sivakami mockingly.

'No, Sivakami. We are pursuing those who are fleeing out of fear of fighting. Thangachi, if you are still here when we return, you will see me return with the Gangapadi king, Durvineethan, tied to the wheels of this chariot!'

'Anna, I will definitely stay here. Please inform Mamallar,' remarked Sivakami. Then she hesitantly requested, 'Please ask him to forgive me if I have erred.'

At that very moment, Kannan wielded his whip on the horses. The horses obediently started trotting. Kannan turned his head around and gestured that he would do so.

The next instant the chariot sped away.

Aayanar, who was inside, asked, 'Sivakami, whom were you talking to? Who was in the chariot?'

'It was Kannabiran, appa! Mamallar and Paranjyothi passed by riding their horses ahead of the chariot.'

'Is that so? It appears they have not forgotten us though we left Kanchi!'

'They did not come for us, appa!'

'Why will they come looking for us? The times when the chakravarthy visited this sculptor's residence are all long past, Sivakami.'

'Don't say that, appa! Apparently Mamallar came to our house as soon as he received permission to leave the fort.'

'In that case, Gundodharan must have stated the truth!'

'Yes. Also, Mamallar was angry that we were not in the house.'

'That's why I wanted to stay in the forest house. You stubbornly insisted on travelling across the country! Look at the outcome of your decision!'

As Aayanar was dejected, blaming others had become a habit with him of late. However, as he had just stated the truth, Sivakami felt very sad.

'Appa, what is the use of discussing past events?'

'It is futile. But couldn't they have paid us a brief visit when they passed this way? Once upon a time, Mamallar was so affectionate towards us . . .'

'His affection for us has not diminished, appa. Isn't war underway? That's why everyone is rushing. Kannabiran mentioned that Mamallar would visit us on his way back, appa!'

'In that case, I'm happy. But why are they all rushing like this?'

'It seems that a big battle was fought in a place called Pullalur.'

'Oh! So they were all fleeing from the battlefield! How times have changed! In the past, people proceeded to war determined to win or to embrace honourable death. For them, nothing was more demeaning than fleeing from the battlefield . . .'

'Appa! Aren't you content that it was our foes that fled from the battlefield?'

'So what? There is pride in defeating valorous warriors and hoisting the flag of victory. Where is the honour in defeating and pursuing cowards who are fleeing the battlefield?'

When Sivakami realized that Aayanar could not be placated, and that there was no use talking to him, she kept quiet. Both of them were immersed in their own thoughts.

That evening, one nazhigai before sunset, Gundodharan suddenly made his appearance. Aayanar and Sivakami eagerly enquired where he had gone. Did he find the bikshu? Was he able to retrieve the horse?

'Don't ask me these things! I chased the bikshu without heeding your words. I was trapped in the battlefield. My god! I have neither seen nor heard of such a terrible battle!' acknowledged Gundodharan.

Sivakami asked, 'What battle? Where did it take place? What was the outcome?'

Gundodharan, in response to her questions, described the historic Pullalur battle.

A few days after the Vatapi army had advanced to invade the Pallava kingdom, the Ganga Nadu king, Durvineethan, accompanied by a large army, had reached the western border of the Pallava kingdom. When news of the Vatapi army defeating the Pallava one spread, Durvineethan's army was waiting to enter the Pallava kingdom. What prompted Durvineethan's aggression is a mystery. The Ganga Nadu army suddenly entered the Pallava kingdom and began advancing towards Kanchi. Hearing this, Mahendra Chakravarthy, who was on the battlefield in the north, commanded Mamallar to lead the army that was stationed at Thirukazhukunram for security purposes and to confront the Ganga Nadu army before it reached Kanchi. Mamalla Narasimhar, who had been itching to receive such a command for the past eight months, immediately went to Thirukazhukunram, along with his commander Paranjyothi, and assumed charge of the army. The two armies met on the outskirts of the Pullalur village, which was two kaadam to the southwest of Kanchi.

The Ganga Nadu army was thrice as large as the Kanchi army Mamallar headed. But Mamallar's brave army pounced unexpectedly on the Ganga Nadu army. The war tactics adopted by Mamallar and Paranjyothi and the brave acts that they performed as they led the army from the front infused immense enthusiasm and courage in the Pallava warriors.

When the battle was at its peak, a rumour that a second army was about to attack the Ganga Nadu army from another side spread. The Ganga Nadu warriors, who had managed to fight courageously till then, lost their nerve and began fleeing the battlefield to save their lives.

News of Durvineethan fleeing westwards on his royal mount (an elephant) spread. Determined to imprison him, Mamallar and Paranjyothi split the Pallava army into smaller forces and despatched them along several west-bound routes in pursuit of Durvineethan. They too hastened westwards.

Gundodharan got hold of a horse that was running loose in the battlefield and followed the Pallava warriors. Unfortunately, the horse he was riding broke its leg on the way. So, he was left behind. Gundodharan concluded his story by saying that he had abandoned the horse and walked to Ashokapuram.

Chapter 25

Thiru Paarkadal

Gundodharan's description of the Pullalur battle stoked Aayanar's and Sivakami's interest. Most importantly, Sivakami was unable to contain her eagerness to hear about Mamallar's valorous deeds on the battlefield. Gundodharan also enthusiastically described Mamallar's brave exploits.

'Ah! When Mamallar entered the battlefield and bravely wielded his sword against our enemies; it did not seem to be a mere weapon. It glittered like Tirumal's discus. Hundreds of flashes of lightning emerged from that sword every second. Every flash of lightning decapitated a foe.'

Gundodharan suddenly paused and then asked, 'Guru! Where is the aged bikshu who was residing in this viharam?'

'Appane, ever since we arrived, he is usually not here. He is mostly at the chaithyam. He comes here twice daily, enquires if we require anything, and then leaves,' informed Aayanar.

'Guru, I need to urgently meet him. I will return after meeting him,' stated Gundodharan and left.

When Gundodharan reached the entrance of the viharam, it was twilight time and the sun was setting. But the twilight did not seem normal that day. Darkness enveloped the sky suddenly from all four sides. When Gundodharan looked up at the sky to ascertain the reason for this, he observed swarms of pitch-black rain clouds approaching from the north. 'Ah! There is going to be a heavy downpour tonight. No wonder it has been so humid all day!' Gundodharan muttered to himself.

The darkness outside cast a shade on the interiors of the chaithyam. Gundodharan, who heard men talking, walked in that direction and hid behind a pillar holding his breath.

'Please leave this very moment and take them along. You should cross the Varaha River before dawn. If you are able to hire a cart in one of the wayside villages, do so. It is imperative that you cross the river before dawn.'

'What if they refuse to leave . . .?'

'That will be troublesome. All my plans have inexplicably gone awry. But by Buddha Bhagavan's grace, everything will be rectified. Please convince them to leave. Tell them that a major battle is to be fought here. If that does not work, tell them that there is a breach in the Thiru Paarkadal Dam embankment.'

'Swami! What are you saying?'

'Yes! As it is, water levels at the Thiru Paarkadal Dam have risen. If it rains tonight, by Buddha Bhagavan's grace, the embankment will definitely be breached . . .' explained Naganandi, and laughed in his deep and fearsome voice.

The bikshu uttered the following words even more softly than before.

'Do you know what needs to be done if they refuse to leave, and the embankment breaks down? Isn't there one more boat available at the viharam? Get into that boat and row to the rocky and elevated area you had visited last month. Swami, irrespective of what happens to the others, we will have to somehow rescue Sivakami.'

When Gundodharan heard the last part of the above conversation, his heart started beating fast. Naganandi's laughter sent a shiver down his spine. He realized that a disaster was imminent that night, and that it was his responsibility to avert it. He prayed to the deity who resided atop the Palani Mountain, Lord Muruga, to assist him.

When the bikshus finished conversing, they stepped out of the chaithyam. Gundodharan followed them. By then, evening had passed and night had set in. Though the clouds that swarmed from the northeast covered the sky, a few stars were visible in the southern and western skies.

One of the bikshus who stepped out of the chaithyam walked towards the viharam. The second bikshu walked around the chaithyam and walked away in the southwest direction.

Gundodharan was confused for a moment. He wondered whether he should go to the viharam and caution Aayanar. But how could he caution Aayanar? From the bikshus' conversation, it was evident that they would somehow be rescued. So Gundodharan decided that the call of the moment was to shadow Naganandi.

Gundodharan followed Naganandi for some distance.

After walking for some time, Naganandi unfastened a horse tied to a tree and mounted it.

Gundodharan thought, 'Ah! I am going to retrieve the stolen horse.'

Due to the strong wind and darkness, Naganandi moved slowly, despite riding a horse. So, it was not difficult to pursue him. Sometimes it was unclear whether the sound of horse hooves was coming from the front or from the rear. It seemed as if the steps of a horse could be heard from both sides. Gundodharan thought that he was fantasizing and walked ahead.

After walking for about three nazhigai, what seemed to be a long range of mountains was visible ahead.

It was then there was a heavy downpour accompanied by lightning.

In the flash of the lightning, Gundodharan saw Naganandi tie the horse to a tree and climb the embankment. He too climbed the embankment at the same place. It was not easy, as the rainwater and mud together formed slush that flowed down the embankment. Finally, Gundodharan climbed a tree adjacent to the embankment and reached the top with great difficulty. Just then, lightning struck, illuminating a horrific sight.

The Thiru Paarkadal Dam that lay on the other side of the embankment was full to the brim due to the rain. Waves rose and ebbed in the dam that then resembled a gigantic ocean. The waves were glistening white in the lightning's blaze. At that point of time, the name Thiru Paarkadal* seemed apt for that dam.

Within a short distance from where Gundodharan stood, he saw a sight that froze his blood.

Naganandi was standing on the banks of the overflowing dam with his arms held aloft and laughing aloud in a ghastly voice. His voice rose above the din of the cyclone and the lashing waves.

Next to Naganandi was a small outlet through which the waters of the dam had started flowing out.

There, next to Naganandi adigal, lay a spade.

---

*Sacred (Thiru) ocean (kadal) of milk (paar). In Hindu mythology, Lord Vishnu's abode is Thiru Paarkadal or Vaikuntam.

Chapter 26

A Voice in the Dark

When Gundodharan saw the bikshu on the banks of the dam with his arms raised and laughing in a ghastly manner, he was paralyzed with fear. Then he mustered courage and walked along the slushy banks with difficulty. As he walked towards the breach through which the water was gushing out, yet another blinding flash of lightning struck. In that light, he observed that the breach had widened. The bikshu had disappeared. But the spade was still there.

Gundodharan felt somewhat heartened. He leapt across the breach, grabbed the spade and shovelled mud to close the breach. Even as he was engaged in this act, he realized that his efforts were futile.

At the same time, he felt someone's breath on his neck. He immediately dropped the spade and looked up. He saw an imposing figure in the dark. He realized that it was the bikshu when the figure tried to strangle his neck with his iron-like hands. Gundodharan's steely grip tightened around the bikshu's wrists.

The next moment, Naganandi's ghostlike laughter washed over Gundodharan.

The short Gundodharan and the tall and lean bikshu started to doggedly wrestle on the banks of the overflowing dam next to the widening breach in the pitch-dark night, intermittently illuminated by lightning that flashed across the sky.

This bizarre scuffle continued for about a quarter of a nazhigai. It was then that a commanding voice that rose above the sounds of the waves lashing against the banks of the dam, the water gushing out of the breach, the rain and the trees precariously swaying in the cyclonic winds calling out, 'Gundodhara! Gundodhara!' was heard.

Both the wrestlers stood stunned for a moment. But neither of them loosened their grip. Gundodharan tried to identify that voice. He recollected hearing a horse's footsteps behind him as he left Ashokapuram.

'Gundodhara! Stop fighting! Don't try to close the breach! It's futile! Hurry up and rescue Aayanar and Sivakami! Can you hear me?'

Gundodharan realized that the voice belonged to his master's master. 'I heard you, prabhu! As you order!' he called out.

As soon as Gundodharan responded, a lightning bolt as bright as a thousand suns struck! Gundodharan realized that this would be followed by deafening thunder. He was reminded of the proverb, 'Like a snake deafened by thunder'. He tightened his grip around the bikshu's wrist.

Thunder struck as he had expected. It seemed as though the entire universe had come crashing down. When the thunder had ceased, Gundodharan was unable to hear the sound of water and rain. There was only a monotonous ringing in his ears. Gundodharan wondered with dismay for a moment if he had gone deaf. But on account of that sound, he could feel Naganandi loosen his grip. That was it. He used all his might to push the bikshu.

Gundodharan saw the bikshu roll down the slope and fall into the breach through which water was flowing out.

Yet another surprise was in store for him. In the absence of lightning, how was he able to see the bikshu roll down and fall? Ah! What was that light? Gundodharan looked around. The top of a palm tree that stood some distance away was ablaze. 'Ah! Lightning must have struck that tree, which then must have caught fire. That is the reason for the light.'

In the light of the burning palm tree, Gundodharan saw a few more sights. He saw a horse galloping away extremely swiftly beyond that palm tree. He realized that it was the rider of that horse who had called out to him some time ago. He observed that the horse on which Naganandi adigal had come was fastened to a tree by the dam. Gundodharan did not wish to see anything beyond this. He hastened towards the horse, unmindful of having slightly slipped while walking.

As soon as Gundodharan unfastened the horse and mounted it, the flame atop the palm tree was extinguished. What had been a slight drizzle till then transformed into a heavy rain. Gundodharan had witnessed several heavy downpours. But he had not seen such heavy rain till that night. It rained as though the skies had given way and all the water stored in the clouds was pouring down.

'Ah! It had to rain just when the embankment was breached. Naganandi chose the right day to break the embankment of the Thiru Paarkadal Dam!' thought Gundodharan.

He resolved to reach Ashokapuram ahead of the water flowing out of the dam.

But he was unable to achieve this. Long before he traced his way and rode back in that dark and rainy night, the stormy waters of the dam had breached a large part of the embankment and the floods had reached Ashokapuram.

Chapter 27

Where Is Mamallar?

One could guess by now the identity of the person who had cautioned Gundodharan before riding away swiftly. It was Mahendra Chakravarthy, who was not only well versed in the fine arts of sculpture, painting and music, but was also an expert in warcraft, and who had succeeded in preventing the ocean-like Vatapi army from advancing beyond the banks of the North Pennai River for eight months.

The war tactics deployed by Mahendra Pallavar ever since he had travelled northwards after leaving the Kanchi fort provide enough material to write several novels. He had suspected that the person who assumed the disguise of Naganandi was a trusted spy of Pulikesi's. The message that Paranjyothi had carried confirmed his suspicion. That message bore Naganandi's handwriting and insignia, which was useful to him in several ways. One such use was to make the Ganga Nadu king, Durvineethan, who was waiting at the borders of the Pallava kingdom, to rush hastily towards Kanchi.

125

Mahendra Pallavar had decided to motivate the Pallava army and subjects by winning a resounding victory before returning to the Kanchi fort after restraining Pulikesi's massive army. He also wanted to use this opportunity to assuage the feelings of the kumara chakravarthy, who was itching to fight a battle.

So, he sent a message to Durvineethan, purportedly written by Naganandi, asking him to immediately advance towards Kanchi. On receiving this message, Durvineethan, accompanied by his small army, marched towards Kanchi.

One can well imagine Naganandi's shock when he read the message Gundodharan gave him. Durvineethan had written that he was proceeding towards Kanchi in accordance with Naganandi's message. As Naganandi had sent no such message, he realized that there was some treachery afoot. He rode away on Gundodharan's horse to the site of the Pullalur battle. Before he reached Pullalur, the Ganga Nadu army had lost and had started fleeing. Naganandi took Durvineethan along and fled southwards, realizing that the only thing he could do in that situation was to save Durvineethan.

Mahendra Pallavar did not trust Mamallar and Paranjyothi so completely as to leave the battle entirely in their hands. A thousand hand-picked horsemen also reached the Pullalur battlefield. As the cavalry arrived unexpectedly at the battlefield and attacked, the Ganga Nadu army lost its nerve and fled. When Mamallar met Vajrabahu, the leader of the cavalry that had just arrived, he recognized his father. But he was even more enraged. After arguing with his father for not having trusted him and leaving the battle entirely in his hands, he sought his father's permission to pursue the fleeing Ganga Nadu army to decimate it. The chakravarthy gave his consent on one condition, which was that Mamallar could pursue the foes up to the banks of the South Pennai River, but that he ought not to cross the river.

Mahendrar did not return after having sent Mamallar southwards to pursue their enemies. How could he leave a naïve youth like Mamallar to counter Naganandi's cruel and treacherous tactics?

After having cautioned Gundodharan, Mahendra Pallavar rode towards the southeast unmindful of the darkness and cyclonic rains. He reached the banks of the South Pennai River one jaamam before dawn. By then, it was not raining so heavily, the clouds were dispersing and stars were visible in the sky. It is impossible to describe how the river and its banks appeared in that dim light. The river was flowing noisily and at a furious pace with frothy waves reaching both the banks. A couple of days ago, the river had not been that visible on account of the groves that grew on its banks. But now all the trees on the banks of the river had been uprooted!

When Mahendrar neared the banks of the river, a horse emerged from amongst the felled trees. The rider was Shatrugnan. 'Prabhu! I have never been as worried as I have been tonight. I regretted my stupidity in letting you go all alone. How did you find your way back in this stormy rain?' enquired Shatrugnan.

'I too have seen several nights, Shatrugna! But no night was as terrible as tonight. Never mind the storm. Was your wait here useful?' enquired Mahendra Pallavar.

'Yes, prabhu! They crossed the river here,' confirmed Shatrugnan.

'Was Durvineethan there? Did you see him?'

'I saw them in close proximity. Durvineethan was seated on an elephant. The others crossed the river in seven to eight boats. The storm hadn't started then. The wind started blowing when the others had almost reached the opposite banks. As they neared the banks, they struggled and reached the shore. The river was also not so flooded at that time.'

'They must have headed to the destination you mentioned. Didn't they leave any boat behind?'

'They left one boat behind. I thought both of us could use it to cross the river and trouble the bikshu. But the cyclone has inconvenienced both of us by washing away the boat!'

'That is also for the good, Shatrugna! There is no necessity to pursue Durvineethan now. There's a more important task. Did you find out where Narasimhan and Paranjyothi are?'

'They are on the banks of this river, about half a kaadam to the east of this place. Ah! I wonder if they are in trouble due to this major cyclone!'

'We should immediately go and meet them. They should cross the South Pennai River before dawn. Does your horse still have some stamina, Shatrugna? My horse is extremely tired.'

'My horse can go further, prabhu. Please ride my horse; I will stay here.'

'No, both of us must go . . .'

'What if the bikshu comes here . . .?'

'The bikshu will not come here, Shatrugna. He will definitely not come here in the next few days.'

'Why, prabhu?'

'Your disciple Gundodharan pushed him into the breach of Thiru Paarkadal.'

'What? What?'

'Don't you hear that noise, Shatrugna?'

Shatrugnan listened intently and asked, 'Yes, prabhu! It sounds like the roar of an ocean! Is it raining again?'

'This is not the sound of rain. There is a breach in Thiru Paarkadal. Before tomorrow night, the area between the Varaha and South Pennai rivers will be flooded!'

'Aiyyo! Mamallar . . .!' cried out Shatrugnan.

'Come! Let's go! Let's caution Narasimhar and Paranjyothi and save them!' remarked Mahendrar.

'Swami, Gundodharan?'

'Gundodharan tried to close the Thiru Paarkadal breach. That's an impossible task. I asked him to rush and save Aayanar and Sivakami and come here. I wonder what he did.'

'Ah! Have they also been trapped? Tonight is truly horrific!' asked Shatrugnan, and urged his horse forward.

'This frightful night has also been fruitful, Shatrugna! I discovered another tactic to defeat Pulikesi!' revealed the chakravarthy.

'Prabhu, you are truly a Vichitra Siddhar!' praised an amazed Shatrugnan.

Both the horses rode eastwards by the riverbank. It was difficult to navigate the felled trees on the way; nevertheless, they reached the Pallava army camp by dawn. The chaotic army camp, on realizing that it was Mahendra Pallavar who had arrived, raised slogans of victory.

Mahendrar, on seeing Commander Paranjyothi, ordered without allowing him to talk, 'Commander! We should leave immediately. We should cross the South Pennai River and reach the opposite bank within the next one nazhigai. Those who know how to swim may do so. Those who don't know how to swim ought to cross the river holding on to logs or anything else! Let the horses and elephants swim across the river. I don't care about weapons and stocks. It is imperative that all the men are rescued!'

Observing that Paranjyothi was standing stunned after listening to this strange command, Mahendrar explained, 'Oh! You want to know the reason? There is a breach in Thiru Paarkadal! Listen to the roar that is growing louder by the moment! The floods will reach here within one jaamam.'

An indescribable fear was then evident on Paranjyothi's face. He stammered 'Prabhu . . . Prabhu!' but was unable to speak further.

Observing this, the chakravarthy asked, 'What's the news, commander? Where is Narasimhan?'

'Last night he left for Ashokapuram! There . . . there . . .' Paranjyothi hesitated to speak further.

'I am aware, commander! Aayanar is in Ashokapuram. Kumara chakravarthy has gone to meet the chakravarthy of sculpting. Good, we are no longer responsible for rescuing Narasimhar! That is the responsibility of Lord Ekambareshwarar! Let's try to save the warriors who are here!' commanded Mahendrar.

Where was Mamallar at that moment?

As dawn was setting in, Mamallar's horse was close to Ashokapuram, struggling to swim in the flood waters that were flowing from the opposite direction.

Aayanar, Sivakami and her athai were standing on the upper storey of the viharam, anxiously watching Mamallar's arrival. Rathi and Suga Rishi were also there.

At the same time, Gundodharan was rowing an earthen boat towards the viharam, which that was surrounded by water.

The road and surrounding areas were submerged in the flood waters, which were rising every moment.

Chapter 28

Suga Rishi's Welcome

There were noteworthy happenings at the dilapidated Ashokapuram viharam that night, while astounding incidents were occurring elsewhere.

The aged bikshu of the viharam returned from the darkened chaithyam after conversing with Naganandi and advised Aayanar that it would be good if he left immediately.

When Aayanar discussed this with Sivakami, she stubbornly refused to leave that place. The bikshu's statement that a battle may be waged there intensified her eagerness to continue staying at Ashokapuram. Sivakami had developed a strange desire to witness a battle. The motive behind that desire was to witness Mamallar's brave deeds on the battlefield. She was visualizing the battle mentally. Sivakami imagined Mamallar swirling his sword and beheading enemies who had surrounded him on all four sides. Unable to withstand the thought of the resultant gore, she attempted to erase that scene from her mind.

One jaamam after night set in, the aged bikshu came again, running, and hurriedly urged in a loud voice, 'Danger, danger! Leave immediately! Otherwise you will not be able to escape!'

'Adigal, what other danger are we going to face?' asked Aayanar disbelievingly.

'I stated that a battle may be waged here because I thought you would not believe the truth. I heard that the Thiru Paarkadal Dam may be breached. That is why I suggested that we leave. Now the dam really has breached. Leave immediately!' he pleaded.

Sivakami asked casually, 'Swami, so what if the dam has breached? Why should we flee because of that?'

'Had you seen the Thiru Paarkadal Dam, you would not speak in this manner. This place will be flooded before dawn,' revealed the bikshu.

Sivakami turned to Aayanar and insisted, 'Appa, I have never seen floods. Let's stay here and watch the floods. The bikshu may leave if he so desires.'

'Lady, your ignorance makes you blabber. Floods are not a spectacle. Water will rise to the height of a palm tree. This viharam and chaithyam will be submerged. Then what will be there to watch?'

'Swami, how are you so sure that this will happen?' asked Aayanar.

'Ten years ago, a similar breach occurred in the Thiru Paarkadal Dam. I myself witnessed the sight then. Several people lost their lives in this low-lying area. The survivors thought that it was dangerous to continue residing here and relocated to an elevated area. It was only after that flood that Ashokapuram fell to ruin.'

When Aayanar and Sivakami heard this, they were perturbed. But they were reluctant to leave in the night. Also, strong winds accompanied by heavy rain had started to blow by then.

Suddenly, Sivakami worriedly enquired, 'Appa! Gundodharan came in the evening. He has disappeared again mysteriously. I wonder where he is trapped amidst this wind and rain!'

'His behaviour is strange these days!' admitted Aayanar.

'Listen to that noise!' warned the bikshu.

Yes! A new kind of noise that had not been heard till then was faintly audible.

Aayanar and Sivakami were even more dismayed. Sivakami asked, 'What is that noise?'

'The dam has been breached. This area will be flooded before dawn,' remarked the bikshu.

'Will water flow down the road? Will water enter even this viharam?' asked Sivakami.

'Water will not only enter the viharam, it will also submerge it!' informed the bikshu.

A concerned Aayanar asked, 'Swami, what is your advice now?'

'What advice can I give now? I had suggested that we leave in the evening. You did not listen to me. I will go to a nearby village and bring an earthen boat. You stay here till then. If we survive tonight, it is due to Buddha Bhagavan's grace. Ah! Naganandi adigal left, giving me this major responsibility.'

After speaking in this manner, that aged bikshu exited the viharam amidst the raging storm and rain.

Within a short time of the bikshu's departure, water flooded Ashokapuram as he had warned. Initially, there was a trickle. Soon the water level started rising. Water seeped into the viharam through the gaps under the doors. Soon the doors crashed open and the water gushed in.

When the water started flooding in, Aayanar and the others went to the porch at the entrance of the viharam. As the rain, storm and lightning intensified, they were unable to stand there. Then they went inside. When the water levels rose, they climbed on to the pedestals and sat there. When the water reached the top of the pedestal, they sat on the stairs that led to the higher storeys. The water levels continued to rise incessantly.

'Appa! I have subjected you to this condition because of my stupidity!' moaned Sivakami as she hugged him. 'Aiyyo! Why did I bring this fawn and parrot along?' she asked with regret and patted them affectionately.

The fawn and the parrot, sensing the imminent danger, came and stood close to Sivakami.

'My child! What can you do? If we are fated to die in this manner, how can we prevent it? We listened to Naganandi and are in this situation,' complained Aayanar, and put his arm affectionately around Sivakami's shoulders.

'Naganandi is not at fault. All this happened because of Mamallar, appa!' blamed Sivakami.

Sivakami thought often about Mamallar that night. When she recollected that he saw her at the entrance and yet rode away without speaking a word, she was furious. Would they have been in this situation if he had stopped to speak to them and taken them along?

'So it would be good if we were to die in this flood. Mamallar is bound to come to know one day that we were drowned in the flood after he rode away without even acknowledging us. Then, wouldn't he recollect this and rue it all his life? Wouldn't he regret not having stopped to speak with Sivakami? Serves him right! Such a hard-hearted man deserves this! We must die here in the flood to ensure he regrets later on. But why should my innocent father, athai, Rathi and Suga Rishi be subject to this fate? God! Why can't a miracle suddenly occur? Everyone excluding me should survive. Why can't I be the sole person who dies? Why should my misfortune affect the others?'

Sivakami was unaware of time as she remained immersed in such thoughts. It seemed as though the intensity of the storm and rain had reduced slightly. Everyone went to the terrace to witness what was happening. The storm had truly ceased and it was no longer raining. There was a slight drizzle. The dim light in the eastern direction indicated that it would soon be dawn.

When Aayanar and the others looked around in that dim light, they saw an astonishing sight, one they had never seen before. They were surrounded by water. The water level was on a par with the roofs of the huts in the villages located a short distance from the viharam. The roofs of houses, hay stacks and large trees were floating by.

Sivakami secretly wished, 'Why can't Mamallar somehow come here to rescue us?' Then she chided herself, thinking, 'Your desire is in vain!'

'But . . . what a miracle! Am I dreaming? Is this a fantasy? Or is it true? Is the impossible actually happening? Is the impossible desire about to be fulfilled? Is it Mamallar who is seated on the horse that is swimming in the flood? Are my eyes telling me the truth? My heart needs to be composed. Yes, yes! There is no doubt that it is him. Nataraja Perumane, Parasakthi thaye! Bless us! He should cross the remaining distance safely! Appa, appa! Do you see who is coming? Athai! Did you see? Are you blind? Suga Brahma Rishi! Why are you dumbstruck?'

Suga Brahma Rishi was not actually dumbstruck. The parrot looked around and squawked, 'Mamalla!' to welcome him.

Chapter 29

The Earthen Boat

Hearing Suga Rishi's welcome, Mamallar smiled imperceptibly. Sivakami raised her hand to spank the parrot. To escape the blow, the parrot circled the place, flapping its wings, and returned to sit on Sivakami's shoulder. This scene amused Mamallar even more.

Mamallar then saw Gundodharan rowing towards the viharam in the earthen boat. He gestured to Gundodharan to stop.

Sivakami, who was watching from the upper storey, pointed to Gundodharan and exclaimed happily, 'Appa! Gundodharan has also arrived! He has fetched an earthen boat!' She had worried about Gundodharan all night. Now all those worries had disappeared and she felt excited, anticipating a lot of amusement.

Gundodharan skilfully manoeuvred the boat to ensure that the boat did not hit the viharam's pillar and rowed towards Mamallar. 'Prabhu, please get into the boat,' he urged.

'Who are you? You look familiar,' remarked Mamallar.

'I'm Shatrugnan's man, swami!' replied Gundodharan, and showed the insignia that he had kept in his turban.

'How did you reach here?'

'Prabhu, I have been with them for the last eight months as ordered by my master,' informed Gundodharan.

'How did you get the boat?'

'An aged bikshu was pushing this boat towards the viharam. I pushed him into the flood and brought the boat.'

'Why did you push the bikshu into the flood? Why did you commit in that sinful act?'

'There wouldn't have been place for him in the boat if you too were in it. That's why I pushed the bikshu out.'

'How did you know that I would come?'

'If I did not know even that, how could I be a part of Mahendra Pallavar's spy force, prabhu?'

Mamallar swiftly leapt down from the horse and skilfully got on to the boat. He then affectionately stroked his horse's face twice and remarked, 'Dhanajaya, try to run away from this place and escape. May god rescue you!'

Immediately that horse whose name was Dhanajaya swam away swiftly towards the road, its head raised above the water.

Gundodharan and Mamallar carefully steered the boat and reached the viharam. It was a difficult task to bring everyone from the upper storey into the boat. Sivakami was the one who caused the maximum trouble. She, who had been ready to die in the flood till some time ago, was now keen to live and extremely scared of the waters.

There was a lot of debate regarding who would get into the boat first. They tried to get Rathi in first, but she stubbornly refused.

Aayanar then forced Sivakami to get in the boat first. Aayanar and athai lowered Sivakami from above into Mamallar's outstretched arms. He then lowered her into the boat. When she got into the boat, it shook, causing her to scream out of fear. Mamallar held her firmly, sat her down and consoled her.

Then when athai and Aayanar got into the boat, it shook. That made her even more afraid.

Suga Rishi, who was circling above, came and sat in one corner of the boat after everyone had got into the boat. Suga Rishi then looked up and called out, 'Rathi! Rathi!' The boat then moved slightly. Sivakami screamed, 'Aiyyo! We are leaving Rathi behind!'

Rathi leapt from above and landed in the boat. When one of her forelegs landed in water, Sivakami again cried out, 'Aiyyo!'

When everyone had sat down and order had returned, Gundodharan requested, 'Prabhu, please hold on to the boat for some time.' He then swam towards the viharam and entered it.

Sivakami was gripped by the fear that danger might befall Gundodharan. As it took time for him to return, she caused a commotion.

Finally, Gundodharan looked down from the upper storey and called out, 'Here I come!' He was carrying a bundle. He handed the bundle down and then lowered himself into the boat. Aayanar asked, 'What's in the bundle?'

Athai felt the bundle and then announced, 'Puffed rice.'

An amused Sivakami quipped, 'Even during these dangerous times, Gundodharan hasn't forgotten about food!'

'Don't you know about me, amma? I can withstand anything but hunger!' confessed Gundodharan.

'You have exercised forethought!' observed Mamallar.

'Gundodharan always appears at the right place at the right time! How did you know that the bikshu had kept some puffed rice?'

After everyone had praised Gundodharan in this manner, Gundodharan and Mamallar each sat in one corner of the boat and rowed.

The earthen boat floated easily on the rapidly flowing waters. But they had to steer the boat carefully to avoid the trees on the way and the logs that came floating by.

The sky was still cloudy. A gentle but cold wind was blowing. An occasional spray of water pricked them.

In a short time, Sivakami felt no fear. She started happily laughing and playing with the waters.

She asked Mamallar, 'For how many days are we going to travel in this boat?'

'Are you finding it difficult?' asked Mamallar.

'No, no. I am worried that this boat expedition will come to an end.'

'Don't you want it to end?'

'No! What if we were to row in these floods for eternity?'

'Probably your wish will come true. These floods will certainly flow into the ocean. If the boat were to head to the ocean ...'

'Then we can float in the boat forever, can't we? I have a doubt.'

'What is it, Sivakami?'

'I wonder if this is a dream or reality.'

'Why do you think it's a dream?'

'I have often dreamt that I will travel forever in a boat. That's why I wonder if this is also a dream. But there's a difference between my dream and what is happening now. In my dream I was alone in that boat with another person. There are several others in this boat.'

'Who's that person?'

'I will not reveal that.'

At dusk, land, rocks and trees were visible in the distance. Even Sivakami, who had wanted to travel for eternity in the boat, felt happy at this sight. Everyone demonstrated their happiness and relief in their own way. Gundodharan's face alone displayed no sign of happiness.

'Gundodhara, do you know which place is this? Should we alight here?' asked Mamallar.

'Yes, prabhu, we have to alight here. But I think that the flood is swift near the shore. There are also rocks there,' pointed out Gundodharan.

There was no necessity for them to steer the boat towards the shore. The boat, trapped in the flow of the flood, automatically sailed towards the island.

The pace of the boat accelerated as it approached the island.

The small rocks that lay scattered on the shore looked like gigantic mountains to those in the boat.

Chapter 30

Mamallar's Ardour

Gundodharan and Mamallar put in great effort to row the boat to the shore without ramming it against the rocks. But the boat continued to rapidly head towards the rocks.

Those in the boat decided that death was was awaiting them. Suga Brahma Rishi shrieked as he flew away, sat on a rock and looked worriedly at the boat.

The boat hit a rock and split. The bamboo rods cracked. The boat swirled around once before sinking in water.

When the boat hit against the rock, Sivakami exclaimed 'Ah!', and tried to stand. The next moment, she was flung into the water.

Light as bright as a thousand flashes of lightning appeared before her. Then darkness prevailed. A monotonous buzzing kept ringing in her ears.

After losing consciousness for what seemed to be a long time, she gradually regained her senses. She could feel the sand beneath her toes. Memories of her travelling in the earthen boat that rammed against the rock returned to her in a moment. Immediately, she recollected sinking in the water and struggling to breathe.

'Ah! Wouldn't Mamallar too have sunk? Didn't both of us sink together in the floods? Can't we die holding each other's hands?' These thoughts struck her like lightning. At that very moment, she felt a hand clasping hers. Ah! That was Mamallar's firm grip. There was no doubt about that. 'Is my last wish going to be fulfilled? Are we going to heaven leaving this world filled with war, treachery and cruelty? What is this? My feet are firmly planted on the earth. I can feel the pebbles under my feet!' Suddenly, there was light.

The water levels rapidly receded and went below her neck, chest and finally her waist. But as the flow of the water continued to be swift, it felt as though Sivakami was being dragged by it. For some time, water flowed out of her nose and mouth, causing her great inconvenience. Amidst all this, Sivakami observed her father firmly holding on to Mamallar and him, along with her athai and Gundodharan, struggling to navigate through the floods. She saw Suga Rishi flying around, chirping in a shrill tone. Rathi had somehow crossed the flood and had placed her head on a rock on the shore and was kicking her feet in a struggle to climb the rock.

At the point where the earthen boat had hit the rock, a big pit had formed due to the swift flow of water. But soon the water flowed over an area that was slightly elevated. It was because of this that everyone had escaped.

As everyone, struggling, reached the shore, Gundodharan lamented, 'Aiyyo, it's gone!' Everyone looked at him with surprise. When Aayanar asked, 'What has gone?' he lamented, 'We lost the bundle of puffed rice!'

Everyone burst out laughing. Then the men and women headed in different directions to wring the water out and dry their clothes.

When Gundodharan and the kumara chakravarthy went away together, Mamallar asked, 'Gundodhara! You are mourning the loss of the bundle of puffed rice. The boat is broken. What will we do now?'

'Prabhu, I am glad that the boat broke in this rocky area. Otherwise we would have headed to the ocean. What would have been the fate of this boat amidst the ocean waves?' asked Gundodharan.

'Nevertheless, we ought to have saved the boat too. If only you had moored the boat slightly more skilfully . . .'

'There seems to be a village at a distance. We can buy pots there and construct a boat, prabhu. But why do we need a boat now? It will be safe for us to stay here till the floods cease.'

'That's excellent, Gundodhara!' shot back Mamallar mockingly. 'Are you suggesting that I abandon my army and stay here? I was thinking of leaving in that boat once we had found a safe place for them to stay.'

'What's the use of leaving, prabhu? Where can we go in this great flood? What can we do? The army is unlikely to remain where you had left it. The banks of the South Pennai River must be heavily flooded by now!'

'That's why it's imperative for me to leave. What will Paranjyothi and the others think of me?'

'What will they think? They will be thinking of your safety. You don't have to worry about them. The news of the breach in the dam must have reached them.'

As their clothes were drying, Gundodharan related to Mamallar what had transpired. He described everything from the chakravarthy doubting Naganandi and Shatrugnan posting him to monitor Aayanar's house to the events of the previous night, when he had shadowed Naganandi and fought with him. He concluded by mentioning the authoritative voice that had cautioned him. It was on account of that command that he had returned, pushing the aged bikshu into the flood and rowing the boat to the viharam.

Hearing Gundodharan's account, Mamallar's regard for Mahendra Pallavar's foresight and statesmanship increased multi-fold. He was also impressed with Gundodharan's ingenuity, and praised him.

'But I did not like your pushing the aged bikshu into the water, Gundodhara. Why did you commit that sin?' he asked.

'That's not a sin but a good deed, prabhu! He is not a bikshu. He was a guard at the southern entrance of the Kanchi fort. He fell into Naganandi's trap and became a traitor. I should not have stopped with pushing him into the flood. I ought to have dropped a boulder on his head,' remarked Gundodharan.

'Then why did you spare Naganandi, who was the force behind everything? Why didn't you kill him too?' asked Mamallar.

'Prabhu, I had decided to kill Naganandi at any cost. But I was unable to flout that authoritative man commanding me to stop fighting. That's why I pushed him into the breach and left. Who knows? That fake bikshu may have drowned and died.'

'Never! Gundodhara, I hope that did not happen! That sinner must not die so easily. Weren't Aayanar and Sivakami in great danger because of that fake bikshu?'

'Prabhu, pardon me. It will be good if we don't mention anything about Naganandi to these people. They don't know anything. If they come to know about him, they will be distressed.'

Mamallar concurred. Then he asked, 'Don't you know who commanded you to leave the Thiru Paarkadal dam?'

'I guessed, prabhu! But I don't have the courage to tell you. Pardon me,' explained Gundodharan.

Mamallar was already wondering if it had been Mahendra chakravarthy who had cautioned Gundodharan. Now, it was evident that Gunodhan thought likewise.

Mamallar felt happiness, shame and sorrow at the same time. 'If it was Mahendra chakravarthy who cautioned Gundodharan, then there was no need to be worried about the army. Everyone would have been rescued. But he must have followed me because he does not trust me enough. Doesn't my action justify his distrust? Didn't I leave the army unattended on the banks of the river and get trapped all by myself in the flood? How can I face the chakravarthy when I meet him again?'

A contradictory thought also occurred to him. 'I don't care what happens. I don't care if I face insult and disrepute. For this one joyous day I can face anything. Won't I recollect this one blissful day for the rest of my life and be happy?'

'Prabhu, let's not worry about the past. Let's think about what needs to be done next,' suggested Gundodharan, disturbing Mamallar's thoughts.

'What is there to think about? We are caught in the flood. We should search for our way back . . .'

'Prabhu, first let's think about where to stay tonight. We can't stay in an open area, can we? What will we do if it rains in the night?'

'Where do you think we ought to stay?'

'There! There is a village at a short distance from here. I will go there first, enquire and return.'

'Do so,' instructed Mamallar.

It was then that Suga Rishi called out, 'Mamalla! Mamalla!' Mamallar walked in the direction from which the voice came and saw Sivakami sitting alone by a rock under a magizham tree. He sat down next to her.

Chapter 31

Under the Magizham Tree

Only the sound of swiftly flowing waters was heard then.

Mamallar was gazing at Sivakami's face without even batting his eyelids. Sivakami alternated between looking at the ground, the floodwaters and the sky. Intermittently her dark eyes dwelt on Mamallar for a moment and then looked away.

Observing this silence that was similar to the uneasy calm before the storm, even Suga Rishi was tongue-tied and alternated between looking at Sivakami and Mamallar. Finally Suga Rishi, losing his patience, flapped his wings as if to say, 'I don't want to associate with these people who are maintaining a vow of silence' and flew away.

As soon as the parrot flew away, Mamallar, attempting to break the silence, asked, 'Sivakami, what are you thinking about?'

Sivakami looked up at Mamallar and remarked, 'I wish I had been swept away in the flood when I sank some time ago.'

Mamallar responded, 'That means that my coming here in search of you was all in vain. Even now nothing is lost. The flood is only a short distance away from here.'

'True! The flood is nearby! But I am unable to voluntarily jump into the flood and die, especially when you are next to me.' When Sivakami uttered these words, her eyes were brimming with tears.

'What is this? I was hoping to converse happily with you. But you are in a completely different state of mind.'

'Prabhu, I have never been as happy as I am today. That's why I wish that today is the last day of my life!'

'The way you demonstrate your happiness is unique!' observed Narasimha Varmar.

'You wouldn't speak in this manner if you knew how much sorrow and distress I have felt in the last one year!' remonstrated Sivakami.

'Sorrow? Why were you sad? Were you unwell? Why didn't you inform me?'

'I had no bodily affliction, prabhu! My body was comfortable consuming three meals a day and wearing clothes and jewellery. It was my heart that was experiencing all the sorrow and distress!'

'Ah! Why should you experience sorrow and distress? Did anyone trouble you? Why didn't your father, Aayanar, ensure no one troubled you?'

The Pallava prince understood why Sivakami was talking in this manner. But as he wanted her to state the reason, he spoke as though he had not understood her.

Sivakami responded saying, 'No one troubled me. I am a helpless girl brought up in a forest. I don't know the art of speaking, prabhu! The reason for my sorrow is my inability to forget you!' Tears then flowed copiously down her cheeks.

Mamallar eagerly looked at her and enquired, 'Is that all, Sivakami? Why are you crying now? I too felt untold sorrow thinking about you! Didn't you read my messages?'

'I've memorized every word you wrote. I've read each message to Rathi a hundred times. I would feel happy while reading the message, but afterwards my sorrow would increase multi-fold. I would feel angry with you . . .'

'Sivakami! You at least had the comfort of feeling angry with me. I did not even have that. Now you tell me who experienced the greater sorrow?'

'If you weren't angry with me, why did you ride away without stopping even for a moment when you saw me at the Ashokapuram viharam? Was that out of your affection for me?'

'Yes, Sivakami! I was slightly annoyed that you people left despite my asking you to continue staying at the forest residence. But didn't I come that very night, unmindful of the storm and rain? Didn't I leave several important tasks unattended and come? Even now I don't know what is happening. Setting aside everything, I am waiting for a slight smile on your golden face. But you make me sad by shedding tears!'

'All this change is because of you. Two to three years ago, I was perpetually happy. I used to play like a carefree deer frolicking in the forest. My father used to caution me saying, "Don't laugh a lot, Sivakami. The Bharata War broke out because of Panchali's laughter. Women should not laugh a lot." Where did all that fun and frolic go? When I think about it, I myself am surprised . . .'

'Sivakami! You describe the times you were happy; tell me about your childhood. I am eager to know about those days!' urged Narasimha Varmar. Sivakami started talking.

'When I was a young girl, my father doted on me. I ruled the palace of sculpture in the middle of the forest like a queen. My father's disciples were my deferential citizens.

They came running at the batting of my eyelid. "May we be of some service to you?" they used to ask. Those days, I didn't know what worry and sorrow meant. Everything in this world filled me with happiness and wonder. When I woke up in the morning, the sight of the golden-hued rising sun would make me happy. I would enjoy the sight of tender red shoots on trees. Colourful flowers that grew on trees, plants and creepers would be a source of boundless cheer. I used to chase the butterflies flying amidst the plants. I used to burst out laughing when they escaped my grip. I used to feel intoxicated listening to the buzz of the honeybees. I was ecstatic listening to the mellifluous songs of the birds in the forest.

'In the night, I used to imagine that all the stars in the wide sky were blinking their eyes and inviting me to join them. Accepting their invitation, I used to soar higher and higher in my imagination. Sometimes, I thought that the moon resembled a swan. I used to sit on it and circle amongst the stars. Sometimes the moon would assume the shape of a small, beautiful boat. I used to climb into that boat and sail around the sky that resembled the blue ocean. I used to scoop up all the stars on the way and collect them in my lap.

'It was during such happy times that my father started teaching me dancing. From then on I became crazy about dancing. I would dance all the time. Even when I went to the forest to play, I used to dance on the way. My legs would perform rhythmic steps when I went to the lotus pond to bathe. Those days, the earth and the sky seemed to be a sprawling stage to me.

'When I saw lotuses swaying in the gentle breeze, I used to imagine that they were joyfully dancing. The stars in the sky appeared to swirl around, dancing to different rhythmic beats.

'It was during such a joyful period of my life that you came one day to the forest residence with your father . . .' Saying this, Sivakami stopped relating her story.

Chapter 32

A Bud Blossomed!

A beautiful lotus bud slowly raised its head above the water. A delicate fragrance had troubled the bud all night in its attempt to emanate from it. By dawn, the escapee's struggle intensified. Light had appeared on the horizon. The tender rays of the rising sun streamed through the lake-side trees and fell on the lotus bud. That gentle nudging caused the bud to tremble and the petals opened. The fragrance that had been trapped all night was set free. It wafted across the lake and its banks and filled the air.

Likewise, all the thoughts and feelings that had lain suppressed within Sivakami's heart surged out when she got the opportunity to talk with Mamallar alone. It was only when Sivakami mentioned Mamallar's first visit to the forest residence that her flow was interrupted.

When Sivakami paused, Mamallar observed, 'Yes! I remember that day vividly. When the chakravarthy and I first came to your forest residence, you were dancing amidst the statues of gods that your father had sculpted. Aayanar was singing the notes and was keeping the thalam. Seeing us, Aayanar stopped the singing, you too stopped dancing. Your large eyes widened further when you saw us. My father persuaded you to continue dancing. Aayanar then resumed singing and you started to dance. When you finished, I clapped loudly. You looked at me with joy-filled eyes. There wasn't an iota of bashfulness in that glance.'

'Prabhu, all what you said is true. Then I was a twelve-year-old girl. I was not worldly-wise. I did not understand that you were the lustrous sun glowing in the sky while I was merely a dewdrop at the tip of a blade of grass on earth. So there was no inhibition when I looked at you in the eye. I did not realize that the eyes that dare to look at the sun will soon feel the heat and look down . . .'

'Sivakami! I am neither the sun nor are you the dew drop. You are like the flame of a lamp and I am like the moth that is drawn to the flame . . .'

'Prabhu, it was a mistake to deviate from what I had initially started talking about. Please forgive me. As soon as I finished dancing, you clapped. I was then unimaginably happy. Your father then told you, "Play with Sivakami for some time. After I'm through with Aayanar, I'll call you." You immediately approached me. Both of us ran to the forest, holding each other's hands.

'After showing you the beautiful fauna around my forest home, I took you back and showed you the parrots and doves I was rearing. When you saw statues of dance postures, you insisted, "I too want to learn dancing." You struck the same pose as one of the statues. Seeing this, I burst out laughing. Our fathers observed, "The children have befriended each other so quickly!"

'From that day on, I eagerly awaited your arrival. I felt happy whenever I heard the sound of a horse or a chariot, thinking that it was you. When I saw you I felt the same joy I did when I saw the rising sun, full moon, colourful flowers, chirping birds and butterflies flying around. But one cannot converse with the sun, moon, birds and parrots. As it was possible to talk with you, I used to chatter incessantly whenever I saw you . . .'

'True, Sivakami! Those days, whenever I saw you I experienced the same joy I did when I saw your father's sculptures. But a statue won't talk, and you spoke without a pause. I used to think that your words had as much meaning as the chirping of birds did. Even though I did not understand a word, I used to listen to you for a long time . . .'

'My friendship, like my speech, came from my heart. After some time, you travelled with the chakravarthy across the country. You did not visit the forest residence for three years. I used to yearn to see you time and again. Then I consoled myself thinking that you would definitely come again one day. I resolved to become a dance exponent before you returned, and to impress you with my dancing. I tried imagining how you would look when you returned after years. But I was unable to conceive of any image . . . Finally, one day, you came! You were a transformed man!'

'You too had completely changed, Sivakami. Both your appearance and character had changed. You did not come running out and take me into the house holding my hands, as I had expected. You bashfully stood behind a pillar and looked at me from the corner of your eye. Your tinkling laughter was replaced by a slight smile. The look from the corner of your eye and the mischievous smile killed me.'

'Something prevented me from running towards you and welcoming you. My legs refused to move. I wanted to talk, but my tongue refused to cooperate. I stood rooted to that spot. I asked myself, "Sivakami! What happened to you?" At the same time, my father remarked, "Sivakami! Why are you standing behind the pillar? Come and prostrate to the chakravarthy! Meet the Pallava kumarar. See how tall he has grown!" I hesitantly came and prostrated. Then the chakravarthy observed, "Aayanar, Sivakami has also grown up. At first, I was unable to recognize her. I wondered if you had started sculpting golden statues along with stone statues." Hearing this, I felt even more shy. After standing silently for some time, I slipped out of the house and went into the forest. I sat on the banks of the lotus pond and wondered what had happened to me.

'Within a short time, I heard the sound of gentle footsteps from behind. But I did not turn around. You came and closed my eyes with your hands. Three years ago, I would have called you by your name, laughed aloud, removed your hands and looked around. Now when your hands closed my eyes, I felt paralyzed. A thousand waves rose and ebbed in my heart.

'You then sat next to me and held my hands. I sat still, unable to move. "Sivakami, are you angry with me?" you asked. I looked at you silently. "You do seem to be angry," you observed, and then described your travels to me. But I did not hear a word of what you said. That you were sitting next to me and our hands were linked was the only consciousness that filled my heart. This feeling took me to ethereal heights. I felt as though I was floating above the clouds. Soon, I felt I was dancing on the lotus leaf floating on the pond. The overpowering feeling almost suffocated me.'

'You made such a fool of me! I thought you were listening intently to what I was saying as I described my travels in detail.'

'Finally, when you took leave of me, you promised, "I will return soon." After that, for some time, I did not walk on the ground. I was floating in a sea of happiness. I felt as though I had been blessed with a miracle, a rare occurrence, a fortune no one had ever been blessed with. So, my eyes saw the world in a new perspective. I saw the beauty I had never previously observed on earth and in the sky. Jasmines and champas exuded the kind of fragrance I had never inhaled before. The blue sky glowed with a new lustre, and there were new melodies in the songs of the birds. The sound of bamboos swaying in the wind used to sound mournful previously. Now that sounded like a joyful melody to my ears. It seemed as though the plants, creepers, birds and insects were telling me in myriad voices, "Sivakami! You're blessed, you're fortunate!" In the night, the stars in the skies smiled at me even more joyfully than before. When I sat in the boat made of the ivory moon and sailed amidst the stars, I felt I was not alone. You were in that boat along with me! I was not alone in the boat of life that sailed through the ocean of infinite thoughts; you were next to me. Then, I felt like singing to myself. Soon, there was tremendous exuberance in my dancing. My father was stupefied at the amazing progress I made in dancing . . .'

'The chakravarthy and I were amazed too. My father often observed that you had attained the artistry that the sage who authored Bharata Shastram had not. He was the one who wished that your arangetram be staged at the Kanchi royal court.'

'Prabhu, during the time of that unfortunate arangetram, I was in a completely different state of mind. I myself am surprised by the changes I underwent. All the happiness and exuberance I had felt when I met you after three years dissipated within a few days. Thoughts about you gradually started inflicting sorrow on me, rather than making me happy.

I despised everything around me. The moon and the stars put me off. I rued the onset of the dawn. I felt like crushing the flowers and throwing them away. I started hating the fawns and parrots that I had so dotingly reared. I started thinking, "What is the necessity of music and dance?" It was during this time that my arangetram was held. I was happy when it abruptly ended.'

'When we met at the lotus pond after the arangetram, sorrow was evident in your speech. You asked me for a promise . . . I found that extremely surprising.'

'Prabhu, I heard talk of your marriage. That news pierced my heart, which was already drowned in sorrow, like a spear. I wanted you to belong solely to me. Every moment I spent away from you seemed to be an epoch. I persuaded my father to visit Navukkarasar Peruman at Kanchi. You know what happened that day . . .'

'Sivakami, I not only know what happened but also understood your state of mind that day. That's why I sent a message through Kannabiran the very next day.'

'I understood from that message that you did not want me to come to Kanchi. The eight months I spent without meeting you seemed to be eight yugams to me. My sorrow and heartache increased by the day. I would be somewhat happy for a day or two when I received your messages. Then I would feel sad again. I thought that I would never meet you again, and that my fantasy would never come true. In such a situation, I lost all interest in life. I frequently thought of ending my life. I thought that if I continued in that state of mind for some more time, I would go mad.

'Prabhu, now do you understand why we left the forest house and embarked on this journey?' asked Sivakami as she concluded her monologue.

'I know, Sivakami! I understand! You embarked on this journey because both of us were destined to get trapped and suffer in this destructive flood and to be marooned in this deserted island! Don't I realize this?' Even as Mamallar was uttering these words, his description of the island was contradicted by the sounds of musical instruments and human speech heard from a distance. Both of them looked around with a start.

Chapter 33

The Reception

Hearing the sound of musical instruments and commotion, Aayanar and athai came to the spot where Mamallar and Sivakami were sitting.

A crowd of people were approaching them. A figure detached itself from the crowd and rushed towards them ahead of the other people. No one harboured any doubts regarding the identity of that figure. It was Gundodharan!

The kumara chakravarthy was extremely angry. 'Ah! What has this fool done? He has told the villagers, "The kumara chakravarthy got trapped in the flood. He has now reached here!" He has ensured that I cannot spend the short time I am here talking to Sivakami. There is so much to convey and to hear from Sivakami. What will the people think of me for not being with my army but with Aayanar and Sivakami instead? Ah! This fool Gundodharan has placed me in such an embarrassing situation! But there is no point in getting angry with him. The damage has been done. This embarrassing situation will have to be managed.'

As Mamallar stood slightly behind, thinking along these lines, he observed Gundodharan talking to Aayanar, instead of coming to him. Then Aayanar whispered something into Sivakami's ears. Both of them looked at Mamallar and smiled.

By then, the crowd had neared them. The man who seemed to be the leader of the crowd placed a plate containing purnakumbham, flowers and fruits in front of them. Gundodharan pointed out the sculptor Aayanar to them.

One of the village leaders remarked: 'People say that there emerges some good even from extreme evil. Similarly, fortune has favoured our village in the form of the breach in the Thiru Paarkadal Dam. We now have the opportunity to welcome the emperor of sculpting, Aayanar, and the queen of Bharata Shastram, Sivakami devi. Welcome, aiyya! Welcome, devi! We will do our utmost to ensure that you and your disciples are comfortable. We request you to stay here as our guests for as long as you desire.'

When the leader finished speaking, Aayanar replied, 'Dear village elders! My daughter, disciples and I are indebted to all of you for your affection! We have no alternative but to stay here with you as your guests till this flood subsides!'

Then the villagers, Aayanar and the others started walking towards the village. Mamallar, who was hesitantly standing at the back, was shell-shocked. The happenings here had directly contradicted his expectation. Except for Sivakami, who occasionally looked at him from the corner of her eye and smiled, the others completely ignored his presence.

It is unnecessary to mention that this surprise was a happy one for Mamallar. 'How wrong I was to think that Gundodharan was a fool. He has a razor-sharp intellect!'

As he was thinking along these lines, Gundodharan came from behind and whispered into his ears, 'Prabhu, why are you standing here? Come, let's go.'

'They have not invited me. How can I go to a place uninvited?' asked Mamalla Narasimhar.

'Of course they invited you! Didn't they say that they will make the necessary arrangements to ensure Aayanar and his disciples are comfortable? Both of us are Aayanar's disciples!' stated Gundodharan.

'Gundodhara, are all of Shatrugnan's men as smart as you? In that case, we can defeat even a thousand Pulikesis invading our kingdom!'

Aayanar's two 'disciples' walked slightly behind the crowd. However, Mamallar did not fall too far back, and he was always at a distance within which Sivakami could look at him from the corner of her eye.

When they had almost reached the village, the crowd became even larger. It seemed as though the entire village had congregated there. The entrance of every house in the village was decorated with colourful kolams. The procession periodically stopped and the village womenfolk performed arathi to Sivakami. Finally, they reached the Shiva temple that was located in the eastern part of the village.

Though the temple was small, it was beautiful and clean. When one entered the temple crossing the outer wall constructed with brick and lime, it was evident that the large inner praharam was spotlessly clean, devoid of even a blade of grass.

Beyond the sacrificial altar, dwajasthambam and the Nandimedai,* was the artha mandapam for devotees to

_____

*An elevated area in a Shiva temple on which the idol of Lord Nandi is instated

congregate and worship. This mandapam had a roof made of brick tiles. Beyond this mandapam was the sanctum, above which there was a beautiful thoonganai madam built in accordance with a newly developing custom in Tamizhagam those days.

As they entered the temple, the fragrance of incense, sandalwood paste, lavender, champa and jasmine mingled with smoke from ghee-filled lamps and the smell of broken coconuts, peeled bananas and sugarcane juice. This created an impression that one had reached another world that was entirely pristine.

When Aayanar, Sivakami and Aayanar's disciples reached the artha mandapam, the deeparadhanai was performed to the deity. Then they were offered the holy water and vibhuti. Similarly, a deeparadhanai was performed at the sanctum of goddess Ambika, and vermillion and flowers were offered to the devotees.

When the prayers were completed, the village headman who had welcomed them humbly requested, 'Aayanar, we have heard a lot about your daughter's dancing skills. It is our good fortune that all of you have unexpectedly come to our village. We will not trouble you today. Your daughter should honour us by dancing in this temple tomorrow!'

Aayanar looked at Sivakami, not knowing how to respond. His confusion increased when he saw her face. Sivakami had already figured out where Mamallar was standing in that hall. She had been extremely careful not to look in Mamallar's direction thus far. Now her eyes immediately darted towards him. The smile on Mamallar's face and the sparkle in his eyes was the answer to Sivakami's query.

The next moment, Sivakami softly told Aayanar, 'So be it, appa!'

The village head remarked, 'Aayanar, we too heard your daughter's response. We're delighted!'

The news of Sivakami's performance on the following day spread across that mandapam and there was commotion.

Amidst all this festivity, Aayanar told the village head, 'Aiyya, Sivakami has not been practising for the last seven to eight months. But that is all right. Sivakami is overwhelmed by your affection. So she has agreed to fulfil your wish tomorrow. But I am amazed that you have heard so much about Sivakami's dancing. How did you come to know? Is this the work of my disciple, Gundodharan?' He then looked towards Gundodharan.

The village head stated, 'No, aiyya! No! It was Navukkarasar Peruman who told us about your daughter!'

'Ah! Did Navukkarasar come here? You are fortunate!' exclaimed Aayanar.

'We are indeed fortunate. Six months ago, Navukkarasar Peruman visited this blessed village. He wielded the hoe with his sacred hands and cleaned the temple praharam. We too participated in that sacred task. That night, Navukkarasar Peruman's disciples sang his nectar-like verses. When they sang the verse

At first His name she heard
About His image then she heard . . .

Navukkarasar Peruman shed copious tears.'

When the village head was speaking thus, Aayanar, Sivakami and Mamallar simultaneously experienced goose bumps. The village head continued.

'Once they completed singing this verse, Peruman told us about Sivakami's dancing. He also told us that you had visited his monastery with your daughter, who danced to this verse and then fainted. We did not even imagine that we would have the fortune of welcoming you so soon.'

'We are blessed that Vageechar Peruman remembered us!' admitted Aayanar.

'After Navukkarasar Peruman visited this village, we built a rest house here named after him. You and your daughter will be the first to stay in that dwelling. This is also our fortune!' stated the village head.

Chapter 34

Nandimedai

That night, in the middle of the second jaamam, Mamallar and Gundodharan were engaged in a conversation at the entrance of the rest house.

By evening itself the clouds had dispersed and the skies were clear. The moon's beautiful rays had transformed that ordinary village into Gandharva Loka. The golden pillar in the village temple that was a short distance away was glowing in the moonlight. There were coconut trees beyond the temple, swaying gently. The moonlight was performing alchemy on their leaves, changing them from green to silver and back to green.

'Prabhu, you, who ought to be sleeping in the upper storey of the palace on a feather-soft bed, are lying down at the portico of this rest house like a pauper. I find the very thought repulsive,' countered Gundodharan.

'Gundodhara, I debated with Aayanar for so long regarding this and have just resolved the issue. Now, you're singing the same tune,' complained Mamallar.

Gundodharan was about to say something, but Mamallar spoke without giving him the opportunity. 'My father's upbringing did not expose me just to the luxury of the palace. I am not only used to sleeping on soft mattresses covered with jasmine flowers, but also on the ground in the midst of a forest, using the aerial roots of trees as my pillow. The smooth surface of this portico is so comfortable!' insisted Mamallar.

'Prabhu, you're mocking me. I feel sad. When I think that all this misery is because of me, I feel distressed. If only I had revealed your identity to the villagers ...'

'Gundodhara, I have seen people who are sorry after committing a mistake. I have not seen people being regretful after performing good and intelligent acts. You're the first such person. I was keen to mingle with the people without revealing the fact that I am the chakravarthy's son. My desire has been fulfilled because of you. Ah! Today I am very happy after realizing that Sivakami's fame has spread far and wide.'

'Prabhu, it's not only the news of Sivakami's dancing skills that has spread. News of the Pullalur battle has also reached here!'

'Is that true, Gundodhara?'

'Yes, prabhu! Everyone here knows about the kumara chakravarthy's brave feats in that battle. The villagers asked me to describe those feats in detail. I have promised to tell them everything at length tonight. They will be waiting at the temple praharam. Do you want to come?' asked Gundodharan.

'I'll come. But you should not engage in any mischief by revealing my identity!' warned Mamallar.

Gundodharan and Mamallar sat on the steps that led to the Nandimedai at the temple praharam. There were platforms constructed using brick and mortar in the area around the Nandimedai and the sacrificial altar. Several people were sitting there. Gundodharan provided a vivid description of the Pullalur battle to all of them. He specifically described the brave role played by the kumara chakravarthy in that battle.

'Do you know how Mamallar fought the battle? One moment he was here; the next moment he was beyond that wall. It was easy to find out where Mamallar was fighting in that vast battlefield at any point of time. The place where a glittering sword that resembled Mahavishnu's discus was swirling around, beheading our enemies, was the place where Mamallar was. Who else could decimate our foes by wielding the sword at lightning speed? Yama himself was residing in Mamallar's sword that day. As he swirled his sword all around that day, one, ten, hundred and thousand foes fell to the ground, lifeless!'

'Ah! Didn't he fight like Abhimanyu?' observed one person in the crowd. Even in that village, people had been reading the Mahabharata for some time. So everyone was reminded of Arjunan and Abhimanyu!

Gundodharan remarked: 'Yes, Mamallar fought like Abhimanyu that day. But there is one difference. Abhimanyu died in the battlefield. At the Pullalur battle, the foes fled, unable to counter Mamallar's sword. The person who led all those who fled was the Ganga Nadu king, Durvineethan!'

'In which direction did Durvineethan flee?' asked one villager.

Mamallar's eyes glinted with anger.

'Good question; it seems as though I cannot refrain from telling you the truth!' Saying this, Gundodharan got up and went and stood a short distance away from Mamallar. 'This man who is next to me, he ... it's he ... why are you staring at me, aiyya? He is truly Aayanar's foremost disciple. I am a soldier in the Pallava army. I had accompanied Mamallar, who was pursuing Durvineethan. I had to stay back as my horse broke its leg on the way. Then I was trapped in the floods, got into the boat with them and saved myself!'

Immediately, the listeners pulled each other's legs and their attention was diverted. They whispered amongst themselves that they had guessed even before that Gundodharan could not have been Aayanar's disciple.

'Probably Mamallar is also trapped in this flood,' speculated one person.

'I'm worried thinking about that!' replied Gundodharan.

'Probably he too has reached here,' opined another person.

'Probably!' agreed Gundodharan.

Chapter 35

Are You a Thief?

The next evening, the Shiva temple at the Mandapapattu village was a feast for the eyes. The front entrance of the temple was decorated with lush green plantain trees, festoons and fabric curtains.

A large pandal covering the area between the artha mandapam and the outer temple tower had been erected. The sides of the pandal were decorated with ivory coloured tender coconut leaves interspersed with pink lotus buds.

In those days, every village in Tamil Nadu with ample water supply had a lotus pond. The water in the pond was not visible as it was completely covered by lotus leaves, flowers and buds. So, while the idols in the temples were adorned with other flowers, lotus leaves and buds were used to decorate the temple.

All the villagers congregated in the beautifully decorated temple before sunset. Even women and children turned up, and there was a rush to occupy the front rows in the pandal.

Once the sun set, the temple was illuminated with thousands of earthen lamps. At the same time, the full moon also rose, as though he wanted to witness Sivakami Devi's divine performance.

The crowd cheered on seeing Aayanar and Sivakami coming into the temple through the main entrance. There was pin-drop silence when Sivakami came and stood on the stage erected at the southern end of the pandal. Even children who had been crying fell silent.

The residents of the Mandapapattu village had not seen such divine beauty till then. Once they had gotten over their initial amazement, they started expressing their appreciation.

'Celestial dancers like Rambha and Urvashi would surely resemble her!' observed one person.

'Never! They could not be so beautiful!' commented another person.

'It's a mistake to compare this girl with the celestial dancers. She is the very incarnation of goddess Sivakami who danced in competition with Nataraja Peruman at Thillai,' quipped a devotee.

'If it were not so, Navukkarasar Peruman wouldn't have praised her so much!' pointed out another ecstatic devotee.

As if instructed, complete silence descended on the pandal. Sivakami started dancing!

Sivakami danced to the thalam Aayanar performed with his hand and the notes he sang.

A local matthala vidwan played with an enthusiasm he had never demonstrated before. The *kum kum* sound of the matthalam mingled with the *kal kal* sound of Sivakami's anklets as she danced.

The swiftness of lightning, the sprightliness of a fawn and the grace of a peacock were evident in her dancing.

Sometimes, Sivakami danced on earth and sometimes it appeared as if she were dancing in the sky on the rays of the white moon. At times she appeared to dance among the stars, swirling around like a top.

When Sivakami swirled around, the eyes of the audience also swirled. The stage and the earthen lamps swirled. The temple and its towers swirled. The golden pillar at the thoonganai madam also swirled. The moon and galaxy of stars came swirling around.

After dancing in various tempos to different beats, Sivakami went backstage to take a break. At that time the audience applauded enthusiastically.

Despite having lived in Aayanar's house for eight months, Gundodharan had not seen Sivakami dance. So he too was euphoric like the rest of the audience.

As he was in a trance even after the dancing had stopped, he addressed Mamallar who was sitting next to him as 'Prabhu . . .' and started to say something. Though Mamallar had been completely engrossed in Sivakami's dancing, he was still alert. So when Gundodharan addressed him as 'Prabhu', Mamallar gave him a nudge. By then, the attention of five to six people sitting next to them turned towards Gundodharan, who in turn became fully alert. He looked towards the sanctum and exclaimed, 'Prabhu! This divine dance is dedicated to you!', exuding devotion.

Those next to him agreed saying, 'There is no doubt. This dance is dedicated to God!'

Sivakami returned to the stage and performed to the following verse of Navukkarasar Peruman:

The perfect trident glitteringly appears
The crescent on matted hair glowingly appears

The audience was immersed in an ocean of joy as though they had seen Lord Shiva himself. Then everyone expected

Sivakami to perform to the verse *'Munnam avanadhu naamam kettal'* (At first His name she heard, About His image then she heard ...).

But contrary to everyone's expectation, Sivakami sang and performed to the following verse:

Are you merely a grey-haired wayfarer who lost his way;
Or a thief after the hearts of unsuspecting damsels.
With ashes on my body and Ganga in my locks
And the crescent adorning my hair;
I have a blameless heart within,
I speak evenly but with a whiff of mischief
So a thief I can't be.
Do look past my veneer to know who I may be'

Lord Shiva assumes the disguise of a grey-haired old man and comes to a naïve girl's house to enquire about something. That girl, who had been sleeping, wakes up with a start. She rubs her eyes and looks at him. Seeing a stranger, she asks, 'Aiyya! You entered my heart without informing me. Who are you, a thief?'

The visitor looks at her intently in the eye. Then he smiles and asks, 'Am I the thief? I am a pure-hearted person unaware of falsehood. I have vibhuti smeared all over me. Don't you recognize me?' It was Lord Shiva who had plucked the moon from the sky and adorned his head with it, who was feigning in this manner! Ah! There were no words to describe the beauty of the crescent moon, his deceit and his consummate acting like a naïve person.

Sivakami enacted the above piece exquisitely through her expressions, body movements and mudras.

The singing and abhinayams enthused the audience who appreciatively exclaimed, 'Ah!' several times. But the audience was still not satisfied. One of the viewers bravely stood up, went to the stage and whispered something in Aayanar's ears.

Sivakami also heard that. She hesitantly commenced singing and dancing to the verse 'Munnam avanadhu naamam kettal'. She skilfully performed several abhinayams to convey the emotion in the song.

By the time the singing and dancing had drawn to a close, several people in the crowd were in a trance!

An aged man stood up chanting, 'Nataraja! Nataraja! The charming dancer Nataraja!' and started dancing with one leg raised.

The audience rejoiced and whispered amongst themselves, 'Never has anyone witnessed such soulful abhinayams before, nor is it going to happen in the future!'

Only three people knew that the abhinayams Sivakami performed to that verse that day were not as effective as her performance at Navukkarasar's monastery. Those three were Aayanar, Mamallar and Sivakami.

Nor did Sivakami fall down on the floor unconscious at the end of her performance!

Chapter 36

A New Birth

Three days after their arrival at Mandapapattu village, Aayanar, Sivakami and Mamallar stepped out of the village for a stroll. They reached the spot where the boat had hit a rock and sunk.

That day, the flood had subsided considerably. Water levels had receded in the area that had been submerged three days ago, and the rocks were visible. More than half the trees on the shore had been previously submerged. Today, water was flowing past the aerial roots of those very trees. As it was a rocky area, it was very clean after the floods.

Aayanar was extremely keen to walk around the rocks and study them closely. He was visualizing those rocks that could be sculpted into temples and others that might be carved into statues.

Sivakami and Mamallar seemed to be very content sitting silently on the rock under the magizham tree.

At the cusp between day and night, Aayanar half-heartedly asked, 'Shall we go, Sivakami?'

Sivakami asked, 'Appa, today won't the moon rise two nazhigai after darkness has set in? Why don't we view that and then go?'

'Why not? Let's do that!' replied Aayanar. He sat down next to the two of them.

Silence prevailed for some time.

'I don't feel like leaving this village at all!' revealed Aayanar.

'This village is fortunate. The villagers spoke the truth!' remarked Mamallar.

'Why do you like this village so much, appa?' asked Sivakami.

'When I see all these rocks, my hands itch to sculpt divine temples.'

'There are rocks in several other villages!' pointed out Sivakami.

'The residents of this village are such connoisseurs. Yesterday, they were so happy watching you dance!'

'Aiyya! Are you saying that the audience is not appreciative in Kanchi?' asked Mamallar, feigning anger.

'How can there be no connoisseurs in a place where Mahendra Pallavar and his son reside? I did not imply that. We were headed elsewhere when we embarked on this voyage. God led us here. I think that it's God's wish that we stay here!'

'Appa, Naganandi bikshu left on the night of the floods. What became of him?' asked Sivakami.

'Poor man! I don't know what happened to him and that aged bikshu!'

At that point of time, Mamallar wondered about the fate of the army that had accompanied him. Gundodharan, who had left in the morning saying that he would buy pots to make a boat, had not yet returned.

Shortly, an almost circular moon rose in the horizon. The waters assumed a glowing white colour in the moonlight and resembled the milky ocean the devas had churned to obtain the nectar of immortality. When the moon rose higher in the sky, it appeared as though a golden pot of nectar was emerging from the water.

For some time, the three of them discussed the beauty of the moonrise. Then Aayanar became restless. 'I will view these rocks in the moonlight and return,' he stated and left.

Mamallar and Sivakami sat silently for a long time. But their conjoined hands conversed silently with each other.

The fragrance of the magizham flowers spread all around, almost choking them.

Their hearts were overflowing with joy and suffocating them.

Within a short time, they felt as though the ground beneath them had slipped away and that they were floating in the air. The sky above them along with the moon and stars had disappeared!

They were sailing towards an unknown destination in an unending flood. Their ecstatic journey was timeless, making it impossible for them to ascertain whether they had travelled for a moment or for several yugams.

Suddenly, a gentle breeze caused the leaves of the magizham tree to rustle. The tree showered magizham flowers on their heads.

Both of them returned to earth with a thud. They realized that they were sitting on a rock under a magizham tree at Mandapapattu village.

When Mamallar asked, 'Sivakami, what are you thinking about?' it seemed as though his voice came from a long distance away.

'Prabhu, please hold my hand tightly! I'm scared I'll fall!' pleaded Sivakami.

'Why are you shivering, Sivakami? Is it because of the cold breeze?' asked Mamallar.

'No, prabhu! It's not the cold. See how hot my body is!' When she said this, there was a tremor in her voice.

'Then why are you shivering like this?'

'I am scared. Am I still alive?'

'What kind of a question is this? If you're not alive, how can you talk to me?'

'Some time ago, I felt as though I was travelling in the sky. Divine music was streaming in from somewhere. My soul was dancing to its beat and was travelling towards heaven. Was that a fantasy? Haven't I died?'

'Yes, Sivakami, in a certain sense, both of us did die! But we were born again. This is indeed a new birth for both of us. When we arrived at this village three days ago, our bodies and souls were not joined together. Today, you are not the same Sivakami, nor am I the same Narasimha Varman. You have merged with my life and soul. Similarly, I have merged with your life and soul. So within three days, both of us have died and been reborn . . .!'

'Is it truly only three days? I find this unbelievable. It seems to be such a long time!'

'That's also true. These three days are not a mere three days. For several births before this one, we had seen each other, fallen in love with each other, were separated and then united. We lived through all those experiences again during these three days.'

'Has everything come to an end with this?'

'How will it end? How can a relationship that has lasted several births end with this one?'

'I am not asking about our future births. I was asking about this birth. Will things be like this forever during this birth?'

'What are you asking about?'

'I am asking about your affection for me!'

Mamallar collected all the magizham flowers that lay scattered on the rock around him and placed them in Sivakami's hands.

'Sivakami, my affection is not like the jasmine and lilies that spread fragrance for a day and then wither away. My affection is like the magizham flower, whose fragrance increases by the day. Even if these flowers dry and wither away, their fragrance intensifies. You asked me for my word by the lotus pond the other day. Do you remember?'

'Yes, I do.'

'Do you ask for my word now?'

'No, prabhu! Your promise is not necessary. I only seek your pardon,' explained Sivakami.

'Why pardon?' asked Mamallar.

'I doubted you. Please forgive me for believing the venomous words uttered by a wicked snake about you!' requested Sivakami.

As a slight rustling noise was heard then, Sivakami got scared and looked around. The shadows of tree branches and moonlight alternately fell on that area, and a snake slithered past.

'Aiyyo! Appa! Snake!' screamed Sivakami, as she stood up. Mamallar also stood up quickly and reassuringly hugged her.

'Don't be scared, Sivakami! Why are you scared when I'm with you?' he asked.

Chapter 37

Race to Sacrifice

Hearing Sivakami scream, the snake was stunned and remained still for some time. Then it went on its way. Aayanar's voice was heard from a distance, 'Sivakami, did you call me?' He was standing amidst the rocks.

'No, appa!' replied Sivakami in a loud voice. Sivakami could understand Mamallar's happiness and gratitude from his tightening grip.

Both of them walked a short distance and then sat on a rock in an area that was as well-lit as the dawn. 'Why did you want to apologize, Sivakami?' asked Mamallar.

'I apologized for tolerating someone uttering slanderous things about you, for believing those words!'

'Is that all? I forgive you. But who bad-mouthed me?'

'Weren't you talking about a bikshu called Naganandi? He was the one who called you a "cowardly Pallavan". He said that you were hiding inside the Kanchi fort because you were scared of the battlefront. He mentioned a lot of other things.'

Mamallar, who was listening to Sivakami, asked, 'I am not angry with Naganandi on this count. I am angry with my father. If I were to remain inside the fort when the kingdom is being invaded, why wouldn't the people call me cowardly? I am not worried about that. But did you believe those rumours, Sivakami?'

'Yes, prabhu, I believed those words. Unable to bear the sorrow of being separated from you, I believed those tales. I comforted myself thinking that it did not matter if such a debased person did not love me. Though I was swayed by his words, my heart kept telling me that this could not be true. My heart told me that Mamallar was a brave man and that I was not worthy of his love. My heart firmly asked me not to think lowly of you, and that was close to my true character. Prabhu! Will you forgive me?'

'Sivakami, you have not committed any mistake for me to forgive you. It is I who have subjected you to so much sorrow and so should ask for pardon. In future, will you believe such rumours about me?' asked Mamallar.

'I will never again believe such rumours. I will not spare the bikshu if ever I meet him again,' quipped Sivakami. Suddenly, Sivakami thought of something and hesitantly asked, 'Prabhu! Have you heard of the soul migrating from one human body to another? Do you believe in that?'

'Why do you ask me if I believe in that?'

'Is it possible for a soul to move from one body to another? That is, can a human assume the form of a snake?'

Mamallar observed that Sivakami was again shivering when she asked this question. He embraced her against his broad chest and asked, 'Why this unnecessary fear? How can a man assume the form of a snake? If a man were to assume the form of a snake and try to bite you, I will assume the form of a kite and kill him. Or I will pull out his poisonous fangs and fling them away in your presence. Why are you scared when I'm around?'

'Prabhu, are you always going to be by my side and protect me? Is it your sole job to safeguard this poor girl? Doesn't Rajya Lakshmi* need you for her protection?' asked Sivakami.

'Sivakami, if you agree, I will leave the kingdom to its fate and stay with you. You are more important to me than the kingdom . . .!' As Mamallar was speaking in this manner, Sivakami interjected.

'Prabhu! I am not such a selfish woman. I don't expect you to pay attention to and shower love on me alone. You have the sole right to ascend the ancient throne of the expansive Pallava empire. Citizens of this kingdom live here, trusting the strength of your shoulders and sword. The responsibility of driving away wicked foes and safeguarding the citizens rests with you. It is on account of the good deeds that I did in my previous birth that you embraced me today. But this good fortune has not gone to my head. I have not lost my common sense. I would never think that the strength and valour of the sole heir of the Pallava dynasty should be used only to safeguard a mere sculptor's daughter. I don't even expect such a great sacrifice from you. Do you know how elated I was when I heard the villagers discuss your brave deeds at the Pullalur battle?'

'Sivakami, I too was ecstatic when the villagers praised your dancing. I feel ashamed thinking of my selfishness.'

'I have not observed any trace of selfishness in you, prabhu!'

'You will not observe it, Sivakami! You see me clothed in the golden fabric of your love. So, you will be blind to my faults. But I am aware of my selfishness. God has endowed you with amazing remarkable talent. But I am trying to

---

*The goddess (Lakshmi) of the kingdom (Rajya).

appropriate all that talent just for myself. Who can be more selfish than me? Your wonderful talent of dancing is worthy of god. My father says that it is not meant for mere humans. I understood the import of his words when I watched you dance at the village temple yesterday. I often wonder if I am not committing a sin by trying to usurp an offering meant for God!'

Sivakami then stood up and observed Mamallar's face closely. Before Mamallar could ascertain her intention and stop her, Sivakami touched his feet and then her eyes with her hands. Then she sat facing him and replied, 'Swami, if my dancing is worthy of God, then you are that god. I enthusiastically learnt dancing from my father so that I could dance for you and make you happy when you visited us. It is your love for me that infuses emotion and life in my dancing. My dancing in ecstasy, forgetting myself, stems from the thought that I am worthy of your love. When I sang and performed abhinayams to Thirunavukkarasar's nectar-like verses, it was your sacred form that appeared in my mind. The proficiency I acquired in this art is on account of you. I can dedicate this to none but you. Even if my art is not worthy of the almighty, I am not affected. You are more than the art to me. If you agree, I am willing to dump all my talent in this river and never dance again.'

Mamallar closed Sivakami's open lips that resembled pomegranate seeds with his mouth. 'Sivakami! I feel increasingly embarrassed when I hear you speak in this manner. I feel unsettled when I think that you would have to give up this art one day. It is unacceptable that the chakravarthini of the Pallava empire render public performances on the stage. When I think about that, I wish that I were your father's disciple learning sculpting from him. If that were the case, couldn't we lead our lives in the same way we spent the last three days? What is the purpose of a kingdom? What is the necessity of war and bloodshed? I am stating the truth, Sivakami! I will send a message to the chakravarthy that I do not want the kingdom. Your father, you and I will travel in a boat. We will take Rathi and Suga Rishi along. We will go to an island in the middle of the sea. We will happily spend the rest of our lives there. What do you say? Please say yes!'

'I will never say that!' insisted Sivakami and continued:

'I have read of brave women who fought along with their husbands in stories. Kaikeyi and Subhadra rode chariots for Dasarathar and Arjunan in the battlefield. I was not born in such fortunate circumstances. I cannot come to the battlefield. I faint at the sight of blood. I am a naïve girl born to adorn myself, sing and dance. But I will not allow you to become like me. I will not allow you, who are destined to ascend the throne, rule the kingdom and decimate enemies, to wield a chisel. I will not allow hands that were meant to wield swords and spears and overcome enemies to perform thalams for singing and dancing. Swami, you're questioning the necessity of a kingdom and war. If you speak in this manner, I will think that it is due to me and give up my life.'

'Sivakami! It is not just the blood of a sculptor who wields a chisel that flows through your veins. The blood of the brave women of ancient Tamizhagam also flows in your veins. You possess the steely heart of the heroic Tamil women who willingly sent their husbands to the warfront as soon as they were married. You are truly worthy of becoming a warrior's wife! You do not have to accompany me to the battlefield. You do not even have to ride my chariot. Henceforth, whenever I head to the battlefield, you will be in my heart. The valiant words you just uttered are echoing in my ears. The thought of your love will be a source of unparalleled bravery and courage to me.'

'Swami! You, the scion of the valorous Pallava dynasty and the winner of the title "Mamallar", don't have to think of me to muster bravery and courage. Were you thinking of this poor girl when you decimated the foes and won a victory that impressed the entire world at Pullalur? The sight of a mere spider scares me. Do you remember, when we were children, we were playing behind my father's statues. I saw a big cockroach and screamed. You came running from your hideout, hugged me and consoled me. "What is it?" you asked. I was initially embarrassed, and then I told you about the cockroach. You did not believe me. "How can a cockroach scare you? Lies! You pretended to be scared to make me leave my hiding place," you remarked. I was truly scared then. I was also scared when I saw a snake here some time ago . . . See, even now I'm shivering!'

Mamallar once again hugged Sivakami, brought her close to his strong chest and enquired, 'Why this foolishness, Sivakami? Why are you shivering?'

'I don't know. Of late, I often feel scared. I feel as though some indescribable danger is in store for me. Swami, I will tell you a secret. You should not reveal this even to my father.'

'Tell me, Sivakami!'

'At Thirunavukkarasar's monastery, when I regained consciousness, you bid farewell to me through your eyes and left. After some time, my father and I took leave of Vageechar Peruman and were going to Kamali's house. Then Navukkarasar held my father back and said something softly that reached my ears too. "Your daughter is very fortunate! She is endowed with a divine aura no one in the world is endowed with. But I don't know why I feel sad when I look at her. I feel that great danger will befall her. Please take care of her carefully." Ever since I heard that . . .'

'The great soul spoke the truth, Sivakami! Weren't you in great danger? Can there be a danger that is greater than this flood? You escaped by God's grace! Henceforth, you will not be in any danger!' remarked Mamallar confidently.

'How can I call the flood that united us and transported me to the heavens for three days a danger? That's why I think something else is in store for me. But I don't care if I face danger in future. The confidence that there is a secure place for me in a corner of your large heart will embolden and motivate me. I will contentedly stay here till you are done with the war and come to fetch me with your father's permission. Your love will shield me from all danger and I will be unharmed.'

'Is Mandapapattu so fortunate? Have you decided to stay here?' asked Mamallar. It was evident from his voice that he also preferred this.

'Yes, prabhu. I cannot live peacefully in any other place. This village temple, rocks and the Varaha River are sources of such happy memories to me. My father is also very keen to carve temples out of the rocks. He will also be at peace. But one issue alone worries me. That Naganandi should not come here,' Sivakami revealed.

'Naganandi will not come here. You don't worry about that!' assured Mamallar confidently, on account of what Gundodharan had informed him earlier.

At the same time, the bikshu who had been hiding behind the rock on which they were sitting and conversing, carefully stood up and walked away.

Chapter 38

With the Moon as Witness

When Mamallar, Sivakami and Aayanar returned to the village at night, they observed a big crowd outside the rest house.

In the middle of that crowd, swords, shields and spears gleamed in the moonlight.

The trio was taken aback and stood by the temple wall at the street corner. All three of them were wondering about the identity of the soldiers who stood outside the monastery.

Gundodharan and Mamallar had had a minor argument that morning about what to do next. Mamallar had opined that, since the Varaha River had subsided, they ought to build an earthen boat in which he and Gundodharan could row across the river. Mamallar wanted to disembark on the opposite bank and head to Kanchi. He thought that Gundodharan should return to Mandapapattu and stay with Aayanar and Sivakami to provide them security.

Gundodharan disagreed with Mamallar and offered the river first and find out about the whereabouts of the Pallava army. He opined that they could decide on a future course of action once he returned. Mamallar, who wanted to spend another day with Sivakami, agreed.

But he often panicked that day. As evening set in, he was troubled thinking, 'Why hasn't Gundodharan returned yet? For how many days can I remain idle here?'

Even when he was conversing with Sivakami in the beautiful moonlight, he occasionally wondered if Gundodharan had returned and what news he had brought.

Seeing the crowd outside the monastery armed with swords and spears, several questions occurred to him simultaneously. 'Who are these people? Are they our enemies or Pallava soldiers? If they are Pallava soldiers, have they come here knowing about my presence? If they do know about my presence, they will raise slogans on seeing me. Then won't the villagers come to know who I am?'

Understanding the reasons for Mamallar's hesitation, Aayanar offered, 'Prabhu, you and Sivakami stand here for some time. I will go ahead and find out who has come,' and walked ahead.

Sivakami and Mamallar stood by the corner of the temple wall under the mandara tree with widespread branches that grew from within the temple wall. But Mamallar listened attentively to the sounds that were coming from the crowd that had congregated outside the monastery. The villagers were talking simultaneously. Amongst those voices, he could hear the firm voice of Paranjyothi and also Suga Brahma Rishi's shrill voice chanting 'Mamalla! Mamalla!'

Mamallar's confusion disappeared in a flash.

'Our commander, Paranjyothi, has come! Come Sivakami, let's go!' he exclaimed enthusiastically and started walking ahead. Sivakami gently touched his hand and muttered,

'Prabhu!' Mamallar observed two teardrops glistening like pearls in her eyes in the milky-white moonlight that streamed through the branches of the mandara tree.

'My dear! What is this?' he asked affectionately and wiped her eyes with his angavastram.

'Once you heard your commander's voice, this helpless girl has become unnecessary,' moaned Sivakami in a choked voice.

Mamallar, who did not even have an inkling that such a situation would arise, stood stunned, not knowing how to console her. Then he asked, 'My dear life! Why do you speak in this manner? Didn't you encourage me with your brave words and ask me to go to the battlefield sometime ago? If you shed tears when I am about to leave, how can I proceed bravely?' and raised Sivakami's beautiful chin. The moonlight fell directly on Sivakami's face and her naturally golden complexion glowed like ivory.

Sivakami removed his hand from her chin and asked, teary-eyed, 'I don't know why I'm feeling so scared. It seems as though happiness has come to an end in my life today. Prabhu! You won't forget me, will you? You won't forget this humble sculptor's daughter even when you are decimating our foes seated on an elephant and after that at your coronation when you're seated on the jewelled throne, will you?'

Mamallar pointed to the full moon glowing in the sky and promised, 'Sivakami, I swear with the moon, which showers beautiful light while travelling in the sky, as the witness. Listen to me! It is redundant to say that I will not forget you during this birth. Such a thought would never cross my mind. There can be only one reason for your fear. If I were to die in the battlefield . . .'

'Aiyyo! Don't say that! Don't ever say that!' cried out Sivakami as she wept.

Mamallar assured: 'If that does not happen, there's no question of my forgetting you. When the war is over and the time comes for me to sit on the jewelled throne as the chakravarthy of this expansive Pallava empire, you will be seated by my side. But when one goes to the battlefield, one must be prepared to accept victory or honourable death. So what if I lose my life in the battlefield, Sivakami? There is no room for worry. Will our love end with this birth? Never! If I am conscious when my life is leaving me, I will pray to the god who wears the moon, "I should be born again in the sacred Bharata, in Tamizhagam where the Palar, Pennaiyar and Kaveri flow." I will be born in Tamil Nadu and wander from place to place. I will search for the beautiful form, the golden statue endowed with life I had loved in my previous births. I will see you again in this very month of Karthikai in the moonlight. I will recognize you the moment I see you. I will realize, "The beauty that is brimming in this girl's face is not hers. It is my love for her over several births that endows her with such beauty." I will recognize my soul in the sparkle of your eyes. "This is Sivakami! She is the joyous glow that has merged with my life in several births. This is the beautiful face that I have admired in the magnificent moonlight. My eyes have been hovering around these black, hyacinth-like eyes and consuming the nectar!" Sivakami, is this vow sufficient? Are you content?'

The flow of words from Mamallar's poetic heart rendered Sivakami breathless. She shivered and felt goosebumps. She could not fathom if she was standing on the earth or floating in the sky.

Suddenly, she returned to reality hearing voices exclaim, 'There's Mamallar!' 'There's the Pallava kumarar!' 'Long live Mamalla Pallavendrar!' 'Long live!'

'I am satisfied. Please go ahead before the people come here!' she urged.

Chapter 39

Row Forth the Boat!

Commander Paranjyothi walked ahead of the others towards Mamallar, bowed to him and asked, 'Prabhu, why did you act in this manner? All of us were distraught!'

Mamallar enthusiastically hugged Paranjyothi and asked, 'It is true that my departure worried all of you. What did you do after I left? Were there a lot of casualties in our army due to the floods?'

Paranjyothi replied, 'By the grace of Lord Soolabani, we were cautioned in time. So there was no loss of lives. There is so much to tell you and to discuss with you. Please come, prabhu. Let's go to that temple and talk.' Both of them walked arm-in-arm into the temple through the main entrance, while the soldiers stood guard and stopped the crowd of villagers from following them.

Sivakami, standing unobserved behind a tree, sorrowfully watched Mamallar and Paranjyothi walk away, talking animatedly, leaving her all by herself. Aayanar, accompanied by Rathi and Suga Rishi, walked up to where Sivakami was standing.

Sivakami stroked Rathi and Suga Rishi as if she meant to say, 'From now on, you are my true friends.' When the commotion caused by the crowd had abated, all of them walked towards the rest house.

As they walked past the temple entrance, Sivakami could hear the conversation amongst the villagers who were standing there.

'How the Pallava kumarar deceived us!'

'Didn't I tell you that he looks regal? He didn't look like a mere sculptor!'

'The son, like his father, is adept at assuming disguises!'

'I heard that he was trapped in the floods when he came with the express purpose of rescuing Aayanar's family!'

'Even though he holds them in high regard, he ought not to have gone to that extent. If something had happened to him, what would have been the fate of the Pallava kingdom?'

'Is it true that Paranjyothi is more adept at warfare than Mamallar?'

'Not at all! Both of them are equally competent!'

'Who said so? Mamallar is peerless in this world. The chakravarthy had taken Paranjyothi along to the battlefield. So his valour became renowned. Wasn't the Pullalur battle the first battle Mamallar fought? Paranjyothi was nowhere to be seen there!'

'Apparently there is no difference between them. They are such thick friends. Why should we discriminate between them?'

'All that does not matter. We must throw a feast for them in our village before they leave.'

Sivakami reached the rest house while listening to such conversations. She felt immense pride and inexplicable sorrow.

Acquiescing to the villagers' wishes, Mamallar, Paranjyothi and the other soldiers partook of the feast hurriedly prepared and lovingly served.

The feast ended well past midnight. The village elders requested them to stay back till the morning; but nothing came of it. It was essential for them to leave that night itself.

When it was time for them to go, Mamallar visited the rest house to bid farewell to Aayanar and Sivakami.

'Aayanar, I feel troubled taking leave of you. But what can I do? It seems that Pulikesi's army is advancing towards Kanchi. The chakravarthy has sent a message asking me to come immediately,' confessed Mamallar.

Aayanar, who had a lot of affection and respect for Mamallar, replied, 'Prabhu, it's our good fortune that you stayed with us for so long. We should not desire for more. Please leave. May we also come up to the riverbank to see you off?'

'It is not necessary for you to come so far! But please come if you want to,' replied Mamallar.

When Mamallar glanced at Sivakami, she was looking in another direction. It seemed as though a curtain had fallen between the extraordinary lovers.

Towards the end of the third jaamam of the night, when the moon was glowing in the western horizon, Mamallar, Paranjyothi and the others boarded the boats that were waiting for them by the Varaha River.

The villagers, Aayanar and Sivakami were standing on the riverbank. Gundodharan, who had not been seen for a while, came running and stood behind the others.

There was no opportunity for Mamallar to speak with Sivakami on the banks of the river. Once he had got into the boat, he looked intently at her. Sivakami too looked at him eagerly. Mamallar's lips itched to say something. But he was unable to speak. Commander Paranjyothi ordered, 'Row forth the boat!' The boat moved. It seemed to Sivakami as though the boat sailed away carrying with it all the happiness in her life.

Chapter 40

Argument

In the milky-white moonlight that transformed night into broad daylight, the boats sailed across the Varaha River and reached the opposite bank. Mamallar did not speak till they had reached. His love-filled heart was wandering in a dream world.

He was dreaming of the time when Sivakami and he would spend their time happily at Kanchi once the war was over—when the demonic Vatapi forces had been annihilated. He was dreaming of the nights when he and Sivakami together would sail down the Palar River in the moonlight.

Mamallar returned to earth from the world of fantasy with a thud when the boat hit the riverbank and came to a halt. He observed the rishabha flags that were fluttering at a distance away from the riverbank and the Pallava forces that surrounded those flags. He felt elated seeing a majority of the soldiers who had accompanied him there.

Mamallar was reminded of Kannabiran. As he was alighting from the boat, he asked, 'Commander, where is Kannabiran? Didn't he insist on accompanying you?'

'Wouldn't he insist? He was adamant about coming. I was the one who commanded him to stay here, feed the horses, and look after them. Don't we have to cover a distance of six kaadam in one stretch?'

As both of them neared the Pallava forces, the sound of a thousand voices raising slogans such as 'Long live the Pallava kumarar!' 'Long live the brave Mamallar!' and 'Long live!' echoed all around.

One soldier stepped forward from the forces that were standing at attention. Paranjyothi asked, 'Varathunga, what's the news?'

'Shortly after you left this place, two horsemen came here. They took Kannabiran, his chariot and ten soldiers along with them.'

'What? Did they take Kannabiran with them?' asked an agitated Paranjyothi.

'Yes, Commander! They said that they had to go to Kanchi on an urgent task.'

'Do you know who those warriors were?'

Varathungan hesitantly replied, 'One of the emissaries said that his name was Vajrabahu. The second was the head of the spies, Shatrugnan. As they showed me the lion insignia, I sent Kannabiran and the soldiers. This is the royal decree they left for the commander!' and extended a communiqué.

The moment he uttered the name Vajrabahu, Mamallar and Paranjyothi exchanged glances. Both of them realized that the chakravarthy had come there. Paranjyothi hurriedly took the missive and read it in the moonlight. The missive contained the following message:

'This message is for Commander Paranjyothi from Mahendra Potharaiyar: I am well. Durvineethan has been imprisoned at the Mazhavaraya fort. I heard that the Vatapi forces have crossed Tirupathi. Come to Kanchi along with Narasimhan without delaying for even a moment. If Narasimhan refuses to come, show him this order, imprison him and bring him along.'

Beneath this message was embossed the royal symbols of the rishabha and spear. There was a postscript below these. 'If the fort gates are sealed before your arrival, meditate on Buddha Bhagavan.'

Paranjyothi handed over the message to Mamallar, who also read it and looked at Paranjyothi.

'Pallava kumara, will you come without giving us any trouble? Should I order them to imprison you?' asked Paranjyothi in a teasing tone.

'Yes, Commander, imprison me and take me along. Being imprisoned is far better than fearing our invading foes and hiding within the fort,' remonstrated Mamallar. He then removed the ornaments that adorned his chest and the sword at his waist and flung it on the ground.

Paranjyothi also flung his sword and headgear down and retorted: 'I too have no need of this commander's post. I would rather chant devotional hymns and travel from place to place than work as a commander under a kumara chakravarthy who abandons his army midway and runs after a dancer whom he loves. I am leaving now! I don't care what happens to you and your army!'

Mamallar stared at the ground and then at the sky for some time and then reasoned, 'Commander, come, let's go. This is not the time for us to argue. Our enemies are nearing Kanchi. What is the use of us wielding swords if we are unable to stop them? I am going to ask my father not to seal the gates of the Kanchi fort and tell him that we ought to wage the war right outside Kanchi. You will support me, won't you?'

Paranjyothi thought for a moment and replied, 'Aiyya, Mahendra Pallavar is your father, he gave birth to you. You have the right to argue with him and ask anything of him. But Pallavendrar is not only my father, my chakravarthy and my senathipathi, he is also my god. His command is my wish. I can neither speak nor act against his wishes. But in the event of you waging a war against our enemies after obtaining your father's consent, I will remain a foot ahead of you. I will not break this vow as long as I'm alive!'

The two friends mounted their waiting horses and rushed towards 'Kalviyil Karaillada Kanchi Managar', Kanchi, the great city that is peerless in education.

Chapter 41

The Survivor

While Sivakami was staring at the boats that were sailing across the Varaha River, Aayanar turned around to see who had come running and was standing breathlessly behind him.

Seeing Gundodharan he asked, 'Appane, where were you all this time?'

'Don't ask me about that, aiyya! I crossed the river and conveyed the news that Mamallar was safe at Mandapapattu to the commander. I rushed back hoping to reach this place ahead of the commander and the warriors, who were then procuring boats. But I was unable to find the earthen boat I had left fastened on the riverbank. In the dim evening light, I could see someone rowing the boat towards this bank. His tonsured head and ochre robes indicated that he may be a bikshu. Thinking that it was Naganandi adigal, I repeatedly called out to him. But the bikshu did not look around. I was furious. I abused all the ochre-clad bikshus in the world aloud. Hearing my voice, two people who were walking by the riverbank enquired what the matter was. I told them. I then came to know that they too had come in search of Naganandi bikshu. The three of us built a raft using logs and creepers and then reached this place. I immediately rushed to the monastery. I came to know that Mamallar was leaving and that you were seeing him off. By the time I came running here, everyone had boarded the boats. See, aiyya! One must never trust members of the royal family. Mamallar left without even telling me. Did he even remember we were inseparable for the last three days?'

Gundodharan incessantly chattered in this manner. Sivakami, who was only half-listening, replied, 'Yes, Gundodhara. It's true that one must never trust royalty!'

Aayanar interjected, 'That's all right, Gundodhara! You said that Naganandi had come to this village. I never saw him!'

'A cobra will never raise its hood so easily. It will hide in an anthill,' quipped Gundodharan.

'Don't speak disparagingly of elders, Gundodhara! Naganandi is a great soul. If he also stays back in this village, I will be truly happy. He will guide me in sculpting rock temples,' observed Aayanar. Then he asked, 'You said that two more people had come here looking for Naganandi. Who are they?'

'Guru, it seems that those people are also extremely interested in sculptures. We reached the same spot where the earthen boat had broken. Do you know what one of them said on seeing the rocks? He echoed what you had said, "One can carve such beautiful temples out of these rocks." That man asked me, "Who is your guru?" He was amazed when I revealed that you were my guru. It seems that he too knows you, guru!'

'Who is this person known to me? I know of only one person who will think of temples as soon as he sees rocks.

But it's unlikely he will come here! Who else could it be?' wondered Aayanar.

'They are sleeping somewhere in the vicinity of the riverbank. I will search for them and bring them along. You go on ahead, guru,' advised Gundodharan.

By this time, the boats had crossed more than half the distance between the two banks. The villagers took leave of each other and started walking back towards the village. Aayanar and Sivakami left with them.

As they walked, Sivakami listened to the villagers' conversation about Mamallar's good nature and his friendship with Paranjyothi. The impact of those words on her heart that was numb after Mamallar's departure was akin to raindrops on a desert.

Gundodharan had detached himself from Aayanar and the others and was looking around in the moonlight as he walked down the riverbank. As he approached a rocky area, he was even more observant. When two people unexpectedly emerged from behind the rocks, he was taken aback. On recognizing them, he stood deferentially in front of them.

'Gundodhara, you work well! You made us wait for so long and disappeared. We wondered if you were alive, or had disappeared to Yama Loka!' rebuked the head of the spies, Shatrugnan.

'Master, by your grace, I escaped. Had I been slightly careless, I would have truly gone to Yama Loka. This sharp knife would have pierced by heart!' exclaimed Gundodharan, as he handed over a rare and small knife whose grip was shaped like a snake.

Chapter 42

Poisoned Knife

When Shatrugnan was about to take the knife from Gundodharan, Mahendra Pallavar, who was disguised as Vajrabahu, called out, 'Careful, Shatrugna! Take the knife carefully!' He then told Gundodharan, 'Why did you carelessly fasten this knife to your waist? This knife does not have to pierce your heart. If its tip were to slightly scratch your body, the poison would enter your bloodstream and kill you within one muhurtham!'

'Aiyyo!' exclaimed Gundodharan.

'Never mind! Where did you leave the bikshu? Tell us quickly!' asked the chakravarthy.

Gundodharan, without responding to his query, murmured, 'I was saved by God's grace!' His body trembled.

Shatrugnan rebuked, 'Yes, Gundodhara! It was by god's grace that our task did not go awry despite your delay. Respond to Pallavendrar's query quickly. By now, we would have covered half the distance back to Kanchi.'

Gundodharan, who was still unsettled, asked, 'What do you want to know?' Looking at the knife Shatrugnan was holding, he shivered again.

'What! What happened to you today, Gundodhara? Reply immediately to the question Prabhu asked. If you don't, this knife will pierce your chest!' threatened Shatrugnan and raised the knife.

'Master, that's the correct punishment for my stupidity. Nothing will happen if I lose my life. By Lord Shiva's grace, nothing happened to Pallava kumarar!' exclaimed Gundodharan.

Hearing this, even the unshakable Mahendra Pallavar trembled.

'Gundodhara! Was this poisoned knife about to strike Narasimhan?'

'Yes, prabhu! The bikshu aimed this poisoned knife at Mamallar's back five to six times. I kept quiet despite observing this. It was all on account of your command. Otherwise . . .' confessed Gundodharan and gritted his teeth.

Truly, Mamallar was saved that day on account of Tamizhagam's prayers and penances.

When Mamallar and Sivakami were sitting under the magizham tree engaged in romantic conversation and silent communication, the bikshu had been standing behind the rock on which they were sitting, aiming the poisoned knife. For some reason, though, he had hesitated to climb the rock. Had he hesitated because Sivakami was sitting beside Mamallar and he was concerned that the knife might accidentally strike her? Who knows?

Then, Lord Shiva's ornament, the snake, had slithered past. That resulted in Mamallar and Sivakami leaving the shade of the magizham tree and sitting on a large rock that was illuminated by the moonlight.

The bikshu had come out of his hiding place and had hidden elsewhere.

Gundodharan, who had been observing all this hiding behind another rock, itched to fight. He was eager to strangle the bikshu from behind. The reason for his refraining from doing so was Mahendra chakravarthy's unequivocal command.

That evening, when the chakravarthy, Shatrugnan and Gundodharan had rowed across the Varaha River in the log boat they had observed the bikshu standing on a rock, surveying the area. Then the chakravarthy had told Gundodharan: 'Gundodhara, I am now going to assign you a task that is more important than all the tasks you have performed thus far. You should carefully execute this task without any mistakes. You should shadow this bikshu all the time, without leaving him alone even for a moment. You should not give him the opportunity to move away from your sight. He should also not realize that you're following him. We have some work to do on the other side of the river. We will go back to complete that and return to the same spot. We will wait for you here. By the time the moon reaches its zenith, you should come here and let us know what happened. You should tell us where the bikshu went and what he did. But he should never see you.'

After commanding thus, the chakravarthy had asked, 'Did you carefully listen to my instructions, Gundodhara? Will you faultlessly execute everything?'

It was due to this command that Gundodharan had suppressed his mounting anger against the bikshu and had done nothing.

When Aayanar, Sivakami and Mamallar had left the rocky area and headed back to the village, the bikshu had followed them at a distance, hiding himself behind the plants and bushes by the side of the road. The bikshu had been unaware that Gundodharan was following him.

When the trio had returned to the village, Aayanar had walked ahead to find out who had congregated outside the monastery. Then Sivakami and Mamallar had had another opportunity to exchange loving words and express their steadfast love to each other. They stood in a corner at the turn of the temple wall. The bikshu had been standing just around the corner of the wall, aiming his poisoned knife. But he had not got the opportunity to fling the knife because Sivakami was standing beside Mamallar. The bikshu had waited for Sivakami and Mamallar to change their positions.

Gundodharan had been hiding behind the fence of a garden that was located opposite the temple, observing them. When the bikshu had raised his hand twice or thrice to fling the knife, Gundodharan had been unable to control himself. He had been ready to pounce on the bikshu when, fortunately, Commander Paranjyothi and the other soldiers had hastened towards Mamallar. The bikshu had immediately beaten a hasty retreat.

Gundodharan had watched Mamallar and Paranjyothi entering the temple and also Aayanar and Sivakami heading towards the monastery. Shortly thereafter, the bikshu had returned and stood again by the turn of the temple wall.

Then the bikshu had done something that Gundodharan had not anticipated. The bikshu had gently held the branches of the tree that grew in the temple praharam, climbed the wall and jumped into the temple compound.

The next instant, Gundodharan had reached the spot where the bikshu had been standing. For a moment, his heart was in his mouth because a snake slithered past quite close to the spot where he was standing. When he had retreated slightly and then returned to where he had originally been standing, he had been nonplussed. That was because the snake had lain still. He had then looked at it intently and chuckled to himself. He realized that it was not a snake, but a knife whose grip was shaped like a snake. He had quickly fastened that knife to his waist and had looked up with the intention of climbing the wall.

The crackling noise of the branches had raised some suspicion in Gundodharan's mind. He had immediately walked around the corner and stood close to the wall. As soon as Gundodharan had moved away, the bikshu's head had emerged at the top of the wall. The bikshu had not taken long to climb down. When he landed on the ground, he had started searching for something.

Realizing that the bikshu was searching for the knife, Gundodharan had noiselessly climbed the temple wall and jumped inside the temple. The temple madapalli was located quite close to the spot where Gundodharan had landed. He had hidden behind the madapalli wall.

Soon, the bikshu had jumped inside the temple again. He searched for something under the panneer tree that stood inside the temple.

Realizing that his efforts were in vain, the bikshu had stood erect and sighed. The sigh that resembled a cobra hissing had made even the steely hearted Gundodharan tremble.

The bikshu had alternated between standing under the panneer tree for some time and walking down the temple praharam and looking out.

The soldiers shouting slogans of victory and the commotion caused by the villagers had been heard intermittently from outside the temple.

It had been almost midnight by the time the noise subsided. The sound of the doors of the temple sanctum being closed and locked had been heard. After this, Naganandi adigal had stood up and walked around the temple praharam.

Gundodharan had seen the bikshu observing the open doors of the madapalli and entering the madapalli. He had immediately reached a decision. He had sprinted towards the madapalli in two long steps, noiselessly closed the doors, and firmly bolted the door shut from outside.

He had immediately climbed the wall, exited the temple, and rushed to the docks on the Varaha River. But he had been slightly delayed and the boats had already sailed.

Chapter 43

Who Is the Bikshu?

Gundodharan trembled when he realized that the knife he had stolen from the bikshu was poisonous. The chakravarthy asked him, 'Where did you leave the bikshu? Tell me quickly!'

'Prabhu, I locked him up in the temple madapalli and came here!' revealed Gundodharan.

'Well done! Come, let's go! Show us the way to the village!' commanded Mahendra Pallavar.

Shatrugnan worriedly enquired, 'Prabhu, why do we have to go to the village now? The task for which we came is accomplished. Gundodharan will take care of the bikshu. Please come, let's go!'

Mahendra Pallavar contended, 'No, Shatrugna! The task for which we came is not yet over. We have a job on hand that is more important than stopping the advance of the Vatapi forces. Imprisoning that traitor Durvineethan was not that critical. If we are able to imprison Naganandi bikshu, we have won three-quarters of this war.'

'Prabhu, if imprisoning the bikshu was so important, we could have easily done so long ago. We could have nabbed him at Aayanar's house itself!'

'As the bikshu was a lone man till now, it was essential for him to remain free for me to accomplish the tasks I had in mind. Henceforth, we will be in danger if he remains free.'

'Prabhu, please leave the job of imprisoning the bikshu to me and Gundodharan. You leave immediately. Kannabiran is waiting for you with the chariot on the opposite bank of this river.'

'Shatrugna, I cannot hand over this task even to you and Gundodharan! I myself have to complete it. Gundodhara, you walk ahead!' instructed Mahendra Pallavar.

Shatrugnan spoke no further. By the time the three of them reached the outskirts of Mandapapattu village, it was almost dawn. They scaled the outer wall of the temple and jumped in. The doors of the madapalli were still bolted from the outside. Gundodharan proudly opened the door. The three of them entered the madapalli and looked around.

The madapalli was empty! The tiles that had been removed from the roof and the resultant aperture indicated the bikshu's escape route.

'I thought as much, Shatrugna! Now do you understand why I was unwilling to assign the task of capturing the bikshu to the two of you?' asked Mahendra Pallavar.

'Gundodhara, did you hear that? You have brought indelible ignominy to Kanchi's spy forces!' accused Shatrugnan.

'Master, I will erase that ignominy today itself. Kindly give me the knife you now have. Naganandi bikshu must still be in this village. If I am unable to find him and stab him with this knife by dawn tomorrow, I will kill myself with this knife,' swore Gundodharan.

When Shatrugnan was about to hand over the knife to Gundodharan, Mahendra Pallavar intercepted it.

'Gundodhara! Never ever make such stupid vows again! You will not be able to stab the bikshu with this knife. His body is hard like a diamond. If you stab him, the tip of this knife will break. Even if you manage to injure him, the poison in this knife will not kill him!' explained Mahendra chakravarthy.

'How is that possible, prabhu? Is the bikshu a sorcerer? Do you believe in sorcery?' asked Shatrugnan.

'It has nothing to do with sorcery or magic. Poison will not affect poison, will it? The blood that flows in the bikshu's body is poisonous. That great soul consumed poisonous herbs for several years and transformed his body into a poisonous one!'

'Aiyyo! How terrible!' exclaimed Shatrugnan.

'If the snakes in the vicinity felt the bikshu's breath, they would flee out of fear!'

'True, master! I have observed that too. I now know the reason!' remarked Gundodharan. He shivered as he spoke.

'Shatrugna, do you remember the fearsome cave on the banks of the Kedil River in which snakes dwelt?'

'Prabhu, how can I forget that?'

'Did you unravel its mystery?'

'Despite thinking a lot about it, I was unable to guess.'

'I will tell you. If they are unable to capture the Kanchi fort by all other means, they intend poisoning the drinking water . . .!'

'How cruel! Is a bikshu doing all this in the name of the embodiment of kindness, Buddha Peruman? I cannot believe this!' observed Shatrugnan.

'It is indeed unbelievable. But the bikshu is not a true bikshu. He is an extremely astute spy who dons ochre robes and uses Buddha sangams to achieve his ends.'

'Why don't you want to kill such a cruel murderer?'

'We don't stand to gain by killing him. If we imprison him, he will be a critical pawn in the war we are waging against Pulikesi.'

'Prabhu, who is the bikshu?' asked Shatrugnan.

'I have a suspicion. When it is confirmed I will tell you, Shatrugna. You and your disciple, Gundodharan, have rendered valuable service to the Pallava empire thus far. But a mission that is far more important than all what you've done so far is awaiting you. If both of you listen to me attentively and act accordingly, the mission will be successful. What do you say?'

'As you wish, prabhu! We will act as per your command without committing even one small mistake,' assured Shatrugnan.

It was dawn now, and a pleasant fragrance emanated from the fresh blooms of the panneer tree.

The almost circular moon had lost its golden glow and had assumed the shade of a white lotus and was setting in the west.

Mahendra chakravarthy sat in the temple praharam at the entrance of the madapalli and made Shatrugnan and Gundodharan sit next to him. He then told them about the tasks they had to complete. The two spies listened attentively.

Chapter 44

Lion Insignia

On the following day, even two jaamams after sunrise, there was no sign of human movement or activity on the streets of Mandapapattu. After participating in the entertainment of the previous two nights and losing sleep by animatedly discussing the extraordinary incidents that had occurred, the villagers were slightly inactive that day. The front doors of several houses remained shut. The doors of the rest house were also bolted from the inside. But the sounds of human conversation could be heard from within.

Gundodharan, Shatrugnan and Vajrabahu reached the rest house then. Gundodharan knocked on the door. The sound of talking heard within immediately ceased. They could hear people walking and doors being opened and shut. Then the front door was opened.

Aayanar came out and asked, 'Is that you, Gundodhara? Where were you all night? If we were to rely on you . . .'

Seeing Vajrabahu and Shatrugnan he asked, 'Who are these people?'

Gundodharan replied, 'Didn't I tell you a duo interested in sculptures arrived last night? I searched for them all night and found them at dawn. I brought them here because they wanted to meet you.'

'Is that so? Please come in! Sivakami! Arrange the wooden seats!' invited Aayanar.

Sivakami, who was standing behind Aayanar, immediately took out and arranged the wooden seats. Aayanar and the two visitors sat down.

Though they insisted on Sivakami sitting, she did not do so. She looked at the two visitors curiously.

'Gundodharan told me that you were interested in sculptures. Where do you two hail from?' asked Aayanar.

'Guru! Don't you recognize me?' asked Shatrugnan.

'I'm unable to recognize you. Did you ever learn sculpting from me?'

'Yes, aiyya! Why don't you ask Sivakami ammai? She will remember.'

'Yes, appa. He was your disciple for two to three days!' recalled Sivakami.

'My luck is such! Within a few days of my arrival, you left for Mamallapuram . . . ,' commented Shatrugnan.

'Then, all work came to an end. I wonder what the purpose of this disastrous war is and when it will come to an end!' wondered Aayanar, and heaved a deep sigh.

'Please be a little patient, Aayanar! The war will get over soon. You can then return to your forest residence,' said Vajrabahu.

Hearing that voice, Aayanar was taken aback. He looked at Vajrabahu intently and asked, 'Aiyya, please tell me who you are!'

'Don't you recognize me, Aayanar?'

'I recollect seeing you before.'

Sivakami whispered into Aayanar's ear, 'It's the chakravarthy, appa! Don't you recognize him?' An astonished Aayanar stared at Vajrabahu for a moment.

He then hurriedly stood up from his seat and exclaimed, 'Prabhu! What kind of a disguise is this? I'm unable to recognize you!'

'I am satisfied with my skill at assuming disguises now. I was not so happy even when I stood in the presence of Pulikesi and delivered a message to him on the battlefield!' confessed Mahendrar.

Aayanar remarked, 'Pallavendra, Gundodharan told me last night itself that two visitors were talking about carving temples out of the rocks in the village. I immediately thought of you. I was wondering who else was endowed with such imagination regarding sculptures besides our chakravarthy. Finally, it turned out to be you. Prabhu, did you come so far to visit this poor sculptor? It has been ages since I saw you. It seems as though a yugam has passed.'

'Aayanar, it's true I am visiting you in disguise. I do not also wish to lie. I did not come here to visit you. I came in search of my son, Narasimhan,' confessed the chakravarthy. Sivakami looked down bashfully.

Aayanar hesitated before saying, 'Pallavendra, Mamallar left last night itself. Didn't Gundodharan inform you?'

'By now, Narasimhan and Paranjyothi must be heading towards Kanchi. Since I was here, I wanted to meet all of you and thank you for saving him,' replied the chakravarthy.

'Prabhu! When did we save Mamallar? It was he who rescued us from the floods in a timely manner!'

'Yes, Aayanar, I know that too. But it is also true that you saved Narasimhan's life. By you, I specifically implied your daughter. Look at this knife!' emphasized the Chakravarthy, and showed them the knife with a snake-like grip. Both Aayanar and Sivakami stared at that knife with inexplicable fear.

'Someone was about to stab Narasimhan with this poisoned knife. But since Sivakami was by his side, Narasimhan escaped.'

Sivakami trembled. When she realized that someone had tried to stab the god who resided in her heart, she felt the agony of being stabbed by the same poisoned knife. She was also incredibly happy that the danger had been averted as she had been present with Mamallar. But she was stunned, unable to comprehend how she had saved Mamallar.

'Prabhu, what are you saying? Was someone about to stab the kumara chakravarthy with a poisoned knife? Who was the sinner who attempted this heinous act? This is such a mystery. Sivakami! Do you know anything?' asked Aayanar.

'It's no use asking Sivakami. She is unaware of this. I will tell you everything at the appropriate time. The danger no longer exists. Narasimhan must have travelled far down the Kanchi highway by now. I too must leave. Aayanar! Don't you like this Mandapapattu village? Why don't you stay here till the war ends?'

'Yes, prabhu! That's my intention. The villagers are extremely good-natured. They are conoisseurs of art. They promised to assist me in carving rock temples.'

'I too will make the necessary arrangements for that. I will command the chief of the Thirukovalur kottam to provide you with the necessary funds, men and implements.'

'Pallavendra, please stay here for at least a day. Why don't we take a look at the rocks this evening and decide the types of temples that may be sculpted?'

Mahendra chakravarthy laughed and stated, 'Aayanar, the Vatapi army is three kaadam away from Kanchi. I must reach Kanchi before that army arrives.'

'Is that so? But Kanchi must be seven kaadam from here. How will you reach in time?' asked a worried Aayanar.

'Don't worry about that. Kannabiran is waiting for me with the chariot on the opposite bank of the river.'

Sivakami then told Aayanar, 'Appa, please ask if all is well with Kamali.'

'Kamali is fine, amma! Kannabiran was keen to meet you and inform you about Kamali. I was the one who stopped him.'

Sivakami reiterated to Aayanar, 'Appa, please ask them to inform us as soon as Kamali delivers the child.' For some reason, she was shy to look at Mahendra Pallavar.

'I will do so, Sivakami. Aayanar, I will take leave. Shall we take a look at the rocks on my way back? Will you come along?' asked the chakravarthy.

Aayanar stood up saying, 'Yes, prabhu! I don't have any other work more important than this.'

'I forgot one more thing,' remarked Mahendra Pallavar as he took out a hexagonal medallion from his pouch. He showed it to Aayanar and asked, 'Do you know what this is?'

Aayanar responded, 'I do, prabhu! It's the lion insignia.'

'Correct, Aayanar. Only eleven people in the Pallava empire possess this insignia. I am giving you the twelfth insignia. If you show this insignia to a functionary in any nook or corner of this kingdom, he will carry out your orders. The doors of all forts will open immediately. With this in hand, you can meet me and Narasimhan any time. I think you should have this during these times of war. You should keep this extremely carefully. Do not use this except when it's absolutely necessary,' instructed the chakravarthy, and handed over the insignia.

'Prabhu, why should this poor sculptor possess this insignia?' asked Aayanar, hesitating to take it.

'Aayanar, I don't consider any treasure in this vast kingdom more valuable than you and your daughter. You may need it at some point of time. So, keep it safely.' When Mahendra Pallavar uttered these words and extended his hand, Aayanar was unable to refuse.

He accepted it deferentially and instructed, 'Sivakami, keep this safely in your wooden chest and come with us.'

Sivakami took the insignia and went to the adjacent room. The wealthy women in the village had given her a beautifully carved chest to store her clothes and ornaments in. Sivakami kept the lion insignia in that chest.

In that very room was Naganandi adigal, hiding behind a pillar, watching Sivakami place the insignia into the chest!

Chapter 45

The Bikshu's Volte-face

Sivakami accompanied Mahendra Pallavar, Aayanar and Shatrugnan to the front entrance to see them off. Mahendra Pallavar asked her casually, 'Sivakami, why don't you come with us?'

Sivakami hesitated. Aayanar then urged, 'Come, Sivakami! Let's go. What are you going to do here all alone?' So, Sivakami left with them, accompanied by Rathi and Suga Rishi.

There was a reason for Sivakami's hesitation. When Sivakami had placed the lion insignia in her chest and looked up, she had seen a flash of an ochre fabric behind the pillar. She had realized that the bikshu was hiding behind the pillar. The bikshu had visited them early in the morning and was talking to them when the voices of strangers were heard outside. Immediately he had left saying, 'I will leave through the backyard.' Sivakami was surprised, wondering how he had returned and why he was hiding.

Had such an incident occurred till the previous day, she would have been alarmed and screamed. But her opinion of the bikshu had completely changed ever since she had conversed with him that morning. All the doubts she had previously harboured about him had vanished and she had started thinking highly of him. She had changed her opinion about the bikshu because the bikshu's opinion about Mamallar had also completely changed.

'I called Mamallar a coward listening to ignorant people. I now feel like slashing my tongue which uttered this. I myself saw him in the battlefield. Ah! We should stop exemplifying Arjunan for bravery and start saying that Mamallar is bravery personified. Do you know how courageously he fought all alone in the midst of a thousand people, swirling his sword around? Only Mamallan can perform such impossible tasks.'

Not only had the bikshu described Mamallar's brave acts, but he had also praised his character. The bikshu had confessed that he had committed a mistake by calling Mamallar a womanizer; that Mamallar was so virtuous that he did not even look in the direction of women; and that the princess who won Mamallar's love was indeed fortunate. Hearing this, Sivakami had not only been ecstatic, but had also felt a sense of respect and devotion towards the bikshu that she had never felt before. When Aayanar had asked about the reason for the bikshu's sudden disappearance from Ashokapuram, Naganandi had replied, 'Don't even ask me about that unfortunate incident. I know the Ganga Nadu king, Durvineethan. He is affiliated to the Buddha sangam and is devoted to me. Didn't Gundodharan give me a missive the other day? That missive contained the message that Durvineethan was about to invade Kanchi. I rushed in the middle of the night to prevent him from committing

such an act of grave stupidity and convince him to return.
I used Gundodharan's horse for this purpose. My efforts were
in vain. By the time I reached the battlefield, the battle was
over. The brave Mamallan had defeated Durvineethan as I
had expected, and Durvineethan had fled. I don't know where
he fled and what became of him!'

Listening to the bikshu praise Mamallar in this manner,
Sivakami had felt extremely happy, and her confidence in
the bikshu had grown. When she requested, 'Swami, please
stay with us in this village,' the bikshu had responded,
'No, amma! It is against my faith to stay in one place. The
southern country is no longer the right place for bikshu-
travellers like me. The Pandian is invading from the south.
The Chalukyas are invading from the north. I was concerned
that I should take the two of you to a safe place. This village
is the right place for you. If Buddha Maha Prabhu deigns,
I will meet you again once the war is over. Aayanar, I will
have learnt about the Ajantha secret by the time I meet
you next. I will share it with you. Sivakami, I would love
to stay here and watch your divine dancing. But I am not
fortunate . . .' The bikshu's kindness and his gentle tone had
caused Sivakami's heart to melt.

It was at this moment that Gundodharan had knocked on
the front door. Then the bikshu had remarked, 'Aayanar, your
disciple, Gundodharan, is unnecessarily suspicious of me. If
he sees me here, he will try to quarrel with me. I also think a
few more people are with Gundodharan. I will leave through
the backyard. Please give me leave!' and had left. As he was
going, he had stated in a gentle tone, 'Sivakami, I don't know
when I will see you again. But I will never be able to forget
you no matter where I go and what I do. Even if I were to
forget you, I will not be able to forget your dancing.'

Sivakami had been taken aback when she saw the bikshu, whom she thought had left, hiding behind the pillar in the inner room. Nevertheless, she thought that he had stayed back to tell her something and that she would ask him about it after the chakravarthy's departure. She returned to the outer chamber. It must be said that Sivakami was a little pleased that the bikshu had not left and had stayed back. When the chakravarthy asked her to accompany him, she thought of the bikshu hiding behind the pillar and hesitated for a moment. But when Aayanar also invited her, she was unable to refuse. She replied, 'Yes, appa,' and accompanied them. She thought that Naganandi bikshu would probably remain at the guest house till she returned.

Chapter 46

Trimurthy Temple

As they were walking towards the rocks, the chakravarthy neither spoke of Mamallar nor the danger that might have befallen him. He started discussing sculptures with Aayanar. Both of them lost all consciousness of this world as they spoke. They continued with their conversation even after reaching the rocky area. They were identifying the rocks that could be sculpted into an elephant, lion, chariot and engraved mandapam. They finally pinpointed a rock that could be carved into a temple and decided that the temple would be the first monument that would be sculpted.

'Aayanar, let's dedicate this temple to all the three gods! Please carve out three sanctums,' ordered Mahendra Pallavar.

'Swami, wouldn't it be good if we created three separate temples to appease those who follow the three major religions? Then there would be no room for controversy,' suggested Aayanar.

'People who follow the three religions? I did not imply that. Whom do you think I referred to as the three gods?'

'Shiva Peruman, Buddha Devar and Rishabha Devar, isn't it?'

'No Aayanar! I was referring to the Trimurthys, Brahma, Vishnu and Shivan.'

'Is that so?'

'Yes, for some time don't even talk about Buddhists and Samanars* to me, Aayanar. I am so annoyed with them!'

'Aiyyo! What have they done to upset an enlightened person like you?'

'Ah! I had treated the Samanars and Buddhists so honourably! I did a lot to appease them! Everything was in vain. Durvineethan sought refuge in a Samana seminary at Pataliputram. The Pallava army had to raze that seminary to the ground to capture Durvineethan, who was hiding in an underground chamber there. Do you know what they are going to do now? They are going to bad mouth me all over the nation saying that Mahendra Pallavan of Kanchi ordered the demolition of a Samana seminary! Never mind, Aayanar. I can't stay here much longer. I will take leave. When I return here after the war is over, the temple should have been completed. Shatrugna, where did we leave our raft? Please look for it and fetch it quickly!' He then instructed, 'Aayanar, will you also look for it? I don't know where we moored the boat on this riverbank. If two of you search for the boat, we may find it soon!'

Shatrugnan and Aayanar went in search of the boat. All this time, Sivakami had been standing in a corner gently patting Rathi and softly muttering a word or two. After Aayanar and

---

*A term, meaning 'wandering reunciates', that was used at the time for Jains.

Shatrugnan had left, the chakravarthy sat on a rock close to her and remarked, 'Sivakami! I need to have a word with you. Please sit on this rock.' Sivakami's instincts told her that the chakravarthy was going to speak of a sombre issue. So she continued standing with her head lowered. 'Sivakami, raise your head and look at this knife!' urged Mahendra Pallavar. Sivakami looked at that knife. 'Sivakami, do you remember what I had mentioned about this knife some time ago?'

'Yes, prabhu!' murmured Sivakami. The thought that the knife had been about to pierce Mamallar's back distressed her.

'I lied, Sivakami!'

Sivakami was astounded and confused. In that confusion she felt some solace, happiness and also some disappointment. Sivakami was also unable to comprehend the reason for the chakravarthy lying previously and admitting to his lie now.

'Yes, Sivakami! You will be bewildered. I do not want to tell your father what actually transpired. That's why I sent him away under the pretext of searching for the raft. But it is essential for you to know the truth . . .'

Sivakami felt even more confused. What was the truth he was going to state? Why was he saying that she alone must be aware of it? 'Sivakami, this knife whose tip is dipped in poison was about to pierce my only son's back. Do you know who was responsible for this danger?'

'Prabhu! You said that it was a lie . . .' stammered Sivakami.

'It's a fact that Narasimhan was about to be stabbed with this knife, Sivakami. That danger was about to befall the Pallava empire. It is untrue that the danger was averted because of you. Sivakami. You're not a coward like other average girls of your age. I am telling you the truth because you are a courageous girl. Narasimha Pallavan was about to be stabbed by this knife and die in this Mandapapattu village yesterday. His desolate corpse would have lain beneath this rock under the magizham tree. It was by the grace of Lord Shiva, who consumed poison ages ago to protect mankind, that Narasimhan and the Pallava dynasty were saved yesterday . . .'

Sivakami felt faint when she recollected that Mamallar had sat on that very rock last night, whispering loving words into her ears.

'Listen to me, Sivakami. No one as valorous as Narasimhan has been born thus far in the ancient and illustrious Pallava dynasty. Neither has this vast Pallava kingdom ever been as dependent on anyone as it is on Narasimhan today. Such a person was about to be treacherously stabbed in the back with a poisoned knife while sitting on this rock. I would have lost my only son who was born after several prayers and penances. The Pallava kingdom would have been bereft of an heir. Kanchi Sundari, extolled in poetry and novels, would have been desolate. Do you know who is responsible for the occurrence of this disastrous incident . . .?' The chakravarthy paused for a moment and heaved a deep sigh. 'It is Sivakami, the daughter of the sculptor, Aayanar, for whom I have more regard than my own life!'

Listening to this, Sivakami felt as though her head had been struck by lightning. Thousands of light rays emanated from that lightning and spread in all four directions.

Chapter 47

Rain and Lightning

When Sivakami regained consciousness, she observed that she was leaning against a rock and that the chakravarthy was consoling her. When she deferentially tried to stand up, Mahendrar firmly held her hand, sat her down and exclaimed, 'Don't!'

Sivakami shot a questioning glance at Mahendra Pallavar, as if she meant to ask whether what she had heard some time ago was real or a figment of her imagination.

The chakravarthy confessed, 'My child! You have demonstrated the depth of your love for Narasimhan. You fainted when you realized that he was in danger because of you. I am forced to hurt a heart as tender as yours.'

Sivakami began sobbing and asked, 'Aiyya! What else?'

Mahendrar remarked, 'Sivakami, I have not yet told you an important matter. I am going to ask you for your word! I am asking this for Narasimhan's well-being. You must promise me without fail.'

Clarity started emerging in the depths of Sivakami's confused heart. The doubts she had already been harbouring about the chakravarthy surfaced. She thought, 'He is trying to mislead me and trap me. I have to be careful!' She also started doubting the chakravarthy's claim that she was the reason behind the danger that had been about to befall Mamallar. Why did he isolate her and speak to her in this manner? What were his motives? She asked with her head bowed, 'Pallavendra, I am unable to register what you're saying. You stated that Mamallar was in danger because of me. How did that happen?'

'My child, I refrained from mentioning this to you as I did not want to upset you. I'm divulging this at your behest. Didn't I visit you at your forest residence two days after your arangetram at Kanchi? Then you must have heard a few things I mentioned to your father. Do you remember I had declared that your art is divine and that it ought to be dedicated to god?'

Sivakami recollected that conversation and wondered why he was repeating it now. She replied with her head lowered, 'I remember.'

'My child, if humans try to appropriate something that is meant for god, won't the outcome be harmful? It is the Pallava kingdom's good fortune that Narasimhan escaped!'

At that point, Sivakami looked up, faced the chakravarthy with tear-filled eyes and sobbed as she pleaded, 'Pallavendra! You are speaking in riddles. I am the uneducated daughter of an impoverished sculptor. Please don't put me to test!'

Mahendrar affectionately ran his hand down Sivakami's untied hair and remarked, 'Sivakami, I am not testing you. Don't you know the intimacy of the friendship between your father, Aayanar and me? Aayanar's daughter is also a daughter to me!

I will not harm you even in my dreams. You are as renowned for dancing as your father is for sculpting. It is my wish that you further enhance your artistic talent and become renowned all over Bharata Kandam. I wish that nothing and nobody impedes that. I will not brook my own son obstructing your progress.'

Sivakami shot a look, which conveyed shock and disbelief, at Mahendrar. 'Please be patient, my child. I will tell you all I have to say. Then you may decide as you please. You accused me of speaking in riddles some time ago. True, I spoke in that manner as I was embarrassed to speak to you directly. I thought you would understand because you are clever. But you're confused at the moment for various reasons. So, you are unable to understand the import of my words. For your well-being, I will state what I have in mind plainly. Please forgive me if you're hurt by what I'm going to say,' remarked Mahendra Pallavar, and heaved a deep sigh. His expression indicated that he was preparing himself for a harsh task.

Sivakami again lowered her head and stared at the ground. Her heart beat rapidly, anticipating disaster. A teardrop or two fell intermittently on the ground.

'Listen to me, Sivakami. Your father carves life-like statues out of stone. Similarly, Brahma Devan moulds all living beings out of mud. But it is said that Brahma Devan mixes the tears from his four pairs of eyes with mud to create women of uncommon beauty. It seems that Brahma Devan is aware that extraordinarily beautiful women will face several woes, which is why he weeps as he creates them! My child, I wonder whether Brahma Devan wept profusely when he created you. You are so exquisitely beautiful. As if that is not enough, your artistic talent is immense. When you were a child, I did not realize this. Like Aayanar, I too carried you around and showered love and affection on you. But when you grew up to be a young woman, I became concerned that no harm should befall this world on account of you. The indications of impending disaster appeared two years ago. I observed that the innocent friendship that blossomed between you and Narasimhan had transformed into love. I was wondering how to nip this inappropriate love in the bud without hurting the two of you, when this war broke out. I had to urgently leave for the battlefield. I sternly ordered him not to leave the Kanchi fort to prevent the two of you from meeting . . .'

Sivakami, whose head was lowered, inadvertently looked at Mahendrar angrily. The sparks that her tear-filled eyes emitted resembled lightning that flashed across the dark skies during heavy rain! The chakravarthy hesitated for a moment because of this and then continued, 'Sivakami, when I separated you and Narasimhan, I did not expect your love for each other to diminish. My instincts warned me that if you and Narasimhan met during my absence, there may be other disastrous consequences. People say that ghosts safeguard underground treasures and cobras watch over precious gems. Similarly, I believe a mysterious force is shadowing you either to safeguard or to abduct an artistic treasure like you. That is why I made the necessary arrangements to ensure that Narasimhan does not meet you. As I had expected, the love you felt for each other strengthened during your separation. I understood this from the messages Narasimhan wrote to you.'

'What?' cried out Sivakami as she looked at the chakravarthy with an expression that conveyed surprise and disgust.

'Yes, Sivakami, Narasimhan's epistles, kept by you in the hollow of a tree reached me. I had no option than to act in such a shameful manner. All for the sake of the Pallava kingdom. My child, the moral codes for civilians and royalty are different. Your father will explain this. Had Narasimhan been the son of a trader or a sculptor, I would have never ever come between the two of you. Your divine love would have exhilarated me. But I have the harsh duty of separating the two of you for the good of the Pallava kingdom.'

Sivakami managed to muster hitherto undiscovered courage. Her face and tone conveyed immense pride as she observed, 'Prabhu, you tried to separate us. But fate, which is more powerful than kings, favoured us. It caused the dam to breach and floods to erupt and united us in this village!'

'Yes, Sivakami, the fate that united you also demonstrated the importance of my arrangements. This poisoned knife is testimony to that!' averred Mahendra Pallavar as he held up the poisoned knife again.

Chapter 48

Mahendra Pallavar's Defeat

Sivakami's eyes widened as she looked at the knife with its grip shaped like a snake. She beseeched Vichitra Siddhar in a quivering voice: 'Pallavendra! Which sinner was about to stab Mamallar in the back with this poisoned knife? Please tell me. If this happened because of me . . .'

The chakravarthy interrupted saying, 'Sivakami, don't threaten to do something rash in anger. This grave danger did occur because of you, but you were unaware of it. Do you know who might have possessed this knife?'

'I have never ever seen such a knife, prabhu!'

'Don't you know anyone whose name contains the word "snake"?'

When Sivakami asked, 'Naganandi adigal?' surprise and fear surfaced in her voice.

'Yes! It is indeed him!'

'Aiyyo! Why should he try to kill Mamallar? This is unbelievable.'

'Why should it be unbelievable? Haven't you heard of even worse kinds of hostility than this?'

'Why should Naganandi harbour enmity against Mamallar? Why should a bikshu clad in ochre robes act like this . . .'

'Sivakami, does it matter whether it's a bikshu or a householder? Wouldn't a bikshu be enticed by feminine beauty? Wasn't Vishwamitrar's intense penance disrupted by Menaka's beauty? Why should this surprise you in this day and age when Buddha sangams are steeped in sin?'

'What are you saying? I am unable to comprehend it. Why did Naganandi try to kill Mamallar?'

'The reason was that the bikshu was intoxicated by your beauty, amma! What other reason can there be? Both the harsh bikshu and child-like Mamallan are captivated by your beauty. But you offered your pure heart to Mamallan. This is the reason for the bikshu's hatred. Last night, when you and Mamallan were sitting on this rock and talking, the bikshu was hiding behind the very same rock, armed with this poisoned knife. He followed the two of you up to the village temple. It was on account of God's grace and Gundodharan's extreme caution that Narasimhan's life was saved.'

'How did Gundodharan save Mamallar, prabhu?'

'Unknown to the two of you and the bikshu, Gundodharan shadowed all of you. When the bikshu was scaling the temple wall, this knife slipped and fell on the ground. Gundodharan took the knife. He locked the bikshu in the temple madapalli in the middle of the night and then came and told us everything. By the time we reached the madapalli, the bikshu had disappeared.'

As Mahendra Pallavar spoke, the various expressions that flitted across Sivakami's face did not escape his eyes.

Ever since they started discussing Naganandi, her attention wandered to and fro from the guest house. The image of Naganandi hiding behind the pillar of the guest house's inner chamber kept flashing in her mind. Would that evil bikshu still be at the monastery? She angrily decided to stab him with the poisoned knife if he was still at the monastery.

'Pallavendra, where is my father? I need to immediately go to the monastery,' implored Sivakami.

'Thaye! You have not yet heard my request. You have not yet granted me the boon I am seeking from you!'

'Why do you torture me by speaking in this manner? Please command the sculptor's daughter to do your bidding!'

'It's not a command, amma! I am seeking a boon from you. I am asking it for the well-being of the Pallava kingdom. You are the one who now possesses the power of rescuing this kingdom from a great disaster.'

'What should I do?'

'You should write a message to Narasimhan.'

'What message?' asked Sivakami.

'You should write to Narasimhan saying that you are freeing him. You should ask him to forget you.'

'Prabhu, why are you testing an impoverished girl like me? How can I free Mamallar? How can I write to him asking him to forget me? Even if I agree, my hand will refuse to cooperate, swami!'

'Sivakami, the Vatapi army is within three kaadam of Kanchi. Still I am here arguing with you. Don't you now realize how critical my request is? I will state the truth more plainly, Sivakami. Listen to me. The Pallava kingdom currently does not have the strength to counter the ocean-like Vatapi army. In this situation, the massive Pandya army is advancing from the south to invade this kingdom. If you deign to fulfil my request, the Pandya army will join hands with the Pallava army. If both the armies fight together, the Vatapi army can be defeated. Sivakami, will you render this great service to the Pallava kingdom?'

'What is the connection between me and the Pandya army, prabhu? What assistance can this humble sculptor's daughter render to the Pallava kingdom?'

'I don't want to hurt you, Sivakami. But you give me no other option. The Pandya king had asked Narasimhan's hand in marriage for his daughter. As Narasimhan did not agree, the Pandya army is invading us. The moment we accept their proposal, the Pandya army will join hands with us. If you free Narasimhan, I will convince him to accept this proposal. What do you say, thaye? Will you grant the boon of life to the Pallava kingdom?' pleaded Mahendrar.

Sivakami immediately sat on the ground and shrieked, 'Never, never! I will not be able to do this!' Then she sobbed as she exclaimed, 'Pallavendra, why don't you kill me with the poisoned knife you're holding? Then your son will be liberated. The Pallava kingdom will also be saved. There is nothing wrong in killing a helpless girl to save a vast kingdom. Wield the knife, prabhu! If you lack the courage to do this, give me the knife. I will stab myself.'

'Sivakami, you win! I lose!' implored Mahendra Pallava chakravarthy.

One nazhigai after this conversation, Aayanar and Sivakami returned to Mandapapattu village. The moment they reached the monastery, Sivakami hurriedly entered the room and looked around. The bikshu was neither hiding behind the pillar nor was he seen anywhere else in the monastery.

She became slightly doubtful . . . She hurriedly opened the chest that contained her clothes and ornaments. She ran her hands inside the chest several times. She rummaged through her clothes and jewels. Despite searching carefully, she was unable to find the medallion bearing the lion insignia the chakravarthy had given them.

Around the same time, the bikshu was showing the charioteer, Kannabiran, the lion insignia. He then commanded Kannabiran to quickly drive him in the chariot to Kanchi. Kannabiran hesitantly asked the bikshu to seat himself in the chariot. The chakravarthy and Shatrugnan were observing this from a distance, hiding behind trees. When Shatrugnan was about to leap forward and stop Kannabiran, the chakravarthy gestured to him not to do so.

The two of them silently watched the bikshu mounting the chariot, Kannabiran reluctantly driving it away and the soldiers following them.

Anger erupted on Shatrugnan's face. The chakravarthy was, however, smiling.

Chapter 49

Revelry at Kanchi

It was almost midnight when Mamallar and Commander Paranjyothi started riding swiftly towards Kanchi. Replacement horses had been arranged for them at the state lodges located at every second kaadam of the highway. Arrangements had also been made for food and for rest at these lodges.

Additionally, at every lodge, a hundred horsemen were standing on guard. These horsemen replaced the horsemen who had accompanied Mamallar till that point, thereby accelerating the pace of the journey.

Mamallar was greatly surprised by these arrangements. He was impressed thinking that his father, who had preceded him down the same highway, made these arrangements. Repeatedly commenting about this to Paranjyothi made him happy.

Paranjyothi responded saying, 'Ah! You're impressed with just this. It is easier to ascertain the depth of an ocean than to guess the extent of precaution, much to the dismay of his foes, that Mahendra Pallavar exercises. I have observed

233

this during the eight months I was with him. That is why, when the chakravarthy says something, I don't contradict him even in my thoughts.'

Paranjyothi then described the various tactics the chakravarthy had employed when camping on the banks of the North Pennai River with the Pallava army, to stop the advance of the Vatapi army. Somehow, the ruses did not find favour with Mamallar.

'Commander, you may be impressed, but I don't see any glory in restraining and deceiving adversaries and retreating and escaping from them,' retorted Mamallar.

Paranjyothi replied, 'There are times in a battle when retreat is necessary. There are also times when aggression is necessary. Did you observe one thing? The chakravarthy forbade you from pursuing Durvineethan beyond the South Pennai River. This disappointed you. But was Durvineethan able to escape? No! Hadn't the chakravarthy also made arrangements to capture him? Didn't he ask the chief of the Thirukovalur kottam, Anandhan Mazhavarayan, to remain alert on the opposite bank of the South Pennai River? Though Durvineethan sought refuge in the Samana seminary, he was unable to escape. Isn't he now imprisoned in Mazhavarayan's fort? Prabhu, there are several people who have won wars with large armies at their disposal. But there is no one like our chakravarthy, who with a small army has defeated awe-inspiring enemies.'

'Yes, there is no doubt about that! Isn't every Pallava warrior as mighty as ten Chalukya soldiers? Didn't we observe this in Pullalur?' quipped Mamallar. The Kumara chakravarthy was bitter about the fact that Mahendra chakravarthy had adopted subterfuge, rather than direct warfare, to win the war. He was unable to accept or appreciate this.

The close friends travelled through half the night and the whole of the following day and reached the southern entrance of Kanchi at sunset.

Paranjyothi was reminded of a day nine months ago, when Naganandi bikshu and he had reached that very entrance at sunset. That day, Paranjyothi had unobtrusively entered the city through a smaller door set within the fort gate. Today, he did not have to enter Kanchi in that manner.

When Mamallar, Paranjyothi and the hundred soldiers accompanying them neared the fort gates, the inspiring sound of drums resounded from the upper storey of the fort. Conches were blown. The sound of trumpets echoed in all directions. The sound of celebrations was heard from within the fort.

The fort gates swung open. The sight of the city inside was a feast to the eyes. The wide roads were lined with Pallava soldiers standing attentively.

Young girls were standing in the upper storeys of mansions. Heaps of jasmine, lilies and konrai lay beside them. The girls stood with their palms filled with flowers. Is it necessary to state the reason? They were waiting to shower the victorious kumara chakravarthy with them.

There were two reasons for the festive mood in Kanchi that day. First, the Pallava forces headed by Commander Kalipahayar had returned from the northern warfront. The city, which had worn a deserted look for the last few days due to the exodus of people, reverberated with life on the arrival of one lakh soldiers. They were also enthused by the news of Mamallar's conclusive victory at the Pullalur battle. The person who was responsible for this joy, Mamallar, was returning to the city that day. The citizens were thrilled that they were going to see him in person.

As soon as the drawbridge was lowered across the moat, Mamallar entered the city on horseback. Paranjyothi and the soldiers followed him. The fort gates closed behind them.

As soon as Mamallar crossed the fort entrance and entered the city, thousands of rishabha flags were raised simultaneously. The soldiers who were standing in the streets had been holding the flags down by their side till then. The sight of the flags, that had been kept low till then, fluttering in the sky on Mamallar's arrival, was magical. The flood of humanity that was spread over a vast distance realized that Mamallar had arrived on seeing the flags held aloft. The din that rose when the people joyously communicated the news of Mamallar's arrival to one another resembled the sound of waves rising simultaneously across the seven oceans.

The ministers' council and Commander Kalipahayar were also waiting at the entrance of the fort to welcome Mamallar. The kumara charkavarthy and Paranjyothi got down from their horses. When the prime minister placed a large garland of golden-hued konrai flowers around Mamallar's neck, Commander Kalipahayar cheered, 'Long live the warrior who defeated the Ganga Nadu king at the Pullalur battle! Long live!' The sound of people cheering, 'Long live! May we be victorious!' reached the heavens.

The smile that ought to have appeared on Mamallar's face in response to this welcome was absent. His heart was troubled by an unknown sorrow. It seemed to him that his father, Mahendra chakravarthy, had reached Kanchi ahead of him and had arranged for this reception. What was the necessity for this victory celebration when the army of the arch enemy of the Pallava kingdom was nearing Kanchi?

Mamallar was keen to meet his father that very moment. He and Paranjyothi mounted on the waiting horses and swiftly rode to the palace. When they crossed the front entrance as well as the nila muttram and reached the anthapuram, they saw Bhuvana Mahadevi surrounded by her ladies-in-waiting. She was waiting at the entrance to the anthapuram. After performing the arathi and drishti kazhithidal[61] to her son who had returned victorious from the battlefield, the chakravarthini observed, 'My child, I feel ecstatic hearing of your brave deeds on the battlefield. But why are you downcast? Is it the fatigue from travelling a long distance?'

'Yes, amma, that is also a contributory factor, but not the sole reason. I did not like the celebratory reception. Is the Pullalur battle victory a significant one? While the Vatapi army is as large as an ocean, the Ganga Nadu army is akin to a small pond. I was not entirely responsible for defeating that small force. The person truly responsible for winning the Pullalur battle is my father! Leave that aside, amma. Where's the chakravarthy?' asked Mamallar.

Surprise was evident on Bhuvana Mahadevi's face.

'What is this, my child? I was about to ask you the same question. Where is your father? Didn't you meet him? Didn't he accompany you?' asked Bhuvana Mahadevi. That was when Mamallar realized that Mahendra chakravarthy had not yet reached Kanchi.

'He left for Kanchi before me. Why hasn't he reached yet? Could he have met with an accident on the way? What is to be done if the chakravarthy does not reach before the Vatapi forces surround the fort? Won't the responsibility of overseeing the kingdom and conducting the war rest on me . . .?' Several such thoughts occurred to Mamallar.

Paranjyothi did not seem as surprised as Mamallar by the news Bhuvana Mahadevi had conveyed. It seemed as though he was expecting this.

Chapter 50

Ministers' Council

One-and-a-half jaamam into the night, the kumara chakravarthy received the news that the ministers' council had assembled and was awaiting his arrival. Mamallar took leave of his mother to attend the council.

The ministers' council had congregated that night as directed by the chakravarthy, who had sent a message from Pullalur. Ministers and chiefs of the various kottams had been summoned for consultation.

When Mamallar entered the mandapam followed by Paranjyothi, everyone stood up for a while as a mark of respect.

The chakravarthy's throne was empty. Mamallar sat on a throne adjacent to the chakravarthy's throne. Paranjyothi stood behind Mamallar. For some reason, he was reluctant to sit down. He was expecting certain unexpected events to occur. His face reflected the agitation within.

The prime minister, Saranga Deva Bhattar, initiated the council proceedings. His address to the council was as follows:

'The ministers' council has assembled here at this time as commanded by the chakravarthy. But the chakravarthy has not yet arrived. Has our chakravarthy, the Vichitra Siddhar, not reached here as he is engaged in other important tasks? Or has he been prevented by unexpected obstacles? We don't know ... In this situation, we have to decide first whether the ministers' council should be conducted under the leadership of the kumara chakravarthy or be postponed. Nine months ago, the chakravarthy empowered Mamallar to run the kingdom before proceeding northwards to the battlefront. So, I feel that this council may be conducted under Mamallar's leadership. I believe that all of you concur with me.'

Everyone assembled supported the prime minister's proposition.

Then, the chief minister, Ranadeera Pallavarayar, spoke as follows: 'We are in a situation that does not allow us to postpone this assembly. The frontline forces of the Vatapi army are within two kaadam of the Kanchi fort. We now are keen to know the kumara chakravarthy's views and orders. We also expect Commander Kalipahayar, who ensured the safe return of our brave forces from the warfront in the north, to brief us on our duties.'

The chief of the Chenji fort, Sadaiappa Singan, enquired, 'We are desirous of knowing about the chakravarthy. All these days we thought that the Pallavendrar was at the northern battlefront with the commander. Will the commander tell us where the chakravarthy went, leaving the army behind?'

Commander Kalipahayar answered: 'Ten days ago, the chakravarthy left the battlefield in the north accompanied by two thousand warriors. At that time, he ordered me to return to the Kanchi fort along with the remaining army. I did not receive any news after that. I thought he may have headed to the Pullalur battle. Some of those soldiers who went with the chakravarthy but have since returned also claim that is so.'

When the words 'Pullalur battle' were uttered, everyone's eyes turned to Mamallar.

'The commander's guess is correct. My father did arrive at the Pullalur battlefield. But I am surprised that he has not yet reached here. When I met all of you at the entrance of the fort, I thought that my father was waiting for me at the palace. I felt very disappointed that this was not so. The messages my father sent through my dear friend Paranjyothi led us to think he would be here. Commander, state all the details to them.'

Commander Paranjyothi informed the assembly about the Pullalur battle, Durvineethan's defeat, Mamallar's and his pursuit of Durvineethan, the chakravarthy reaching the south through another route, Mamallar getting trapped in the floods and ultimately reaching Mandapapattu, his searching for Mamallar and the chakravarthy sending a message to him after imprisoning Durvineethan. But he did not mention anything about Aayanar and Sivakami.

The prime minister, Saranga Deva Bhattar, subsequently spoke as follows: 'In the absence of the chakravarthy, our responsibility has increased multi-fold. An inconceivably large army is marching towards us. In this situation, we are desirous of knowing the future course of action the kumara chakravarthy has in mind. The chiefs of the kottams are also waiting for Mamallar's orders. Don't they have to return to their respective forts before the Kanchi fort is besieged?'

Mamallar, who was listening to all this, did not respond immediately. He was immersed in deep thought. Observing this, the chief minister, Ranadeera Pallavarayar, asked, 'It would be good if Commander Kalipahayar, who returned from the northern battlefield, stated his opinion first. He may know the reason why the chakravarthy asked us to congregate here.'

Commander Kalipahayar stood up and started speaking: 'The reason for the chakravarthy asking us to assemble here is related to the siege of the Kanchi fort. The chakravarthy expects the siege to continue for even up to a year. During this period, there will be no possibility of communication between those inside and those outside the fort. The chakravarthy wanted to inform the chiefs of their duties during the siege. I am unaware of the exact details he wanted to share.'

'I wish to ask the commander a question. When do you think the Vatapi army will reach the entrance of our fort?' asked one of the chiefs.

'They may reach here by dawn tomorrow. They may surround the fort by sunset.'

'In that case, shouldn't those who have to leave the fort do so before dawn tomorrow?'

'If the chakravarthy does not return tonight, it would be wise for the chiefs to return to their forts by dawn. They may expect the chakravarthy to convey his commands to them at their respective forts.'

Silence prevailed for some time. Everyone was gazing intently at Mamallar.

'Everyone is awaiting the kumara chakravarthy's command,' prompted the chief minister.

Mamallar stood up from his seat majestically. He looked around at those present in the assembly. 'When the chakravarthy left the Kanchi fort nine months ago, he commanded me to discharge all state duties on his behalf till he returned. Don't you all remember this?'

'We remember!' replied some amongst those present. Others nodded in support. The rest kept quiet as if anticipating something undesirable.

'The chakravarthy has not yet returned. May I still retain the powers he granted me? Are you supportive of this?'

'We accept! We accept! We happily accept!' stated the voices that rose in unison in the assembly.

The prime minister stood up and stated, 'Pallava kumara, when the chakravarthy asked us for our counsel, we would state our opinions. Similarly, we will state our views if you seek our advice. We will act as per your command once we conduct an in-depth discussion. We only have the right to offer counsel; the right to command is yours.'

'I agree . . . Please voice your views. I will listen. But I have already decided the course of action. Ministers! Chiefs of kottams! Everyone listen. Hiding inside the fort and fearing the invading enemies will cause permanent ignominy to the Pallava dynasty. As long as I am alive, I will not tolerate any slur being cast on the illustrious Pallava dynasty that traces its origins to Thondaiman Illandirayan. One lakh soldiers who are stationed inside this fort are itching to fight a battle. I have decided to lead them and counter the Vatapi army outside our fort. Commander Paranjyothi will accompany me to the battlefield. I appoint Commander Kalipahayar in Paranjyothi's place to oversee the security of the fort. After seeking your consent for this, I will speak to the chiefs of the other forts.'

The silence that prevailed after Mamallar's speech was akin to the disquiet after a long bout of thunder. The ministers and chiefs looked at each other. They were tongue-tied.

Chapter 51

The Chakravarthy's Emissary

The kumara chakravarthy looked intently at those assembled and asked, 'What is your opinion? Do you agree?'

Shock was evident on their faces. Pin-drop silence prevailed for some time.

In truth, all those who had been summoned to the council had not come to express their opinions on war-related issues. They had come to listen to Mahendra chakravarthy's wishes and commands.

Nine months ago, when the chakravarthy had left for the northern battlefront, they had adopted the same policy and had granted all powers to him. Now they had assembled with the same intention in mind.

In this situation, when Mamallar unexpectedly announced that he was going to embark on a dangerous venture and sought their views, everyone was confused and kept quiet.

Mamallar once again looked around at everyone and asked majestically, 'Why are you not responding? Why this silence? Have I mentioned something that ought not to have been said in your presence? Did I say something that is derogatory to the valorous Pallava dynasty?'

The assembly continued to be silent. Those assembled realized that they were in an awkward situation and did not open their mouths.

'Good. Since none of you objects, I may infer that you accept my decision. Am I right, Commander?' asked Mamallar, looking at Commander Kalipahayar.

Commander Kalipahayar replied, 'I'm duty-bound to obey the kumara chakravarthy's command. But I don't think that this is the most appropriate course of action. What Mamallar is saying contradicts the chakravarthy's wishes. After several rounds of in-depth consultations, the Pallavendrar had commanded the army to return and to remain within the fort. Mahendra chakravarthy is neither a coward, nor is he afraid of war. It is not wise to act contrary to the chakravarthy's wishes.'

Anger erupted on the kumara chakravarthy's face.

'Commander! Did I ever say that my brave father was cowardly or afraid? I would rather cut off my tongue. My father's war strategy and mine are different. In his absence, I have the right to pursue my strategy. Commander, arrange for the Pallava army to leave for the battlefield on a war footing by dawn tomorrow.'

Commander Kalipahayar lowered his voice and pointed out, 'The Pallava kumarar's strategy is not a war strategy but a suicidal strategy. The Vatapi army has five lakh soldiers. The strength of the Pallava army does not exceed one lakh soldiers.'

Mamallar's eyes emitted sparks of anger as he glared and questioned, 'Commander! Are you aware of the strength of the Pallava and Gangapadi armies at the Pullalur battle? Didn't ten thousand of our soldiers defeat fifty thousand Ganga Nadu soldiers and cause them to flee? On the battlefield, does the size of the army matter? Every Pallava soldier is equal to nine Chalukya soldiers. Kalipahayar, have you not realized this yet?'

'The Vatapi army not only consists of five lakh soldiers, but also fifteen thousand war elephants,' replied Kalipahayar.

'So what? It seems that you're not aware that a mad elephant fled down the streets of Kanchi fearing the spear wielded by our brave commander, Paranjyothi. When there are one lakh lions who are as brave as Paranjyothi in the Pallava army, why should we be scared of Pulikesi's war elephants?'

As the argument escalated in this manner, the prime minister, Saranga Deva Bhattar, became worried.

The prime minister asked, 'There is one thing we wish to know. Isn't there still time for the chakravarthy to return? Have the sentries at the entrance of the fort been informed of this? If the chakravarthy were to return tonight, are the sentries prepared to open the fort gates without delay?'

Commander Paranjyothi then replied, 'Yes, I have instructed the sentries. Anticipating the possibility of the chakravarthy sending a message through emissaries, I have made the necessary arrangements for that too.'

Commander Paranjyothi had barely finished announcing this when one of the guards rushed in and stated, 'An emissary has brought a message from the chakravarthy. He has come with the lion insignia.'

Hearing this, Mamallar was stunned. The others in the assembly were relieved, feeling as if the Almighty himself had arrived.

Chapter 52

Horrific News

When the chakravarthy's emissary entered the mandapam, pin-drop silence prevailed in the assembly.

The man who entered was tall and well built. It seemed as though he had come directly from the battlefield. The crown of his head and his face were bandaged. His clothes were blood-stained.

Everyone was keen to know the message he carried; no one thought of anything else. Everyone in the assembly including Paranjyothi was staring at the emissary without blinking. He was not only eager like the others but was also taken aback. He felt that he had seen this emissary before.

The emissary turned around and looked at everyone in the assembly. Finally, his gaze dwelt on the kumara chakravarthy.

'Pallava kumara! I bear a message from your father. May I announce it in this assembly itself?' he asked.

Mamallar looked at the prime minister, who understood the gesture and declared, 'It is necessary for all those who are gathered here to be aware of the chakravarthy's message. You may announce it here.'

'In that case, hear me. I bear horrific news. Nevertheless, it has to be told ... The chakravarthy of the Pallava empire has been imprisoned ...'

Everyone in the assembly felt as if they had been struck by a bolt of lightning. Some shrieked, 'What? What?' A few others jumped up from their seats. People's jaws dropped as they gaped at the emissary.

Mamallar let out a terrifying laugh, which sent a chill down the spine of all those present.

'Has the chakravarthy been imprisoned? When? Where? Who imprisoned him?' roared Mamallar. His hand unconsciously pulled out the sword fastened at his waist.

'The frontline forces of the Vatapi army imprisoned the chakravarthy last evening. He rode northwards from the southern front to ascertain the position of the Vatapi army. The Vatapi soldiers turned up unexpectedly and imprisoned him. Pallava kumara, this is the message that the chakravarthy has sent to you through me. "The time has come for my son to demonstrate his peerless bravery. It is my son's responsibility to defeat the Vatapi army, humble the haughty Pulikesi and liberate me. This is not an impossible task for Narasimhan." This is the message I bear from your father,' stated the emissary and paused.

Mamallar surveyed everyone in the assembly with glowering eyes and asked in a thundering tone, 'Commander, will you consent at least now to lead our forces out of the fort? What do the ministers and chiefs of the kottams have to say?' He then looked at Paranjyothi who was standing behind him and roared, 'Commander! Why are you too standing transfixed like this? Have you all become lifeless?'

Then the chief minister stood up and asked, 'What's the proof that this emissary is stating the truth?'

The emissary immediately held up the lion insignia and declared, 'This is the proof. The wounds on my body and face are witness.'

'Ah! Mahendra chakravarthy has been trapped by our foes, and you are wasting time asking for proof! Commander, come, let's go,' urged Mamallar looking at Paranjyothi.

But a confused Paranjyothi was staring intently at the tall, bandaged emissary.

Prime minister Saranga Deva Bhattar enquired, 'Have any of you seen this emissary before? Emissary, who are you?'

The emissary answered, 'Who am I? The Pallava chakravarthy's personal spy. In the Pallava spy force, I hold a position second only to Shatrugnan. Commander Paranjyothi has often seen me. Don't you recognize Naganandi, who brought you here? The chakravarthy had appointed me to monitor Aayanar and Sivakami who, knowingly or unknowingly, were acting as spies for the Vatapi king. You had headed to the Nagarjuna mountain carrying the secret message that Aayanar had written to Pulikesi. I had tipped off the chakravarthy, who then seized the message from you. Commander! Am I not stating the truth?' the emissary asked with conviction.

Commander Paranjyothi's head swirled. Considering what the emissary was recounting, it appeared that he might be stating the truth.

The emissary continued, 'There was a Vatapi spy called Gundodharan who was staying with Aayanar. Yesterday, he carried a message for the Vatapi army from Aayanar. When the chakravarthy and I pursued him to prevent him from delivering the message, the Chalukya warriors unexpectedly surrounded us. By God's grace, I escaped. That's all the information I have. The chakravarthy has assigned a few more tasks to me. I need to go in search of Shatrugnan to fulfil those tasks. Please allow me to leave! I have stated all that I am supposed to. Discuss thoroughly and act appropriately!'

After speaking in this manner, the emissary left the mandapam. It occurred to none to stop him or question him further.

Mamallar felt as though a thousand scorpions were stinging him. Ah! Were Aayanar and his daughter spies of the Vatapi kingdom? *Was it these people whom I rescued from the floods? Was it on this Sivakami that I showered boundless love? Is it because of them that our enemies have imprisoned Mahendra Pallavar . . .?*

Amongst all those in the assembly, it was only Commander Paranjyothi who could comprehend Mamallar's sorrow. He held Mamallar's hand and urged, 'What are you still thinking about? Come, let's head to the battlefield! We will once again decimate those Vatapi demons, liberate the chakravarthy and bring him back. Mamallar! Think of the Pullalur battle!'

Commander Kalipahayar, who also heard this, snapped out of his reverie and announced as he stood up, 'Yes, what Commander Paranjyothi says is true. There is no more room for thought. Please command the forces to leave!'

All those in the assembly stood up in unison and raised several heroic slogans such as, 'Long live Mahendra Pallavar! Death to the demonic Pulikesi!'

Amidst this cheering, certain confusing noises were heard from near the entrance of the mandapam. The sound of horse hooves, spears and swords clashing, an authoritative voice commanding someone and several people running were all heard together.

Yes, a dramatic incident was unfolding at the entrance of the mandapam. Just as the emissary who came with the news of the chakravarthy's imprisonment was leaving the mandapam, Mahendra Pallavar himself arrived at the mandapam on horseback. The chakravarthy commanded the guards at the entrance of the mandapam to imprison the emissary. They immediately surrounded the interloper.

Chapter 53

The Fire That Bharavi Ignited

Words cannot describe the joy and commotion that erupted in the mandapam when Mahendra chakravarthy entered.

For quite some time, the sounds of people raising slogans of victory echoed all around.

Mamallar leapt up from his seat and embraced Mahendra Pallavar. The ministers and chiefs of kottams, unmindful of protocol, surrounded the chakravarthy. Everyone tried to speak at the same time.

Commander Paranjyothi stood slightly aloof and all alone at a distance. He looked embarrassed. The brave youth was probably ashamed, thinking, 'I too was deceived. Despite knowing the chakravarthy so well, how could I believe that he had been imprisoned by our adversaries?'

When the commotion subsided slightly, the chakravarthy looked around at the courtiers and quizzed, 'All of you seem to be so exuberant! Have we already won the war? The commander of our fort, however, seems downcast.'

Everyone looked at Paranjyothi, which embarrassed him even more.

Prime Minister Saranga Devar revealed, 'Pallavendra! A moment before your arrival, we had decided to lead our forces outside the fort and attack Pulikesi's army. The commander of our fort may be disappointed that there is no need for that now.'

'What? What? Is it wise to lead our forces outside the fort? Whose brilliant idea was this? Commander! How dare you flout my command? Did you also lose your trust in me?' roared the Pallavendrar like a lion.

Commander Kalipahayar responded meekly, 'Prabhu, when we heard that the enemies had imprisoned you, how could we hide inside the fort? Where is the need for a Pallava army if it is unable to liberate you?'

When the chakravarthy asked, 'Ah! Was I imprisoned by our enemies? What kind of a tale is this?' those present in the court were taken aback.

Prime Minister Saranga Devar related how a man had come to the court claiming to be the chakravarthy's emissary, the surprising news he had communicated and the decision the court had reached subsequently.

After listening to everything, Mahendra chakravarthy acknowledged, 'Ah! Naganandi is even more astute than I had thought. Had I come a little later, everything would have gone awry.'

'Prabhu, in that case, did that emissary lie? Weren't you imprisoned by our enemies?' asked Commander Kalipahayar.

Mahendrar responded, 'No—the emissary lied. I was not imprisoned. Even if I had been imprisoned, there is no necessity for you to lead the army out of the fort to free me. I know how to escape. How could you completely trust an unknown envoy? Didn't Narasimhan or Paranjyothi inform you that Naganandi was our enemies' spy?'

'Prabhu, the news of your imprisonment confused me. The Pallava kumarar was also distraught,' confessed Paranjyothi.

'Was he a spy? Then how did he come to possess the lion insignia?' asked the chief minister.

'It was I who gave it to him. It was to capture this extremely crafty spy that I headed to the south from the northern battlefield ...'

'Prabhu, why did you give the lion insignia to our enemy's spy? Were you unaware that he was a spy when you gave it to him?'

'I have known about him for nine months. I suspected it the very day Paranjyothi arrived at Kanchi. I came to know that the Vatapi spies were working all over the Pallava kingdom through the Buddha sangams. I allowed Naganandi go scot-free to apprehend all of them. I decided to somehow capture Naganandi before the siege began and therefore headed southwards. I finally found him at Mandapapattu village.'

'At Mandapapattu?' asked a shocked Mamallar.

'Yes, Narasimha! At Mandapapattu, I even met Aayanar and Sivakami. They informed me that you had rescued them from the severe floods. Both of them are well. I have made the necessary arrangements for Aayanar to carve rock temples there. This was one good thing that emerged from my going to Mandapapattu in search of Naganandi ...'

Mamallar, who had been feeling dejected ever since hearing Naganandi state that Aayanar and Sivakami were the enemy's spies, felt happy on hearing this news. His face reflected the happiness he felt within.

'Prabhu, has the spy been imprisoned?' asked Commander Kalipahayar in a worried tone. Though he was adept at waging wars on the battlefield, matters relating to espionage gave him a headache.

'Yes, Commander! The extremely astute spy of Vatapi has been imprisoned. We have now won half the war,' declared the chakravarthy.

Immediately, with his palms folded, Mamallar pleaded his father, 'Pallavendra, you have won half the war. Please permit me to win the remaining half. Kindly permit me to lead our brave Pallava army and decimate the demons from Vatapi. Please allow my dear friend Paranjyothi to accompany me.'

Mahendra Pallavar embraced Mamallar and urged, 'My child! I laud your valour. But please pay heed to what I have to say.' He then looked at the courtiers and stated, 'I want everyone to listen to me. I will tell you the primary reason for this war. Then you may voice your views.'

The courtiers listened attentively.

'When I was young, the thought of war did not even cross my mind. My brave father Simha Vishnu's fame had spread all over Dakshina Bharata. My father had annexed Chola Nadu in the east to the Pallava kingdom even before my birth. He defeated the Uraiyur Cholas and made them pay tribute. He humbled the Pandyas. The Gangars in the west and the Kadambars in the northwest were deferential and friendly with Simha Vishnu Maharaja. In the north, the king of Vengi is my maternal uncle. So, I grew up without an inkling of war. I spent my time engaged in painting, sculpture, poetry, music and dance. I identified the arts that flourished in various nations, invited exponents of those arts to the Pallava kingdom and tried to nurture those arts here too.

'It was during this time that I heard that a poet from Utthara Bharata named Bharavi had visited Durvineethan's court. He had lived in Asalapuram in the north and was a friend of the Vatapi princes. When Pulikesi and his brothers were hiding in the forest in fear of their uncle, Bharavi also spent some time there with them. Then he sought refuge in the Ganga Nadu king's court. He arranged the marriage between Durvineethan's daughter and Pulikesi's brother, Vishnuvardhanan, and tried to strengthen Pulikesi.

'You all know that Durvineethan was extremely indebted to my father. So, he used to periodically inform Kanchi about the goings-on in Gangapadi. When I heard that Bharavi was at the Ganga Nadu court, I was desirous of inviting him to Kanchi. My father accordingly sent a message to Durvineethan, after which Bharavi came here. Bharavi fell in love with Kanchi Sundari. He was smitten by the temples, wide roads, mansions and flower gardens of Kanchi. After Pulikesi ascended the Vatapi throne, he and his brother sent several messages to Bharavi, asking him to return to Vatapi. But Bharavi refused their invitation. He was reluctant to leave Kanchi. Bharavi responded to Pulikesi's messages, stating his unwillingness to return. He described Kanchi in those messages. In one such message, he wrote:

Jasmine is the most enticing amongst flowers, Vishnu is the most adored amongst men,

Rambha is the most alluring amongst women, and Kanchi is the most vibrant amongst cities.

'I felt extremely happy reading this verse then. But it was the spark that the poet Bharavi ignited then that has become this war. Pulikesi wrote in one of his messages to Bharavi, "I will come to Kanchi one day and see if what you say is true." Even that made me proud. I decided to accord the Vatapi emperor a lavish reception when he visited Kanchi. But courtiers! Contrary to my wishes,

I have to shut the gates of the fort and make the Vatapi emperor stand outside . . .'

Mamallar, who had been listening intently to Mahendrar's story like the rest of the courtiers, interrupted saying, 'Pallavendra! Why do we have to seal the gates of our forts? Why can't we welcome Pulikesi with spears and swords?'

'Yes, we are indeed going to welcome him. Our warriors will stand on the fort ramparts and welcome the Chalukyas with spears and swords. After welcoming them, the Chalukyas will be offered as feast to the crocodiles in our moats! I will complete what I intend to tell you. I myself saw how much that demon Pulikesi is smitten by Kanchi Sundari. Ah! Do you know how his eyes gleamed when I described the beauty of Kanchi . . .'

'What is this? Did you see Pulikesi face-to-face? When? Where?' asked Saranga Devar.

When Mahendrar revealed, 'I saw him in person on the banks of the North Pennai River in the Chalukya army camp,' the assembly was shell-shocked.

'Prabhu! How could you invite danger upon yourself in this manner? This vast Pallava kingdom in solely dependent on you!' exclaimed the chief minister.

Chapter 54

The Court Is Dismissed

When the commotion in the mandapam had finally subsided, Mahendra Pallavar resumed.

'Courtiers, I do not accept your view that the Pallava kingdom is solely dependent on me. Here is my brave son, Narasimhan. He will uphold the honour of the Pallava dynasty. I did not meet the Vatapi king at his own army camp to demonstrate my bravery. There was an important reason for my meeting Pulikesi in person. The man who caused you grief a little while ago, Naganandi adigal, had sent a message to Pulikesi through the commander of our fort. This brave youth, who had come to Kanchi to learn sculpting from Aayanar, carried the missive unaware of its contents. I intercepted the message from him on the way and visited Pulikesi at his army camp. But I did not deliver Naganandi's message to Pulikesi. I gave the message I had written instead. Due to that message and our brave commander, Kalipahayar,

257

we were able to prevent the Vatapi army from advancing beyond the North Pennai River.'

'Prabhu, what was written in Naganandi's message?' asked Prime Minister Saranga Devar.

'The message stated that no other city's defence was as poor as Kanchi's. He further opined that if the Vatapi army marched to Kanchi without stopping on the way, Kanchi may be captured in three days!'

Angry roars echoed all over the court.

The chakravarthy confessed candidly: 'Naganandi's opinion at that point of time was entirely correct. Had the Vatapi army marched directly to Kanchi, we could not have withstood them for more than three days. Fifteen of the fifteen thousand Chalukya war elephants would have sufficed to force open the gates of our fort. Courtiers, Kanchi would have then faced the same fate as Vyjayanthi Pattinam. Don't you know that Vyjayanthi Pattinam, which was ruled by the ancient Kadamba clan for generations, has now been reduced to ashes?'

Sympathetic sighs were heard in the court. Mahendra Pallavar continued. 'Kanchi city has flourished since the time of Lord Buddha, who had incarnated for this world's welfare, for a thousand years. Thirunavukkarasar Peruman has described this city as "Kalviyil Karailladha Kanchi Managaram". This city's fame has spread far and wide to China, Javaha, Greece and Rome. I do not want to face the ignominy of such a city being destroyed during my lifetime. My foremost duty is to safeguard Kanchi. Will you all cooperate with me to fulfil my duty?'

The courtiers responded in unison to the chakravarthy, 'Yes, we will! Yes, we will!'

The chakravarthy asked forthrightly: 'I informed you of the fundamental reason for this war breaking out. As this war is about to occur because of me, I seek your permission to conduct this war as per my wishes.'

The courtiers once again unanimously responded, 'So be it!'

Subsequently, Mahendrar pointedly looked at the chiefs of the southern kottams of the Pallava empire and asked, 'Those of you who reside in villages outside the fort will undergo greater difficulty than those of us within the fort. Are you prepared to withstand all difficulties to safeguard Kanchi?'

The chiefs of the kottams responded in one voice, 'We are ready! We are ready!'

'By dawn tomorrow, the Vatapi army would have reached our fort. All of you ought to leave the city before that. All of you should rush back to your respective kottams. When the Kanchi fort is under siege, there will be no communication between you and those of us within the fort. When Pulikesi is defeated, he will vent his anger on the surrounding villages. You should be prepared for all this. Chiefs of the kottams! Think well before you respond. Are you prepared to sacrifice all you have to safeguard Kanchi? Will you tolerate all the atrocities perpetrated by the demonic Vatapi army? Will you be steadfast even if famine strikes the nation and people die of hunger?' asked the chakravarthy regally.

The chief of the Chenji kottam, Sadaiappa Singan, stood up and replied:

'Pallavendra! There is nothing to think about. Kanchi is the jewel in the Pallava kingdom's crown. If Kanchi were to be destroyed, then is there any use in anything else surviving? We are ready to sacrifice everything to protect Kanchi.

We will act in accordance with your wishes. I am sure everyone else here shares my sentiments!'

The chiefs of the kottams supported him saying, 'Yes! Yes!'

At this point of time, an envoy entered the court. He prostrated before the chakravarthy and announced that a massive cloud of dust was visible at the eastern horizon and that a noise that resembled a wild sea could be heard.

Mahendrar announced in a thundering voice, 'Courtiers! The Vatapi army has arrived! The time has come for every one of us to demonstrate our bravery. Ministers! The court may now disperse. From tomorrow till the end of the siege, the ministers' council will assemble here every day at the second jaamam of the night. Now everyone may leave and attend to their respective tasks!'

The ministers promptly exited the court.

'Chiefs of the kottams! I am extremely pleased with the promise you have made. If you remain steadfast in fulfilling that promise, I am sure I will be able to vanquish Pulikesi and hoist the flag of victory.' He then instructed Commander Paranjyothi, 'Commander! Escort them to the southern gates of the fort! As soon as they cross the moat, demolish the drawbridge. Aren't you working on the tasks we agreed to complete to strengthen the fort's security?'

'Yes, prabhu! All other gates of the fort except the southern gate have been sealed. The drawbridges have also been broken. Sixteen thousand warriors armed with spears have been stationed on the walls of the fort,' replied Commander Paranjyothi.

After Paranjyothi and the chiefs of the kottams had left the court, the chakravarthy and Mamallar were all by themselves. Mamallar was downcast, devoid of fire.

The chakravarthy went up to Mamallar, placed his arm around his son's shoulder and asked, 'Narasimha, do you also approve of this war being conducted as per my wishes?'

'Appa, why do you ask me? I accept your decision!' replied Mamallar.

'I am happy, Kumara! Go to the palace and inform your mother that I have returned safely. I have to complete important tasks before dawn. Once I complete those, I will come to the palace,' remarked Mahendrar. Mamallar walked towards the anthapuram. The chakravarthy mounted a waiting horse and rushed towards the royal viharam.

Chapter 55

The Siege Begins

At dawn the following day, a worried Kamali was sitting in the portico of her house. Her eyes were swollen as she had stayed awake the whole night, crying. Kannabiran's father, Ashwabalar, was sitting next to her, consoling her.

When Kamali heard that the kumara chakravarthy had returned the previous evening, she had expected Kannabiran to return with him. When all the womenfolk had congregated to welcome the hero of the Pullalur battle, Ashwabalar had gone to fetch his son. He had returned late at night with the news that Kannabiran had not accompanied Mamallar.

Since no one in Kanchi had slept that night, the news of the chakravarthy's return had reached them in the third jaamam of the night. By the fourth jaamam of the night, news of the Vatapi army nearing the fort, the gates of the fort being sealed, and the bridges across the moats being demolished had become known.

Hence the chance of Kannabiran entering the fort was naught. This was why Kamali was immersed in an ocean of sorrow and Ashwabalar was consoling her.

Just then, Kannan himself came and stood at the entrance of the house. Kamali immediately stood up and shrieked, 'Kanna!' She was about to run up to him and embrace him when she observed Chakravarthy Peruman riding behind Kannan. A shocked Kamali bashfully stood rooted to the spot.

'Kamali, I have brought Kannan back. Now the responsibility of looking after him safely is yours,' quipped the chakravarthy smiling. Then the chakravarthy stated, as he rode away, 'Sivakami enquired if you were well. She asked you to inform her immediately when you deliver a son.'

Kamali, who felt shy with the chakravarthy around, went into the house, casting a sideways glance at Kannabiran. Kannabiran greeted Ashwabalar and followed Kamali inside the house.

'What is this, Kamali? Aren't you happy that I returned? You came in even without looking at me! Were you unable to see me?' asked Kannabiran.

Kamali responded, 'Yes, I was unable to see. My eyes are swollen after crying all night.'

'Aiyyo! Why were you crying?' asked Kannabiran as he neared her.

Kamali brushed away his hand and asked, 'Where did all this affection disappear to yesterday? Why didn't you come last night itself?'

'Why didn't I come last night itself? I didn't because a wide moat, crocodiles and a high wall separated us!' exclaimed Kannan.

'Is that so? Were you outside for the entirety of last night? Apparently they demolished all the drawbridges last night itself! How did you enter? Tell me all that happened ever since you left!' demanded an agitated Kamali.

'Kamali! What do you want me to say? Should I relate the story of my birth or my upbringing? Should I tell you how I suffered when I got trapped in the flood? Should I relate the story of taking the bikshu in the chariot instead of Mamallar? Or how I wandered outside the fort all night?' asked Kannan. He then related all the astounding experiences since he had left Kanchi.

Kannan related what happened after the bikshu had mounted the chariot on the banks of the Varaha River:

The bikshu had not been satisfied despite Kannabiran riding the chariot as fast as he could. He had repeatedly urged Kannabiran to go faster. They had changed horses twice en route, and had reached the southern entrance of the Kanchi fort one nazhigai after sunset. Then Kannabiran had steered the chariot down the road adjacent to the moat, as directed by the bikshu. After riding down this road for some time, the bikshu had dismounted from the chariot and entered the forest. As Kannabiran heard the sound of a boat sailing across the moat shortly thereafter, he had closely observed the direction from which the sound came. The moon was just rising on the horizon at that time. In the wavering light provided by the moon rays streaming through the trees, Kannabiran had seen two bikshus seated in the boat sailing across the moat. When the boat reached the opposite bank, both of them had alighted. They had stood adjacent to the fort walls. Suddenly, both of them had miraculously disappeared.

Kannabiran had waited for a very long time at that very spot. He had not known what to do. He had thought deeply for a long time, 'How could they have disappeared?' He realized that there might be a secret tunnel within the fort walls. Since the bikshu had asked him to remain there, he thought that they might return. So, he kept staring attentively at the spot where they had disappeared. Somehow, sleep had overcome him and he had closed his eyes. When he suddenly opened his eyes, he heard a sound that resembled waves noisily rising in the sea at a distance. As he had previously heard the noise of water gushing out of a breach in the dam, he was scared. He had agitatedly climbed up a nearby tree and looked in the direction from which the noise came.

In the moonlight, he had seen, at a great distance, an ocean-like army approaching along with elephants, horses, canopies, flags, spears and swords. He had realized that it was the Vatapi army and had hurriedly driven his chariot towards the southern entrance of the fort. Kannabiran had loudly called out to the sentries of the fort. His efforts had been futile. He had stood there hesitantly for some time when an idea struck him. 'I will probably find the secret tunnel the bikshus used if I search for it! I can enter the fort through that tunnel.' Thinking thus, he had returned to the spot opposite to where the bikshus had disappeared. He wondered how to cross the moat. When he considered swimming across, he had shuddered at the thought of the hundreds of crocodiles in the water. By then, the sound of the army approaching had grown louder.

'It's all right if I become food for the crocodiles. But I should not be captured by our enemies.' Thinking thus, Kannabiran had been about to jump into the moat when he suddenly observed an open door located in the fort wall. He had seen a young bikshu running out of that exit. Kannabiran had immediately hidden himself behind a tree. He watched the young bikshu row the boat towards the bank where he stood. Kannabiran's mind had been working hard then. When the young bikshu reached the bank, he had been about to submerge the boat in the water. Kannabiran had leapt out and prevented the bikshu from doing so. He had forced the young bikshu into the boat and got into the boat himself. He had slowly rowed the boat to the opposite bank.

The door in the fort wall was still open. Kannabiran pushed the young bikshu into that entrance and followed him. He remembered the chariot he had left on the other side of the moat. As he had been about to turn around, a vice-like grip had grabbed him and pulled him back into the tunnel. Kannan's surprise knew no bounds when he realized that the extremely strong hands belonged to Mahendra Pallavar. Then the chakravarthy had observed, 'Kanna! This fake bikshu was the last of the Vatapi spies in the Pallava kingdom. You have rendered a great service to the Pallava kingdom by preventing him from escaping. Come, let's go. Kamali will be anxiously waiting for you.' Saying this, the chakravarthy had entered the tunnel and closed the door from the inside. Kannan had soon realized that they had entered the royal viharam at Kanchi.

After relating the above incidents, Kannabiran remarked, 'Kamali! It was your mangalyam that saved me from our enemies and crocodiles. I am unable to believe that I have indeed escaped. Please embrace me with your tender hands and tell me if I am truly alive.'

'I cannot, Kanna! Infant Kannan will be disturbed if I embrace you!' replied Kamali, smiling mischievously.

* * *

To be continued . . .

Glossary

Tamil Months	
Cittirai	mid-April to mid-May
Vaikasi	mid-May to mid-June
Ani	mid-June to mid-July
Aṭi	mid-July to mid-August
Avaṇi	mid-August to mid-September
Puraṭṭasi	mid-September to mid-October
Aippasi	mid-October to mid-November
Karthikai	mid-November to mid-December
Markazhi	mid-December to mid-January
Thai	mid-January to mid-February
Masi	mid-February to mid-March
Pankuni	mid-March to mid-April
Distances	
1 kaadam	Approximately 10 miles or 16 kilometres

Units of Time	
1 nazhigai	24 minutes
1 muhurtham	48 minutes
1 jaamam	2 hours 24 minutes
10 jaamams	1 day